8-98

DATE DUE

Charlotte's
Friends

Also by Sarah Kennedy

Non Fiction

The Terrible Twos
Terrible Pets

Charlotte's Friends

Sarah Kennedy

St. Martin's Press ✻ New York

Library of Congress Cataloging-in-Publication Data

Kennedy, Sarah.
  Charlotte's friends / Sarah Kennedy.
    p. cm.
  ISBN 0-312-18554-5
  I. Title.
PR6061.E598C48   1998   98-3657
823'.914—dc21   CIP

First published in Great Britain by Hodder and Stoughton, Hodder Headline PLC

First U.S. Edition: August 1998

10 9 8 7 6 5 4 3 2 1

For loving families:

Mary, George, 'Hallo dear', Anne,
Richard, Jane, Carolyn, Jemma

Acknowledgements

Special thanks to
Barbara Nash, my editor,
whose help throughout
has been invaluable

and

Dr Graham Robertson
of the Maudsley Hospital, London

and

Lee Durrell BA, PhD
and Kevin Bulley BSc (Hons)
of the Jersey Wildlife
Preservation Trust

PART ONE

— • ◆ • —

Chapter One

꧁

Lord and Lady Pierce had always wanted a boy. The birth of Charlotte, their first child, a mere daughter, had been a massive disappointment. Despite all their wealth and status, they had not got what they wanted and did not bother to conceal their frustration. They had wanted an heir.

Charlotte shifted uneasily in her chair. She had been the wrong sex at the wrong time, the innocent and unwanted arrival. Why, tonight, was she burdened again with this rejection? It had been a wasted day. She had not been able to see her friends, the shopping had not worked, and she was aware she was now wallowing in thoughts of the past. She looked around the room. Perfect taste. The family paintings, the subtle colours, the old family silver – she took it all for granted. Tonight, the luxury of her London house in Eaton Square gave no comfort and worked no magic. She looked down at her forty-two-year-old hands, and felt a flash of anger. From birth, she had been made to feel she was a disappointment to her family. Inside and outside the nursery, she had been known as Grizzle. She had never forgiven them for that mean little nickname.

Normally, she never allowed herself to think about her mother. Whenever she did, she remembered being blamed for the varicose veins, the bulging belly, the subsequent stretchmarks – these had all been her fault. And she had *not* been a boy. How could a mother blame a child for being born? What a wonderful welcome to the world. And what a mother – six foot tall, elegant, graceful, an aristocratic socialite and serious drunk, the latter conveniently passed off for years as postnatal depression.

Charlotte stood up. The memories were making her uneasy. She prowled around the room, trying to dodge a mental image of her father. The tweeds, the brusque attitudes, the commands, his obsession with his lakes, his fishing, running the estate. The dogs had always come before his daughter. What a father! She flinched at the memory of his jubilation at the eventual birth of an heir, thought sarcastically of dear brother Henry who arrived six weeks before her fourth birthday. She remembered the flag being raised on the estate. There had been no flag for her.

Henry had been a perfect baby, giggling, gurgling, dry, smiling, sleeping to order. She, on the other hand, had relentlessly been reminded of her so-called bad behaviour – wailing, whinging, wet. She had been a pain in the neck to a stream of nannies who, undermined by her constant grizzling, had rapidly left.

On the one day her mother had needed to show her off, Charlotte had apparently screamed so loudly and for so long, Lady Pierce had abandoned the gathering and waited, po-faced, for the chauffeur. Mother had been furious and taken it out on the Nanny who had lasted the longest. The mother and child outing had *never* been repeated.

Years later, Natalie, one of her mother's oldest friends, had jokingly mentioned that Lady Pierce always believed that Charlotte had rejected her. Sitting down again in her chair, Charlotte shuddered at the memory. What a joke. How absurd. She couldn't remember her mother ever showing her any affection – no comforting hugs, nothing maternal, the perfunctory moth's-wing kiss at bedtime, so wispy, so quick . . . Had those kisses even happened? She reached for a cigarette. Memories of her mother off to cocktails, to hunt balls, to weekend house-parties. All Charlotte had been left with was the waft of her perfume and the vision of wonderful party frocks. Why had Mummy always been going away, abandoning her to Nanny to scoop up? Nanny was not Mummy.

Papa had not been any better. She had been a mere trophy carried into rooms by Nanny to be presented to his guests: 'Ah, here's Charlotte.'

In her mind's eye, she could still see his chiselled features, the flamboyant gestures, and hear his jovial guffaw as he showed her off. They didn't know that this was the only time he ever bothered with her. Brother Henry had been a completely different kettle of fish – always by Papa's side, being trained up to take over the estate. As he grew up, with Papa's encouragement, he had become more and more confident, smug, dictatorial, always right. Chalotte had been an easy target, feeling ever more unloved, unappreciated and unwanted. Henry had verbally swiped at her at every opportunity. Now sitting in her chair, she realized she disliked her brother intensely. It was not a pleasant thought. She loathed her mother, her father, her brother – the whole bloody lot of them.

Lady Pierce had given up on life. When Charlotte was six years old, her mother had told her she hated pregnancy – the doctor's necessary but intimate intrusions, followed by prolonged labour and forceps delivery. Her mother had also told her: 'Once was bad enough, darling.' Callously – with no attempt at concealment – it had been made obvious to her that the need to go through the whole ghastly business twice was all *her* fault. Her parents had needed an heir but, first time round, had ended up with a spare daughter. Mother had swiftly tucked away her breasts, ordered Charlotte to be bottle-fed and turned to her own bottle – the solace of sherry.

All these thoughts had wearied Charlotte. *She* needed a drink, went to the kitchen and poured herself a vodka. After Henry's birth, Mother had swiftly graduated from sherry to gin, soon discarding the tonic. When she died, it was with a drink-thinned body and gaunt face. The disintegration had taken years and sapped the patience and strength of everyone around her. The excuses, the bad behaviour, the social cover-ups, the daily embarrassments in front of the staff. Mother, she reflected, had not been a great loss to the world. Did she miss her? She was her mother after all. *No. No. No.* She sipped her drink.

On the day of her mother's death she had walked the estate, had circled the lake, followed her favourite trail. She had been out that afternoon for three hours. Had she been mourning? She had certainly found no resolutions, no answers to her questions. Why had it had to be like that? So much money, so much privilege, and, in emotional terms, seemingly nothing to show for it. Zilch. Had she ever mattered to her mother?

She reached for her drink, suddenly aware that she was silently crying.

'What's for dinner?' she had asked Henry when she eventually re-entered the house.

'You're a callous little bitch, aren't you?' he had replied, with a typical fifteen-year-old's venom. 'Your mother has just died and all you can think about is your stomach.'

That, she remembered now, was the moment she started turning inwards. She had kept her feelings to herself, had bitten her tongue, retained outward control. She remembered feeling truly grown-up at that moment. She had deceived her brother, convinced him she didn't care. He knew nothing of what she was feeling. She was in control. Her mother's death had finally released her from everything – the family, the estate. Putting on a silly, smirking expression, she had pushed past Henry, saying: 'Oh, bugger off, you horrible little brat. You don't understand anything.'

Sitting back in her chair, she realized she had never been happy. That afternoon she had gone to see Cook, the only person who had ever taken an interest in her. Her childhood had continued as it had started – empty tear-stained days eked out in empty houses with empty people doing empty things.

The day her mother died – that evening when she was absolutely certain her mother really was dead – Charlotte had entered the bedroom, looked down at the person who had given her life, then, stooping over her, had savagely kissed her on the mouth. She had held the kiss until her lips were as numb and as cold as her mother's.

Aside from her birth, Charlotte realized this was the closest she had ever been to her. That perfume . . .

Chapter Two

The light was beginning to fade on her futile day. Charlotte couldn't be bothered to get up and switch on the lights. Instinctively she knew this would not banish her painful childhood memories. Her mind flickered over her parents' absurdities, the time-consuming life of the estate, the busy home farm, the subservient estate workers: 'Yes, M'Lord. No, M'Lord . . . three bags full of manure, M'Lord.' She bet that was what they had been thinking. Poor sods.

Had they been nice to her? She thought of Greg, the groom's son, and shuddered. She remembered the stocky legs and dirty fingernails. He must have been fourteen and she seven at the time. Strange, after all these years, she could remember him so clearly. He had mesmerized her. He had known everything: where the badgers had their sett, when the fox cubs were about to be born. He had seemed so grown-up as he showed her the tiny dormouse climbing a head of wheat. He knew about dragonflies, newts and hares. He knew what they ate, when they slept, knew their predators – and, one day, he had fixed the combine harvester when all the grown-ups had failed. She had been so proud of him. It was as if he belonged to her. At the end of her school hours when her governess had finally closed the books, Charlotte had been off like a greyhound to find him.

Looking back on it, she realized that, although she had come from the top of the pile and he from the bottom, they had grown up together – had had the estate in common. The Lady Chatterley syndrome? Well, Greg had made it his personal task to introduce her to copulation.

'Look at the donkey, Miss Charlotte. What do you think that is hanging down?'

She hadn't known. She remembered her red face. She had known what he was saying was wrong, but hadn't known what to reply. He had relished her discomfort. The next day, bolder, he had led her to the trees behind the paddock, promising her a secret. Shielded by the foliage, she had seen Magdalene, her favourite horse. She remembered her confusion. She hadn't understood what was going on.

'What's happening to Magdalene?' she had asked Greg.

'He's a stallion. She's a mare. Look at her. She's loving it,' he said.

Magdalene's wild eyes and wide nostrils told Charlotte he was lying. Why, she had wondered, was Greg's father holding Magdalene so tightly by the halter? The stallion was trying to crush her. She remembered trying to run forward to help Magdalene, but Greg had stopped her, clamping his hand over her mouth.

'This is our secret,' he had whispered. 'Don't you be getting me into trouble. This is grown-up stuff, Miss Charlotte. Magdalene's fine – don't you worry.'

Leading her away from the paddock, he had grinned and fished out a grubby Polo mint. Reluctantly she had put it in her mouth and felt she had to eat it.

It was now quite dark. Charlotte lit a cigarette and watched it glow. The sounds of London drifted in. Lights had been switched on in neighbouring houses. Was she the *only* one sitting alone in the dark with her wretched thoughts? Did *they* have family secrets? She realized now that Greg had loved every minute of talking dirty and insinuating sex into a seven year old's mind.

Some time later, he had pointed out the farmyard cats, dwelling on the tom in great detail. She had known those cats from kittens. They had turned into great mousers. Henry had named them Minnie and Mickey after the cartoon. One day Greg had slyly beckoned her into a stable, and she had watched, horrified, as

Mickey tried to kill Minnie. He had her pinned by her scruff to the ground and Minnie suddenly screeched.

'Look at that – just like the horses,' Greg had laughed. 'Don't you worry, Miss Charlotte. That's nature – you'll be doing it one day. She's loving it, so will you.'

Greg had just had his fifteenth birthday. Once again, Charlotte had known he was lying. Minnie was *not* enjoying it – neither had Magdalene. She had walked away distressed. She had not told Cook – not told anybody. This was obviously what grown-ups did.

That night she had lain awake, hating Mickey for what he had done to Minnie. Had she heard Minnie screaming again that night? Sitting there in the dark of Eaton Square, she remembered what had happened next. She had made a plan.

The next day, she had gone to Henry's secret place and 'borrowed' his catapult. Farmyard cats were only ever in one place at one time – feeding time. She knew where Mickey would be at five-thirty – head in the bowl. Four o'clock nursery tea had seemed endless that day. As soon as she could escape, she had rushed down to the farmyard. Loading the catapult, she had got him in one. His tabby head had slumped forward into the bowl. She had been transfixed. Wallop. A seven-year-old bullseye.

She couldn't believe what she had done. She had pulled it off. She had stared at the motionless tabby body. How long had she stayed in her hiding place? Five minutes, perhaps? She had only moved from behind the bushes when she knew absolutely for certain Mickey would not be hurting Minnie again. She recalled her sense of triumph – it had been huge. She had felt like Goliath. Back at the house, Cook had commented on her good mood. Even better, Henry had not missed his catapult, and Mickey's death had remained 'just one of those things'.

What had happened to Greg? She didn't really care. He had probably turned into a nasty piece of work, though he had had his moments. There had been the thrill of his cupped hands, kept close to his body. 'Come over here, Miss Charlotte. I've got something to show you,' he was always calling out, and it had always been something wonderful. She smiled at the memory of the yellow baby chick, the brilliant green of a tiny frog. How had he captured dragonflies? The vision of his cupped hands, full of furry caterpillars and birds' eggs, was so vivid, it was as if

Sarah Kennedy

it were yesterday. She remembered one of his thumbs, the nail
blackened. He had dismissed it with: 'I had a run-in with your
dad's tractor.'

But then there had been that summer's day when, innocently,
she had responded to the usual summons. What had he got for her
today? she had wondered as she crossed the stable yard to him.

'I've got something to show you. Have you ever seen one of
these?' he had said, uncupping his hands.

She had looked down on a flaccid piece of pink skin. It had
looked like a snake. This was not his usual kind of gift. Intuitively
she had felt threatened – uncomfortable. This was wrong. She had
wanted to run away, but had remained transfixed.

The next moment the snake had moved in his hands.

'You goin' to show me yours?' he had laughed.

She hadn't got one. She had fled.

Wryly, she was thinking now, nobody had told *her* the Facts
of Life. There had been no caring parents for her with the delicately balanced prepared speech. The ghastly Greg had come the
nearest.

She had floundered blindly into her first period. The bleeding
had been a *terrible* shock.

Yes, her childhood and teenage years had been a nightmare. She
had felt so alone with her body. She knew now knowledge was
power – ignorance dangerous and damaging. Too late, her parents
had woken up to the fact that their daughter was disturbed and
unhappy. They had called in a psychiatrist, but he had only homed
in on her attention-seeking tantrums, petty thefts and relationship
with her mother. What relationship? Charlotte had been clever
enough to tell him what he wanted to hear. She had played with
him. If he had seen through her, he had not been any help. She
had learned how to block out anything distasteful, threatening and
troublesome. She had become her own best friend – secretive and
withdrawn.

Sitting in the chair, she realized that, since those childhood
betrayals, she had not trusted a soul.

The gloom was beginning to depress her. There were too many
shadows in the room. She stubbed out her cigarette and did the
familiar rounds of turning on the lamps. She poured herself another
half drink. She knew she was being maudlin, but, as she returned to

her chair, there was a slightly masochistic pleasure in the memories. She was not ready to go to bed yet.

Saturday tomorrow. Although she worked only two days a week at the BBC – well, only two hours on air really – the weekend was still a comfort, a buffer zone. With her private income, she didn't need to work at all. Why did she bother? Henry had got her the job as a BBC Radio Agony Aunt.

'After all, Charlotte, your one asset is your voice – it's husky, like Marlene's – and a job will keep you out of trouble,' he had said sardonically.

It was a typical Henry remark. Apart from her voice, he never seemed to appreciate any of her good points. Charlotte mulled them over. He never commented on her immaculately streaked bobbed hair, her beautifully manicured nails. She also had good lips. True, she would have preferred a smaller nose, and could have done without the diminutive cast in her right eye. At least, she comforted herself, her eyes were a striking hazel colour, and she was five foot five, petite – and had never had a weight problem, always hovering around eight stone.

Looking at her briefcase, it was a comforting thought that she didn't have to do anything grown-up till Tuesday. That was something to celebrate. She lit another cigarette, still remembering. What a childhood!

For some reason, her pet snails came to mind. How many had there been? Three? Yes. She laughed inwardly at their names – Simon Snail, Sally Snail and Stephen Snail. How stupid. They had been her secret – given her hours of pleasure. She had never let Henry know about the snails. That would have been fatal. She had spent days watching them eating the bread she had secreted from breakfast. She remembered being fascinated by the way they munched the breadcrumbs, moving their tiny mouths from side to side, like giraffes.

She drew on her cigarette. Perhaps she should have been a zoologist? If only she had had a proper full-time career ... Fat chance of that! Her parents had only ever entertained the thought of a good marriage for her – to one of their own sort, preferably a duke ... well, a title anyway. She felt herself becoming irritable. Oh, no, careers had not come into it. Marriage was her parents' panacea for everything.

One day the snails had ceased to amuse her and she had stood on them, one by one. Stephen, crunch. Simon, crunch. Sally, crunch. *All gone.* She realized she had protected them from Henry, but nobody had protected them from her. Charlotte wriggled her toes.

She stood up and drew the curtains. Was she hungry? No. She walked around the room. She supposed childhood had not been *all* bad. There had been some fun tennis matches, trips to the beach, lovely Somerset days and the picnics. Henry had not always been beastly. Had *she* been beastly? Yes, but he was such a smug little bastard, he deserved everything he'd got.

It was all coming back now. She remembered the time she had removed the crucial pieces of his Lego, and the last sixteen pieces of his jigsaw. He had gone ballistic over that. Then there had been the mysterious disappearance of his fishing bait ... the sudden sagging of the strings of his tennis racquet. She laughed. He had never suspected her. She had also removed the puncture kit from his bike, and, best of all, irritated to a state of madness with his roller-skating on the concrete slope, had stolen out one night and pushed his roller-skates down a badger hole and blocked it up.

Oh, yes, she had determinedly held her own against brother Henry. By the age of sixteen she had been ahead – secretly winning the sibling war. Henry, though, had got his own back in adulthood, had well and truly shafted her. She trembled at the memory.

'Mother,' she had said with emphasis, retaliating to one of his endless jibes, 'once told Papa I was *very* artistic.'

She had been totally unprepared for Henry's guffaw, his sudden spite.

'*Autistic,* Charlie,' he had bellowed. 'She said *autistic – not* artistic, you fool. What have you ever done that could be *artistic*?'

Even now, after all these years, she felt herself stiffen. She remembered feeling winded – emotionally gutted. He had been so busy laughing, he had not registered the impact of his words – her white face and inner howl.

How could he have known that her mother's compliment had meant *everything* to her? It had been the only nice thing she had ever said. Over the years, Charlotte had snuggled the words to her like a hot-water bottle. Mother had praised her, thought she was artistic, had been proud of her. In a sentence, Henry had destroyed the compliment. It had never existed – she had misheard the word. For years, she had believed in a lie. Mother had *never* complimented her, *never* praised her.

After her mother's death, she had gone into Lady Pierce's dressing-room and swept up an armful of ballgowns, still with their lingering fragrance. She had scissored them to shreds for as long as her anger and frustration had lasted. Hoarse from crying for herself, she had stuffed the remains into black bags and thrust them into the hands of the local bag-lady.

The truth was horrible. Her mother had *never* loved her.

Chapter Three

It was midnight – really time to go to bed. Charlotte felt emotionally exhausted by all the memories. The doorbell suddenly ringing was the *last* thing she had expected – or wanted. The shrill noise violated the peace of the room and stung her out of her inertia. Hell, who was that? She leaped up and peered out of the window. A practical joker – the usual late-night drunk? She never answered the bell at this time of night.

By the light of the street lamps, she could see a forlorn group – a woman holding a sleeping child, a weary toddler at her side. Charlotte recognized the hair. Oh, hell. It was Sally, the programme's assistant producer. What the blazes was she doing on the porch with her offspring at this time of night? There had obviously been a disaster. Instinctively, she reached for the small mirror in her handbag. She looked okay.

The bell rang persistently. She would have to answer it. The lights were still on in the house. Sally would know she was there. Charlotte liked Sally, but didn't need her now. Reluctantly, she crossed to the intercom.

'Oh, Charlotte,' Sally said, 'this is a catastrophe. I'm so sorry to bother you, it's unforgivable at this time of night, but the car's died on me and I've got the girls with me. They're exhausted. I can't get them home. Could we *possibly* stay the night? I promise we'll be away by seven.'

'Of course.' Charlotte put on her professional face and voice. 'I'm pressing the buzzer. Come on up.'

Inside, she was furious. She hated children, but had no option. She couldn't possibly say there was no room at the inn.

Sally's embarrassment was tangible as Charlotte ushered them into an immaculate guest room.

'We'll all sleep together,' she said. 'Don't worry, Charlotte. This is an emergency. I really am so sorry. I promise,' she reiterated, 'we'll be away first thing.'

'Can I get you anything?' Charlotte asked.

Briskly, the offer was rejected. All Sally wanted to do was get her girls to bed.

Dismissed, Charlotte went round the house switching off the lights. In her bedroom, she enjoyed the feeling of being a Good Samaritan, but felt faintly disturbed that Sally had been so uneasy with her. Why hadn't she taken up the offer of a coffee, the opportunity to unwind? She could just have put the children to bed. Why hadn't she stayed up a while and had a brandy and a gossip? Why did people, even when she was being *so* nice, seem to be *so* uneasy with her? Charlotte brushed her teeth. Was she imagining it? No. Somehow she sensed that Sally would have preferred to dump on anybody but her.

As she finally drifted into sleep, she knew Sally hadn't felt comfortable with her at all.

She had just been the last-stop motel.

Saturday 7 a.m. Charlotte lay in bed listening to muffled whispers. Sally was as good as her promise, trying to do the impossible and get a two and a four year old dressed without any noise.

'Mum,' Daisy said loudly, letting the side down, 'Joanna's wet her pants and it's gone on the pink stool.'

She heard Sally sigh despairingly: 'Oh, no.'

There was a pause, followed by: 'Mum, she's writing on the wall.'

For Charlotte, this was another world. Last night, she had said she would not get up to see them off. She snuggled down into the pillow, almost enjoying the unravelling drama. Sally was now whispering: 'Joanna, do a wee before we leave.'

There was another pause.

'I know you've done one, but do another . . . Jo-Jo, stop pulling the chain and get on with it.'

She could have fallen back to sleep if Daisy had not had another problem: 'Oh, darling, you've got them on the wrong feet. Come here.'

This was followed by a series of giggles. There was obviously a serious tickling session going on.

True to their word, the refugees left about 7.30, trying but failing to shut the heavy black door quietly. Bang. Secretly, from behind the curtains, Charlotte watched them go. Sally was struggling down the street burdened by child-rearing paraphernalia, the two bouncing demons running on ahead. *Poor Sally.* How did she cope with *them* and a job? Now she would have to deal with the AA man, somehow get them all back to Leatherhead, and then they would want lunch! Thank God, Charlotte thought, I'm single.

She got back into bed. The sight of the happy tight-knit family laughing their way down the street had triggered off more bad memories from the night before. She remembered reading somewhere that Edward VIII had once said publicly that his mother, Queen Mary, was 'An ice-veined bitch!' His poisonous epitaph had struck a chord and lodged in Charlotte's brain. She was not the *only* person with a horrendous mother. Wistfully, she thought again of Sally. When her girls grew up, Sally would be more like a friend or sister to them.

Charlotte felt a pricking of self-indulgent tears. She could never think of her mother without crying, but they were never 'missing-you-Mummy' tears. They were tears of anger and frustration – tears of yearning for revenge for the awfulness of her childhood.

While her mother was alive, she had always been too frightened to stand up for herself, say what she really thought and felt: 'You, Mother, are a drink-sodden, selfish, deluded bitch. You've made Papa's life a misery and your chief fun in life is gunning for me.'

If only she had said it. If only she had said: 'You're not *fit* to be a mother. D'you think anyone believes your pathetic cover-ups? D'you think anyone believes the clinking of glass in your handbag is truly lavender water? D'you *really* think we're all that stupid?'

Why hadn't she said it? Why hadn't she said: 'And what about when you crashed into the glass cabinet, d'you really think we believed you tripped over the rug? Did you ever wonder what you looked like, sprawled there on the carpet covered in shards of glass, your suspenders showing, while, miraculously, you still hung on to the drink in your hand? Did you really believe anyone thought you had 'flu when you hung on to the curtains in the drawing-room and brought the whole lot crashing down, nearly impaling one of your guests?

'Did you really believe nobody noticed your inane stories repeated over and over again? That nobody noticed the night you called for three dinners in one evening, forgetting you had already eaten? Did you ever remember me finding you lying on your bedroom carpet barking like a dog? Did you ever remember hurling that bowl of soup at me?'

Lying in bed, she wept silently into her linen pillow case. The hot tears ran down her cheeks, soaking the neck of her nightdress. Her mother's life could be fitted into periods – the Sways, the Trips and the Thuds. The Thud period had been the most difficult to cover up. Charlotte pulled the duvet over her head. She remembered how she and the rest of the family had followed the trail of Thuds. These usually ended in the conservatory, where her mother kept her 'secret supplies'.

'Pheasants – ruddy pheasants crashing into the conservatory again,' she and Papa would lie to guests.

Oh, yes, her mother had rampaged on, graduating from sherry, to gin, to whisky. Sometimes she had managed to consume a bottle a night.

'Mother's not feeling well, sends her love,' Charlotte had lied and covered up. 'She won't be down tonight.'

Her father's irritation would be followed by an instant: 'Right! Sorry, everyone. Poor old Celia. Let's go into dinner.'

The butler would automatically remove the now superfluous place setting.

She remembered her father's strained face. Sometimes she had felt sorry for him; sometimes her own pain and shame were so great she could not bear to look at him or any of the guests.

She dragged a tissue from the box on the bedside table. Oh, yes, Mother, she thought, you cried so much for yourself you never had tears to spare for any of us. How you 'milked' the postnatal depression after my birth; how I suffered when you made me feel I was to blame for all your problems. How you betrayed me when, occasionally sober-ish, you flirted with me and teased out all my childish secrets. Then, spiteful from a few more drinks, exposed me – and all my vulnerabilities – to the world.

She turned over, trying to find a dry patch on the pillow.

On the rare occasions she had tried to reason with her mother, complimenting her on her wonderful wardrobe, suggesting maybe she should dress up, the slurred reply would be: 'What's the point—? Nowhere to go. Can't be bothered.'

Oh, God, she *had* to get up. Why was she torturing herself like this? But the memories kept coming. Mother had lost all interest in food, had become a hyperactive insomniac. There had been constant tussles to get her out of harm's way and into bed, so the rest of the household could sleep. 'I wanna play the piano,' she would slur at midnight, waving her arms in drunken dismissal. 'I wanna sing . . . dance . . . go for a walk . . .' It had been so awful the way she had lashed out at staff and family alike, become abusive, sometimes foul-mouthed and gross.

Eventually they had all waited for the inevitable Thud. Then – and only then – could she be lifted, sag-mouthed and snoring, into bed. Only then could others sleep. But not for long. A few hours later, Mother would revive and wake up the nearest occupants to her room. They would hear her retching, and sometimes she would even make her way back to the conservatory for yet another drink. Who was kidding who?

Charlotte lay back. Oh, God, if *only* these memories would go away. They had been hovering now for twenty-four hours. But . . . she was already remembering that *awful* night when Mother, having run through her secret hoard, had made her drunken way to the cellar and fallen down the concrete steps. That had been the all-time Thud of Thuds.

Charlotte had got there first, hardly able to believe what she was seeing. She had crouched over the unconscious body, trembling and terrified, while the second on the scene – Kathy, a housemaid – had rushed to summon first Papa, then the doctor. Charlotte had never been able to forget that moment when Dr Balfour first shone his torch into Mother's eyes. Nothing. Blank. Blank. He had taken a piece of cotton wool, gently trawling it along the bottom eyelid, then checked her spine, her neck, and every other bone in her body for damage. Satisfied there was no injury that could render Mother a paraplegic, the doctor, butler and Papa had somehow got her up to her room and into bed. An hour later, she had come round, muttering to Charlotte who was sitting closest to her: 'Be a good girl, darling. Get me a drink . . . Look after Mummy.' Her eyes had not even focused on the others present, and she had fallen back into a drunken torpor before the doctor had time to cross the room.

Oh, hell. She was all cried out now, remembering the egg-sized lump on her mother's forehead, the gashed lip and black-and-blue face, the damaged hands, legs and arms. Her mother had been forced to stay in her room for two weeks after that.

Charlotte had tried to help – had watered down the bottles, hidden the car keys, gone, at the doctor's suggestion, on a first-aid course.

'Catching Thud Courses,' Henry had joked.

Mother had crashed on, wreaking havoc, causing mayhem, refusing all treatment – admitting nothing.

Had she ever been anguished at what was happening to her? Had she ever known what she was doing to herself and to others? If so, she had *never* shown it. She had simply rejected the truth, slammed doors on anybody who tried to help her. London and Somerset had soon become littered with now excluded, once-loved – and loving – friends. Her newspapers, magazines and books had remained unread, her bridge unplayed. A disguised drink ever close to hand, more and more dishevelled, Mother had spent her days alone at her desk gazing with blank eyes at the deer park and lawns, drinking more, eating less and less.

The cellar incident, Charlotte reflected, was the moment she personally had given up pleading with and cajoling her mother to get dressed; given up telling her which of her friends were persevering with phone calls – trying to re-establish their lost friendship and get her back. After her mother had deposited the car into the ha-ha, there had been a family conference and Papa, as pragmatic as ever, had decided to hire a second chauffeur. It had become obvious that Mother had to be protected from herself and equally obvious that the public had to be protected from *her*.

Memories. Memories. As Charlotte got up and slowly started the boring rigmarole of picking out clothes for the day, she put herself into her father's shoes. He must have been desperate to save the family's name and reputation.

What *had* gone wrong? All the advantages and privileges – town and country houses, Nanny, Cook, butler, chauffeurs. As a family they had been endowed with everything they could possibly have wanted. But none of these privileges had worked, had they?

Other children, she thought, could invite their friends home, have parties, chums to stay for weekends and holidays. She couldn't; Henry couldn't; eventually their father couldn't. He had isolated himself in a wing of the house. They had all been terrified at what Mother might do next, all hurt, bewildered, humiliated – ashamed.

She forced herself back into the present. By now, Sally would have rendezvoused with the AA man and should be heading back home.

How do some mothers, she thought, give their all for their puking, incontinent offspring? How do they manage to combine all that stuff – the potty-training, schooling, exams – with the desperate need to earn a living? Some mothers seemed to achieve all this in the most appalling circumstances. She knew this from her Agony Aunt postbag. Husbands, wives, single parents . . . They all seemed to do it on Income Support, existing between paper-thin walls, noisy neighbours and the next Giro.

Who – and what – had *her* mother been? An icy-veined bitch? A two-bottle-a-day Thud? A woman who had never wanted children – and certainly not a daughter? Had Mother been a victim of her class – destined never to work, destined only to breed? Charlotte knew she was in no mood to make excuses for her. Love surely didn't have a class, should never have a price.

Her mother had forced her to grow up alone, unloved, un-noticed, unwanted – surplus to requirements. She thought about the alternative – Sally and her happy girls. She really was a warm and sympathetic mother.

Feeling suddenly sterile, she looked at the clock. It was only 8.15 a.m. Charlotte knew she couldn't face the day just yet, and went back to bed. Early-morning misery. She could not give a damn if she never woke up again.

Chapter Four

❦

'Thirty-four per cent of men suffer from impotence at the age of fifty-eight.'

Charlotte tossed *The Times* on to the carpet, at the same time swinging her legs up on to the sofa. Not bad for forty-two – no veins – and she had good breasts. They had not sagged yet. She was no beauty, but she could, as Papa used to say, 'still cut the mustard'.

Which was more than could be said for thirty-four per cent of the male population at fifty-eight. Why not fifty-seven or fifty-nine? The world was obsessed with ridiculous surveys.

She glanced out of the window. It really had been a glorious day. She allowed her mind to wander. A bath? Put on her robe, catch the last of the evening sunshine, do a spot of watering, then bed?

Stubbornly, her mind returned to the irritating statistic. Giving in, she fumbled on the floor and retrieved the paper. Scanning the health correspondent's report once more, she re-read: 'This pill is not an aphrodisiac but acts by blocking the effect of an enzyme, phosphodiesterase-5, effectively increasing the blood flow to the penis. Available only on prescription. Taken an hour before sex . . .' blah . . . blah . . . blah.

Poor fifty-eight year olds. They could be in for a very long wait for a better erection. The phone rang. Charlotte let the machine take it. Marvellous device – you could hide behind it, but still hear who was calling. It was an invitation. At forty-two, invitations from suitable men – she corrected herself: safe, attractive, single men – were becoming a rarity.

Men . . . what had they meant to her? She found herself thinking back to all those hunt balls, the clumsy fumblings, the kisses she had never wanted to give let alone receive, uninvited tongues probing everywhere – even in her ears. Ugh!

She stood up, stepping over the newspaper, and moved into the garden. Outside, solace came from the night-scented stocks perfuming the air. The soil was very dry. Gardening was so therapeutic. Soothed, she bent down and unravelled the hose. It always seemed to have a mind of its own. As soon as she turned on the tap, it would shoot off, randomly watering whatever it fancied.

She allowed the men in her life to creep back in to her mind. She had purposely kept them at bay; over the years locked them all safely away; had mentally blanketed them – tucked them all up with hospital-tight corners.

The hose had kinked itself again, reducing the spray to a dribble. Irritably, she bent down to straighten it. Damn that article on impotence! Her mind was now buzzing with men and how she had felt about them from twelve onwards. Did she fear men? No. She simply loathed their traditional hold over women, their patronizing superiority, their undisguised farting and schoolboyish sense of humour. She was remembering Captain Nigel Shawcroft and the night of that dinner party. They must have been about twenty-eight – perhaps thirty? There had been ten for dinner that night.

A trail of ants yomped across the patio table. She squashed them.

Her cousin, Annabelle, a newly converted anti-bloodsports' fanatic, had rounded on the belligerent hunting-shooting Captain. Nigel had retaliated with the usual bloodsports justifications: 'Annabelle! Grow up. Foxes are responsible for incalculable damage. For God's sake, why don't you think about the poor bloody farmers and their lambs and chickens? Culling is crucial. It's all part of country life . . .'

Eventually, thanks to badgers, there had been an uneasy truce.

They had both detested the cruelty of badger-baiting. It had not been the jolly evening Charlotte had anticipated – more the dinner party from hell. Three hours of raw tension. The spoons dipped only half-heartedly into the chocolate mousse.

After a polite cup of coffee, all the guests had shuffled off, except Annabelle who had stayed the night. It had only been about half-past ten. All right, it had been mid-week and everybody did have to work the next day, but even so Charlotte's hostess's sensibilities had been offended. She heard later they had gone round the corner to the Grenadier for a nightcap. Dreadful manners. In the bar they had undoubtedly been taking the piss out of her and Annabelle. How dare Nigel launch such a vicious attack on Annabelle – brave, beautiful, principled Annabelle? The man had been a bully. Charlotte felt as cross now as the night it had happened. After that dinner, he had telephoned her, of course. He knew *she* had money and *he* was lumbered with a disintegrating family pile in Cumberland. But she was certainly not going to marry him. He was not going to get his hands on her money. She had pointedly not returned any of his calls.

Charlotte sprinkled the urns and hanging baskets.

A year later she had seen a caption under one of those boring photographs in *Country Life*:

> 'The engagement is announced between Miss Antonia
> Lawrence and Major Nigel Shawcroft.'

The no-hoper in pearls had gazed out from Daddy's-paid-for spread. Antonia, all teeth and ears, looked like a horse. But Daddy had got rid of an embarrassingly plain daughter; Antonia had got her man; Nigel had finally got his promotion to Major and got his hands on an inheritance. Good luck to them – they looked as if they deserved each other.

Savagely, Charlotte shoved the nozzle of the hose down into the roots of her best climbing rose, and checked for any signs of blackspot. She realized she, too, was thirsty. Looking at her watch, she thought: Damn, I've missed the weather forecast. She moved indoors, taking off the gardening gloves, and poured herself a bitter lemon.

Men. When she had been a young thing, they had come and

gone – some keener than others. There had been a handful of service chaps, a quite nice submariner, a baby wannabe politician, a Scottish earl who was one grouse short of a moor. He had seemed to spend most of his time in a shed. Oh, she had forgotten the gorgeous, perpetually skint actor and his constant refrain: 'Charlie, I'm seriously short of cash.' There had also been the dull, the sullen, the flamboyant, her parents' favourites, and the occasional social-climber.

Some had been after her trust fund. Some had concealed it better than others.

Now, her early-twenties seemed such a long time ago. But even then, she reassured herself, she had always been in control. Had she ever been in love?

She dropped some ice into her glass and took the drink back outside to catch the last of the Chelsea sunshine. She mulled over the word 'engaged'. Had she ever wanted to be 'engaged'? It sounded like a public loo at Victoria Station. When she had been twenty-seven, her parents had started putting on the none-too-subtle thumbscrews. Her marriage was their priority.

'Time to get on with WRM – What Really Matters. Settling down.'

Brother Henry had, of course, joined in. Ever alert for a sister-baiting opportunity, he had said of the Earl: 'C' mon, Charlotte. How about a title? He's not *that* bad and you might even get to like his shed. What does he keep in there – Mummy?'

Although four years younger than her, Henry spent most of his time sniggering at her. When he grew tired of her carefully concealed irritation, he usually sloped off with his friends to hunt, shoot, play tennis.

She sipped her drink. Why had he always left her behind? The gang had never once invited her along, not even to sit on the river bank while they fished.

The only man she had ever really wanted had been Hugh, Henry's best friend and best man, now married to someone else. He had never given her a second look. She gave some ground elder another yank and fell back, bruising her bottom on the patio tiles. Hugh had three children now: a girl, a boy and a Down's Syndrome. Serve him right.

David drifted into her mind. Even after all these years, she felt her face redden. It didn't matter. There was no one there to see her embarrassment. She realized she was blinking nervously and her arms were goose-pimpled. After all this time, the memory of Lady McIntyre could still have this effect on her. That conversation had been awful. She had been totally unprepared for it after the lunch in Scotland.

Lady McIntyre, her mother's oldest friend, had watched her closely over the picnic. Charlotte had been only too aware of the raptor's eyes flickering between herself and David, Lady McIntyre's eldest son and heir. After coffee, the stroll around the grounds *à deux* had obviously been carefully planned.

'As you know, Charlotte, our families have been friends for nearly two hundred years,' Lady McIntyre had reminded her.

The rhododendrons had been out, creating a magenta corridor along the path. The sunshine had picked out the dancing midges. Spring in Scotland. They had strolled, supposedly casually, while the men, according to their age, played croquet or slept off lunch. She was wondering now if David had ever known what his mother was about to unleash on her. Surely, *surely* not?

Nearly six feet tall, Lady McIntyre was an imposing figure, known for her straight talking. The estate workers always said: 'Aye, Her Ladyship speaks as she finds. Aye.'

True to form that day, she had come straight out with her carefully prepared speech. Walking slowly, arm in arm, she had given Charlotte only a one-sentence buffer between an innocent sunny afternoon's stroll and abject embarrassment.

'Now, Charlotte, we have a slight family problem. Charles and I have been worrying about David and his future. I don't want you to be shocked by what I'm about to say. But, my dear, there is no way of putting this delicately.'

At twenty-three she remembered how she had frozen inside. What *was* Mother's friend about to come out with?

'Poor David . . .' Lady McIntyre had said, squeezing her arm. 'Poor David unfortunately has a very small willy.'

She had turned slyly to see Charlotte's reaction to this bomb-shell.

'And, Charlotte, when I say small, I mean *very* small.'

To illustrate the point, she had held up half her arthritic thumb.

'Ever since he was of an age for such things to matter, his father

– you know what Charles is like, not exactly a man to let the grass grow under his feet – has been very worried about him and his future. So much so,' she had added conspiratorially, 'he sent David off to some woman in Paris. I won't trouble you, darling, with the sordid details. All Charles said to me is what *little* David has, at least he's been taught to make the most of.'

She had sighed, relieved. She had said it. Charlotte remembered feeling sick.

'It's very much the Edward-Wallis Simpson syndrome,' Lady McIntyre had continued. 'But you, Charlotte, are probably too young to have heard those 1930s rumours.'

She remembered feeling a hundred per cent certain that something was about to be expected of her.

'Charlotte,' Lady McIntyre had said, her voice softening, 'your mother and I always hoped you and David would marry one day. You would be so good for him. I know he likes you, but he's shy and inhibited . . . needs a strong woman to take the initiative.'

She had paused to swat off some midges congregating around her grey hair, adding: 'I felt I owed it to you to speak plainly. But, Charlotte, when you get to my age, you'll appreciate that this sex business really is secondary. David can *certainly* give you children . . . Oh, dear, I should have said that earlier. He's all right in that department, but I don't think you'll ever find him . . .' she had hesitated, groping for the right phrase 'a bull in the lover department. Not a David Niven or a Richard Todd,' she had added incongruously.

Then, for the first time on the walk, Lady McIntyre had stopped and looked Charlotte straight in the eyes, the powdered lines of her own face picked out in the harsh sunlight.

'Darling, you really would be *so* good for him. You're so well organized.' She paused, looking down at a patch of moss. 'You would give him confidence. You would cope so effortlessly with the estate.' She lowered her eyes again. 'You've got the fortune, David's got the title. It could all be so perfect.' She had squeezed Charlotte's arm again, trying to convince her. 'My son is truly a lovely boy – a lovely man,' she had corrected herself. 'Charlotte, it's not been easy for me to say all this. It's truly not easy to admit your son is . . . imperfectly endowed. But I wanted, for your late mother's sake, to be absolutely frank with you. I truly hope you will soon be our daughter-in-law. Now, my dear, don't say anything just now. Take time to think about what I've said.'

Briskly changing the subject, she wafted a hand towards her Angus cattle, grazing by the Spey.

'They're in wonderful condition, aren't they? Better than last year. After London, Ballindalloch must seem so peaceful for you.'

Charlotte remembered she had not noticed the cows – her eyes had been riveted on the bull's massive testicles.

Chapter Five

❦

It was a sunny Friday morning. Bright light was picking up the rosy japonica outside, and the tulips in the window-boxes were grimly hanging on to life. By tomorrow, they would have lost their bravado and their red heads would be dipped in surrender to oncoming summer.

Charlotte had just had a shower and was sitting in the kitchen in her bathrobe, hair still wet, hands round a mug of freshly ground coffee. This aroma was so evocative of childhood. Papa had always adored coffee. She could picture him still at the long oak table, tutting at *The Times*, muttering: 'The Government's gone mad.' He would strike the paper with his signet ring. 'What are they playing at? What a bunch! When I next see Wheatcroft in town, I'll tell him exactly what I think of him and his idiotic agricultural policies. The man's an idiot!'

Lost in his newspaper, he had rarely acknowledged her morning kiss. When he had, it had been with a grunted, 'Mornin', Charlotte.'

She made some toast and sat down again at the table. Father had been born into the era of silly names: 'Fruity Metcalf', 'Bomber Harris', 'Spinky Smythe', 'Wally Wallace'.

When exactly, she wondered, had he tired of Mother's Thuds? When had he absented himself from the marital bed, the nursery and the estate? All she could remember now was that eventually he was at home less and less. He had never neglected estate business, but had done more and more by phone from London. One day, she recalled, during one of his infrequent visits to the country, he had brought home a tall elegant woman with severe dark hair peeping from beneath an exotic snood. This had fascinated her. How did it stay up? How did the netting stay on?

Then suddenly, with no warning, Papa had come back home again.

Now, grown-up, she could understand why he had changed tack. Mother, more and more in the grip of the bottle, had totally withdrawn to her own quarters. Meals went up on a tray. All embarrassments were confined to her bedroom. She was never seen in the drawing-room again. No visitors. It had been safe for Papa to come home again. With renewed enthusiasm, he had thrown himself back into the work of the estate.

Charlotte flinched, swirling the coffee around the bottom of the mug. Well, there had been *one* change – his mistresses. Every Friday night, a crunching of gravel announced the latest arrival. Occasionally the mistresses had become over-familiar with her, trying to take Mother's place, coming out with: 'Charlotte, you *can't* wear that.' Or: 'Why are you so sulky?' And there had been the dismissals: 'Go and see Cook. Your father and I want to talk.'

Eventually, a rumour had flown around the estate: Lord Pierce was *seriously* in love. This mistress was a charming cultured expert on Georgian silver. Mother, if she had known of her existence, had been too busy unscrewing bottle tops to care.

This mistress had thrown herself into making life more comfortable for her lover. The wing of the house he had made his own had been renovated and decorated. Charlotte remembered one day stumbling upon rejected stags' heads and sagging chairs in the courtyard. Vans had arrived from London spilling out sofas, armchairs and curtains in unusually vibrant colours. Strange abstract sculptures had arrived, and trees for *inside* the house. At fourteen, she had found it bizarre.

Sitting there, she wondered if she should have told Mother about all the comings and goings? But Papa had been so happy – almost transformed – and, prodded by the mistress, had even noticed Charlotte more. That period had not been so bad. How long had it lasted? Three years – perhaps four? He had picked up his responsibilities, good works and local politics – faced up to the interminable committees. Father had once again become a solid pillar of the Establishment.

Then one weekend it had all gone sour. The mistress had left. Charlotte and Henry had never been given an explanation.

Looking back on it now, she realized her father had lost the love of his life. Shortly after this, he had learned of the death of his best friend who had broken his neck in a polo accident. Then there had been some kind of financial disaster in the futures market. Of course, Papa had not told her *anything* about this. It had always been left to her to pick up the fag-ends of family news from the only too obliging staff. In country houses there were no secrets.

One lightning-streaked Wednesday in February Papa had called his favourite springer spaniel, Hamish, and strode off at dawn into the woods where he had shot first the dog, then himself. True to form, there had been no note, no explanation, no backward glance. He had been fifty-six.

With sudden decisiveness, Charlotte pushed away the empty coffee mug and stood up.

Had she anguished over her father's suicide? The shock of that day had the power to rock her even now. There had been sleepless nights, nightmares, and all the whys? But had she ever really loved him? He had never encouraged her to love him – never pushed her on a swing, remembered her birthday, even bothered to see her off to school. But he had not been a bad man. He, like Mother, she thought charitably, had been a victim of the English class system. He had not known how to hug, tease or tickle.

She suddenly felt exasperated. A bullet had cheated her of the father she had never known. Brilliant on wine, politics, travel, dogs and horses, Papa had been an ace raconteur and witty joke-teller, but hopeless at *intimate* conversation. Then, by his own hand, he had taken himself away from her. Like an adopted child, she wanted to know who her real father was. But it was too late. For her, it always seemed too late. She would never know now. Maybe there hadn't been anything else to know?

Charlotte felt bleak. Outside the sun was shining. She didn't have to go to the BBC today. She was not – *absolutely not* –

going to waste her free time on unhappy memories, self-pity, or, worse, self-analysis. If she stayed in, by lunchtime she would be blaming herself for her father's death. She could ring Therese? She hesitated. No, she might get Mick. She didn't want to talk to him. She crossed to her bag, checked for credit cards and keys. Get a life. She headed out for the short walk to Harrods.

Walking slowly down Sloane Street, she paused to look at some amber pendants and silver bracelets. She could, of course, afford them, but she had all the trinkets she needed. What she lacked were the real things in life – the things others took for granted. Her parents had left her an enviable trust fund, a bulging bank account, but she knew for certain she was emotionally in the red.

Unbidden, memories rose again of Sally, Joanna and Daisy – their love and acceptance of each other. She remembered Sally's maternal chiding: 'Come back, you two . . . you're as daft as brushes.'

It had all been such innocent fun: love given freely, love received and returned – no charge. Yes, childhood should mean fun.

She crossed from one side of Sloane Street to the other against the lights, weaving between a bus and a taxi, remembering the day her father had called her into his study. The Snood had long ago been replaced by the Young Blonde, who was soon to be replaced by the Redhead, then the next, and the next. They seemed to be getting younger and younger.

'Charlotte,' her father had said, 'it's time you went off to school, young lady.' He had taken a sip of his whisky and poked the fire with his foot. 'You'll like St Margaret's. It's miles away, of course . . . but never mind, can't be helped. Your cousin Annabelle is head of something there – head of house, milk-monitors, hockey sticks . . . something like that. She'll keep an eye on you – show you the ropes. Your uniform's been arranged. Your governess has been told . . . no love lost between you and Govvie, eh!' he had quipped, actually smiling at her. 'You go in three weeks.' He had stood warming his bottom by the fire, a smell of plus-fours and apple-logs pervading the room. 'I'll see you off, of course. I promise.'

Miserably, she had let herself out of the oak-panelled room. She knew he would not. If he had never remembered her birthday, he certainly wouldn't remember the date his only daughter would be going off to boarding school. That would be asking too much.

Father had a conveniently selective memory. Probably he would be out fishing.

She had *never* been to school – had always been educated at home. She had been right, though. On that dreadful day Papa had not been around. Only Miss Frost, her unloved, unmourned governess, who had never liked her anyway, had seen her off. Cook, the only one in tears, had stayed in the kitchen after briskly shoving a bag of home-made biscuits into Charlotte's hand.

'For the journey,' she had said, choked.

In the car, white and pinched, Charlotte had managed a shaky wave goodbye. Goodbye to what? Hallo to what?

A ten-line letter had arrived for her about a month later. Her father had finally remembered her and got round to writing.

The three-hour journey had transported her from the world she knew to a world she did not. As the family chauffeur finally switched off the ignition, she realized how nauseous she felt. She was shaking with nerves – determined not to wet her pants. The biscuits lay uneaten on her lap, crumbled by her anxious fingers. She just did not know what was going to be expected of her. The new uniform felt stiff, like a straitjacket, and had a funny smell. As she waited forlornly in the hall for matron, who was allocating dormitories to the new arrivals, she saw two other late-comers.

Charlotte continued walking along Sloane Street, suddenly remembering something she had learned in a Nature class. The first thing a duckling sees at birth becomes its mother. It could be a boot, a balloon, but hopefully something natural to waddle after, like another duck or chicken.

In her displaced refugee state that first day at St Margaret's she had seen Barty and Therese and had waddled off after them. They had not known it then – did not know it now – but from that first sighting during that terrifying wait for Matron they had become the two most important people in her life.

That moment had been crucial. They were her first real friends. There was nothing Charlotte would not have done then – or now – to safeguard their friendship. Nobody she would not have sacrificed – then or now – if she felt that friendship threatened. She had always known that other people would come and go, zig-zagging in and out of her friends' lives. But what they must not do was threaten her friendship. If they did, any *serious* interlopers would have to be persuaded to go. *She would persuade them.*

Within minutes of arrival at St Margaret's, she had found the Family she had never had.

Now, as she gazed unseeing into one of Harrods' windows, she could put that thought into mature perspective. What counted for her was friendship – *not* passion. Passion was smelly, damp, uncomfortable – embarrassing afterwards. She had seen enough of *that* at home. Passion equalled betrayal. Friendship was what really mattered to her. Friendship lasted. Passion didn't. Seeing her reflection in the window, she knew *that* with certainty.

At long last, at St Margaret's, she had found something worth hanging on to and living for – Barty and Therese.

Reaching for her Gold Card, Charlotte entered Harrods.

Chapter Six

꧁꧂

Some days she woke up wanting to do it. Others days she didn't.
This was a 'didn't' day. Some days she would willingly have returned
the broadcast fee in exchange for sleep.

As she lay in the warm bed, having turned off the seven o'clock
alarm, Charlotte's imagination went into over-drive. Wouldn't it be
lovely if the phone rang and crashed into her sleep-dead brain? The
BBC saying she did not have to come in.

'Darling,' Felicity, her producer, would say, 'the programme's
scrapped. You must have heard the News? The Queen Mum
snuffed it in the night.'

BBC producers were always expecting the Queen Mum to die.

'It's sombre music,' Felicity would go on, 'and black-plumed
horses time.'

Charlotte snuggled down in bed, imagining the exchanging courtesies.

'What a marvellous woman. What a life. What a disappointment
her grandchildren must have been to her.'

On the 'what-a-trooper-during-the-Blitz note' she would be able to
replace the receiver and reward herself with a victory roll in bed.

Unfortunately, the phone on the bedside table remained silent.
Ah, well . . . she sighed. She didn't really wish the Queen Mother
any harm, and grudgingly acknowledged she had to get up. She was
on air at eleven o'clock.

After a shower, she petulantly pulled up one leg of her tights. Anyway, the Queen Mother would never oblige by bowing out on *her* days – Tuesday or Thursday mornings. She tugged at the reluctant gusset of her tights. Bloody things.

When she was actually on air, she was fine. She just, well, let's face it, didn't really like doing it. At the BBC, she kept seriously quiet about being seriously rich. During a recession, it was important to be seen to be doing something. Henry had lectured her on that: 'Charlotte,' he had said, 'if you're not careful, you'll turn into one of those ladies who lunch.' Typical of Henry – Exocet-like – he had thrown in: 'You'll get fat'.

After that, she remembered, she hadn't eaten for three days.

'Concentrate on positive things' – that's what she told her listeners.

Secretly she found the BBC team threatening – especially Felicity. Sally, the assistant producer, was no trouble, but the four researchers were younger, twenty-eightish, no make-up, long skirts, big boots – she suspected unwashed sweaters – cropped heads, brains by the yard.

In the early-June morning, the mirror threw back Charlotte's designer dress and expensive earrings and necklace. She didn't feel it, but the mirror was telling her she looked good. She glanced down at her immaculate black briefcase. The Team carried their lives – personal and professional – in Sainsbury's bags and coffee-stained folders. Brains they might have, but what about breeding? What's the point of an Oxford first in Egyptology if you don't live next to a ruddy pyramid? Charlotte knew she was being grumpy – a tranquillizer might help.

More roughly than usual she dabbed an extra bit of camouflage on the tiny broken vein on her right cheek. A bit of 'lippy', some lacquer, some breakfast, and she would be ready to go. She checked her bag for keys, her shoulders for imaginary dandruff, and made a mental checklist: letters to post, nothing to defrost. She wouldn't be eating tonight – echoes of Henry's 'you'll get fat' – she was having lunch with one of the girls.

Goodbye to privacy. The slam of the door demanded her mask be put on.

Waving to a neighbour, she thought: Next time I put the key back in the lock I will be home safe.

Being an adult was hell.

Chapter Seven

~~~

BBC studios are like wombs. Once you're in, you're in. Only when your allocated broadcasting time is up can you come out.

Fiddling for her dongle, Charlotte flashed the inch of black plastic across the white magnetic square, and flashed a token smile at the Radio 3 continuity announcer coming out.

The security door quickly but slyly opened, allowing the chosen Dongled Ones entrance and exit. This glass door, Charlotte reflected, was meant to provide protection for the gobs-on-sticks working for the five BBC network radio stations, and to prevent unlawful access to the all-powerful microphones. Behind the protective glass, life was so normal that visitors were invariably disappointed. Industrial, made-to-last coffee-stained carpet, chosen by committee, a cooler machine dispensing water and germs, occasional trays of forlorn sandwiches and leftover glasses of white wine. All remnants of post-programme adrenaline, these were automatically left for somebody else to clear up.

As she walked down the corridor to her own studio, the door to the Gents opened. Peering down at himself, a Radio 4 Rottweiler was re-jigging his zip. He knew her but, embarrassed about being seen doing something personal, feigned blindness.

Charlotte heaved her shoulder at the heavy studio door. Reluctantly, it moved inwards revealing neon lights and busy people around the studio console. It always reminded her of an aircraft's flight deck.

Hell, she couldn't remember the studio manager's name and she had worked with him for at least two years. Was it Jason or Robin? The 'How-are-yous' flowed like melted butter. Putting down her briefcase she fiddled around, playing for time. The cavalry came to the rescue. One of the Team, Chrissie – young, confident, eagle-eyed for any weakness in their Agony Aunt – slid in the missing name.

'Jason's doing us today,' she said, adding, 'and, true to form, the gannet has eaten most of the guest sandwiches.'

'On my salary,' he defended himself, 'I need subsidizing! The egg-and-cress ones were *very* good.' He laughed. 'Charlotte, sorry, I can't remember, d'you have a mike shield?'

'Yes,' she said.

She knew she sometimes sounded sibilant.

She accepted a coffee, left the cubicle and went into the studio. There was half-an-hour to go before they went on air. They had talked on the phone the previous day, so she only needed a cursory check that Madeleine's questions tallied with her scripted answers. As usual the researchers had done all the work, ringing up the caring organizations and the usual subject experts.

Jason went into action, asking them for voice-level checks. Madeleine, the presenter, always invited Charlotte to go first. With CDs loaded in the machines, they still had five minutes to go to the green light.

They settled behind their microphones, facing each other. Charlotte watched Madeleine talking on the intercom to the News Desk. She was recounting a silly story about a man with a snake that had bitten his wife's bottom and would not let go. Madeleine, she thought, was rather common and pushy. This was not one of her good-looking days. She seemed worn out. What had she been up to? There had been rumours that she was having an affair with a man in the Sports Room.

The news jingle was Charlotte's cue to concentrate – focus. She knew the first question was from a listener in Blackburn worried about a school reunion where she knew she would meet the boy she had sat next to in class. Later, after a chance meeting, he had become her lover. The affair had nearly wrecked her marriage and she had almost decided to leave her husband for him. She wanted to go to the reunion and meet up with everyone else, but knew that on her side the old flame could easily be rekindled. Sexually, her marriage had never been really satisfactory and she still fantasized about the other man. Was the risk of seeing him again too great?

Madeleine, slowly and caringly – she didn't really give a damn – read out the listener's letter, ending with: 'What advice would you give this listener from Lancashire, Charlotte?'

She looked down at her scripted answer. This one, the experts had advised her, needed a firm hand rather than the more usual sympathy and compassion.

'You're playing with fire, aren't you?' she began. 'And I think you know that. Are you really willing to risk your marriage? Just think of the consequences. In your letter you say you have two children. What would happen to them – and your husband – if you broke up? Maybe the question you *should* be asking me is how to improve your sex life.'

She always hated talking about sex, but it was part of the job.

Madeleine, the star, could never keep quiet for long, always loved playing devil's advocate.

'But, Charlotte,' she interrupted, 'the school reunion could be completely innocent. Provided our listener decides not to pick up the reins of the relationship, she *could* go and have a good time.'

Charlotte came back with her scripted reply. Luckily it fitted the unscripted interruption.

'The very fact she has written to us – and you've got the letter in your hand, Madeleine – is an admission of her weakness. She knows she will be tempted. My advice would be that this is potentially a very dangerous situation. Why put yourself in it? Is a school reunion really worth risking all you've got now, and restarting all the anguish you experienced last time? I really do feel that A: you should not go; B: the question you should be asking is how to improve your sex life with your husband. Do get in touch with Relate – Madeleine will give the address at the end of the programme.'

An hour later – sex, sex, sex – the programme had passed in a flash, and Charlotte and Madeleine had thrown off their head-phones.

Another programme done – and in the ether.

Jason came in, eating the remaining sandwich.

'Here's the "snoop" tape,' he said.

As always, the whole programme had been recorded for posterity in case there was any legal come-back.

Charlotte and Madeleine rarely went out to lunch. The programme was the only thing they had in common. After the usual polite goodbyes, the obliging dongle let her out of the air-conditioned BBC and into a pleasantly warm June day.

From the studio she had cancelled her lunch date. She didn't feel like being with anybody. What she needed was a bit of space, a real cup of coffee and a sandwich that Jason had not fingered. She loved the view from The Heights Bar and Restaurant in St George's Hotel next-door to Broadcasting House. Fergus there knew exactly what she wanted.

By the time she emerged from the Ladies, the plate of sandwiches and the small cafetière were on the glass-topped table. Charlotte sat back on the sofa, feeling relaxed, and reviewed her performance. Only four stumbles, and Felicity had reassured her: 'Don't worry. Nobody would have noticed. You just sounded natural.'

She sipped her coffee. What was it about Felicity? Why didn't she trust what the woman said? Charlotte was quite certain she knew and resented the fact that Henry had pulled strings and got his sister her job.

After the predictable Eton-Oxbridge path, and, of course, with family connections, Henry himself had flourished. She looked back jealously on her brother's career. Big in the City, he was now also a Governor of the BBC – Financial Controller (Radio).

'Not bad,' he said, 'for thirty-eight.'

He was six foot one, had green eyes, thick sandy hair, and, she supposed, was quite attractive to women. Whatever Henry was doing, he was always immaculately turned out. If he was going shooting, he was the country gentleman in tweeds; wheeler-dealing in the City, his shark-like instincts were always perfectly concealed by one or other of his pin-stripe suits. His trademark was the ever-present red silk handkerchief.

She knew there had been a period when he was concerned about her being rudderless.

'The trouble with you, Charlotte, is oodles of money and too much time on your hands,' he had said. 'What you need is a job.'

God, she thought, he was always so patronizing, but she knew she had been a bit wobbly around that time.

A week later, Henry had telephoned to say he had pulled strings and got her a job in the Agony Aunt department of a woman's magazine. She had panicked, but he had insisted.

After about six months, she supposed, she had started to enjoy it. A year later, in another Svengali telephone call Henry considered it would be good for her to get into the BBC – and he had the contacts to make sure she was foisted on to Felicity and the programme.

Today's show had been fine, but the listener's letter about school reunions had rattled her, taken her down a personal path.

What would she feel about being reunited with all her old schoolfriends at St Margaret's? They would be gathered in the hall, would traipse en masse to the biology lab, the cookery wing, the gym. Like a Joyce Grenfell sketch, pupils would meet retired teachers with whoops of 'Mamselle', and 'Good God, weren't you Dippy Dawkins? Did you *ever* become a scientist?'

She shuddered with horror, but comforted herself with the thought that some 'old girls' went to reunions, some 'old girls' didn't.

Out of the corner of her eye, she could see a journalist from the *Daily Mail* entering the lounge. He was obviously meeting someone. If he saw her, he would certainly force a glass of wine on her in the hope of some BBC gossip. It was time to go.

Swiftly she got up, realizing she was not fleeing the journalist but the mental image of a school reunion at St Margaret's.

For her, there were very private reasons why *that* must never happen.

It would be a nightmare come true.

Chapter Eight

⌖

Once back home, Charlotte reluctantly picked up a folder full of unopened bills and mail, and took it out on to the terrace. Analysing herself, she realized it was a quirk of her character that she always put off opening letters unless she recognized familiar handwriting.

The buff folder lay there on the garden table – unopened, accusing. She wanted to wallow in memories of St Margaret's, but knew she would have to make a start on the letters. The Season was in full swing, the boring hamster-wheel of invitations coming in for Trooping the Colour, Royal Ascot, Henley Royal Regatta, the Curragh in Dublin. .

She had done it all before – done it with the same round of people, the same car rugs, the same hampers. She was fed up with going through the grown-up motions.

Most people, she knew, could not wait to grow up. *Not her.* Her schooldays *really* had been the happiest days of her life. Matron had replaced Cook. All the girls had had a crush on Miss Leeson who taught gym and Mr McDougal who taught tennis and maths. Looking back, he could only have been about nineteen. She had thought he was madly in love with her. Looking back closer still, she envisaged herself at fourteen – the eczema legs, braces and perpetually anxious expression. At tennis, she had no ball-sense whatsoever. Once they saw him opening his car door for Miss Leeson. 'We're off to the pictures,' he had called out, as the row of schoolgirls died of jealousy. They would have killed to be in the back seat of that car.

When she had been there, St Margaret's had had an impressive roll-call. The ivy-covered Georgian building, home to the biggest spiders she had ever seen, had held educational court to the Prime Minister of Tobago's daughter, their own Prime Minister's conceited offspring, and a handful of pleasant but plump foreign princesses. Charlotte's group had sneered at the New Money – the brash millionaires' daughters who spoke with a twang. Their fathers had spent a fortune on elocution lessons. The girls had still left with a twang.

Charlotte gave up on the file and shut it. She was enjoying herself. The sun was still shining. When they were seventeen, she remembered, one anorexic had tried to burn down the school kitchens and had nearly succeeded. They discovered years later that her father was a Gnome of Zurich. Greta, the anorexic, had boasted that Daddy had ordered her a Porsche. They had all been terribly impressed by that. In the holidays, she had a grown-up boyfriend – a drummer in a pop group. St Margaret's did not hold much interest for *her*. Burning down the kitchens had been part of her great escape plan.

Charlotte had learned a lot from that incident. If Greta could make things happen, so could she.

After the kitchen débâcle Greta had been expelled and had left in Daddy's Rolls-Royce, winking and grinning from the back seat. She had beaten the public-school Establishment, outwitted the staff and her parents. She had won.

The three of them – Barty, Therese and Charlotte – had hidden behind the hedge and waved her off down the drive, back home to Switzerland and her drummer.

Deflated, they had gone into supper. Despite the fire, the cooks had managed to cobble up the usual Wednesday supper: cow-pats and frogs' spawn.

Chapter Nine

'Two's company, three's a crowd.'

Barty and Therese had been at St Margaret's together from the age of eight. Charlotte's arrival at thirteen, and her determination to make their relationship a triangle, had initially been resisted by both of them. To begin with, they had not welcomed her attempts to ingratiate herself into the tight little duo.

She looked up. There was a spat going on in her bird bath. A robin, territorial little chap, was seeing off a blue tit. Needless to say, he won. And so had she with Barty and Therese.

The sharing of her ample pocket money with Barty had been an inspired idea. Scholarship girls like Barty were always impoverished. It had given Charlotte the *entrée* she had so desperately wanted. It would not have worked with Therese whose family was almost as aristocratic and wealthy as hers. It had taken an interminable term – and an awful lot of pocket money and crawling – to buy her way in. Then – bliss. Eventually even Therese had accepted her.

All right, she had remained at the base of the triangle, always third, the green horn, but she had been accepted. They had soon become known, by staff and pupils alike, as the 'Gang of Three'. They had been reduced to uncontrollable schoolgirlish giggles by the same things, and had done detention together. Yes, detention had been a big bond.

A year later, any initial animosity forgotten, the three of them had been inseparable. They had gone everywhere in convoy, managed to share the same dorm, the same specialist subjects and hobbies. During *exeats*, they had swopped clothes. Therese had always invited them home for half-terms, and school holidays in Wales. That had been a plus.

Because of Mother, Charlotte had lied that her parents were always abroad, that the house was being renovated or someone was sick, and she could not invite them back to her place.

Barty had come out with it straight: 'You can't come to *me*. We've only got a terrace house, bulging at the seams, in Streatham. You two would loathe it. You'd be like fish out of water.'

Charlotte looked back on the young Therese. At fifteen she had been one of the tallest girls in the class – leggy, about five foot eight. She remembered being jealous of her swinging blonde hair – held in an Alice band at the weekend, a pony-tail during the week. Those were the rules.

At eight, Therese had obviously been attracted to Barty's refreshing zest for life and the differences in their backgrounds had not counted. At St Margaret's, in the same uniform, with the same battles to fight, they had gravitated to each other and become best friends. And yet they were so different in character and personality. Even in a gym-slip, Barty couldn't disguise her bullish determination – no one was ever going to get one over *her*. Therese, though, insecure and timid at school, had carried this baggage into her adult life. Crushed by her mother's smug tweedy opinions, she had been quiet at school and never the first to volunteer a raised arm and answer. Vulnerable herself, Therese had always been the first to recognize fear and panic in others, and was always so kind.

It had been Therese who had taught Charlotte to swim in the school pool. She could see Therese now in her black school 'swims' with the badge on the front; could still feel her large, capable, reassuring hands holding her up under her tummy.

'Charlie,' she would say, 'relax. Don't be so tense. I won't let you go. Breathe. Relax. Breathe.'

She had never told Therese why she was so frightened of water; why she went rigid the moment she was in the pool; why she was so terrified of drowning. It was all Henry's fault. Once, on a seaside picnic, behind rocks, where Nanny could not see him, he had dive-bombed her and held her head under the heavy green wall of salt water until she was gasping for breath. As she lay sobbing, choking, and breathless on the shifting sand – her heart bursting – he had run off with a donkey-bray laugh and crashed down on a rug to demolish the waiting picnic.

Therese had never asked why water frightened her so much, had simply spent hours with her in the pool. They had giggled at their water-crinkled skin, their chlorine-red eyes and whooped for joy when she had finally achieved a width without arm bands. Thanks to Henry, she would never feel at ease in the water, would never go under, dive or snorkel. But, thanks to Therese, she could swim.

'You did really well today, Charlie,' Therese would say encouragingly as they stood wrapped in their sodden bath towels by the changing lockers. And, without ever realizing she had earned the eternal devotion of the person shivering alongside her, Therese would grin, break open a bar of chocolate and cheerfully reward her with half.

Yes, theirs had been a friendship forged through mutual insecurities, timidity, lack of self-confidence. But, ironically, her friendship with Therese had been forged first and foremost through what she feared and dreaded most – water.

Her thoughts moved back to Barty – darling Barty. Short dark hair, with hazel eyes flecked sea-green, Barty was five foot six-ish, enviably slim-hipped, flat-bottomed and looked fantastic in jeans. She was the first of their group to wear her father's shirts and sport Chukka boots.

After one holiday, she had returned with the latest idea from Streatham. They had found her, fully clothed in her Levis, lying in stone-cold bathwater.

'When they dry off,' she had said triumphantly, 'they'll be extra tight.'

She had been nearly blue with cold. It was a miracle some of Barty's weirder fashion ploys had not killed her.

The next term, tiring of the cold-water torture, she had been caught sewing herself into her jeans to make them drainpipes.

However much the snobs used to bitch about her, Barty McClaren had certainly thrown herself into all the advantages St Margaret's had to offer. Her father had been a South London builder and her mother, too, had had to go out to work. The parents had read a lot, and passed on their love of books to Barty. Her father had kept up his ban on television for a long time, but they had an upright piano in the front room and Barty had learned to play it.

Charlotte thought of the three grand pianos in her own home. They had been meticulously dusted but never opened, never played, not even at Christmas.

By thirteen, Barty had known what she wanted to be – a photojournalist.

Oh, yes, with her impish sense of humour, quick wits and brains, Barty had always known where she was going. Too much privilege, Charlotte rued, had been the undoing of herself and Therese. It had taken *them* another ten years after leaving school to get themselves sorted out.

Was she sorted out – even now? This negative thought instantly summoned another childhood disappointment.

It had been the end-of-term production of *The Mikado*. Barty, of course, with her beautiful voice, had got the part of Nanki-Poo. All those 'rounds' – *London's burning, London's burning, Fetch the engines, Fetch the engines* – and carol-singing round the family upright had paid off.

Charlotte had tried so hard to get the part of Yum-Yum so she could partner Barty on stage and sing duets with her. But, despite all her after-prep one-to-one singing tuition, she had *not* got the part. Angela had won the role of Yum-Yum. *She* had only achieved understudy status and prickled, even now, at the humiliation she had felt when the roles had been announced. She had also been made head of props. Nobody had entertained, for one moment, the idea that Angela might go down with a sore throat, period pain or 'flu. Red-haired, freckled, piggy-eyed, pubescently budded, Angela would be Yum-Yum.

How could Charlotte oust her from the production?

Lying in the dormitory that night, she remembered how her mind had whirled. If she 'accidentally' tripped her up, Angela wouldn't be able to get up on the stage. They couldn't have a hobbling Yum-Yum, could they? Or, what if, when the breakfast bell went, followed by the usual stampede downstairs, she shoved her enemy in the back?

Lying there in the dark throughout a sleepless night, Charlotte had known she had to do something to stop Angela getting that plum role and stage kiss. She had a terrible vision of Barty and Angela, in Japanese costume, standing hand in hand taking their final curtain-call. She had to do something in the next six weeks – but what?

The performance had drawn nearer and nearer. Everyday life had carried on: maths, geography, history, pottery, hockey . . .

'Keep your sticks *down*, girls. *D.O.W.N.* – down at your side,' Mrs Deveney, the games mistress, had shrieked down the pitch. '*Don't* carry them like lethal weapons shoulder-high.'

This often-repeated instruction, followed by a piercing whistle, had the reverse effect. Hockey, like rugby, became a no-holds-barred arena. Angela, long-sensing the intense rivalry between them, was forever charging up or down the field marking her obsessively. It was all coming back. She had had the ball, was about to pass it when she saw Angela coming to challenge her.

Instantly, she had known what to do. She had *the* answer.

Slowing down, she had let Angela catch her up. One shoulder-high back-thrust swing of her hockey stick, timed to perfection, had done the trick. *Thwack!* Screams. Red hair on the grass. Blood flowing. Other members of the team had frozen, hockey sticks drooping at their sides. The match had been forgotten. Everybody had rushed to Angela panting. Mrs Deveney had been the last to arrive from the sidelines. Blood was pouring down Angela's face from a terrible gash.

'Stand back, girls,' she had said, panicking as she knelt down. 'Are you all right, Angela?'

There had been no response.

'My God,' she had said, 'she's unconscious. Roseanne, go to the office and call for an ambulance. Run, girl! *Run.*'

Charlotte remembered how everyone had turned round and looked at her. Had she burst into tears? Yes. She remembered looking down at Angela. The left side of her face had been a sea of red in contrast to the white of her other cheek. She had been lying spreadeagled on the grass, covered in mud.

After what had seemed an eternity of people coming and going with blankets, hot-water bottles and sweet tea in the hope she would come to, the ambulance had arrived, sirens going, bumping on the pitch. Angela, on a stretcher, covered with a red blanket, had been whisked off to hospital.

That had left Charlotte the centre of attention.

'It was a terrible accident. It could have happened to any-one,' Mrs Deveney had said, shakily putting an arm around her. 'Charlotte, you *mustn't* blame yourself. Come on. Pull yourself together. I'm sure Angela will be all right. Don't cry. Girls – anyone got a hanky?'

'But . . . But . . .' She had heard her own Oscar-winning sobs. 'Will she be all right? Will she?'

Even as she had asked the question, she had been carefully concealing her real thoughts. Suppose Angela recovered in time to struggle into her kimono and hear Barty sing: '*A wandering minstrel I, a thing of rags and patches, of ballads, songs and snatches . . .*'? Would she be back in time to go on?

'*Please*, Mrs Deveney,' she had pleaded, '*please* can we go to the hospital now and see how Angela is? I want to say how sorry I am.'

Really, she had to know if Angela would come back. She had to know if, at the end of term, *she* would be the one in the wings while the whole school held its breath as Barty swept *Angela* into her Nanki-Poo arms, and kissed her in front of the whole auditorium.

'There, Charlotte. Calm down . . .' Mrs Deveney had replied. 'As soon as we receive any news from the hospital, you will be the first to hear. I'll come and find you, I promise. Now, come on, girls, there's the bell. Go and get changed.'

The robin had returned to the bird bath, Charlotte noted absently.

Looking back on that afternoon, she knew the Games Mistress's comforting words must have belied the woman's adult anxieties. After all, *she* had been in charge. How bad was the wound? How would the parents take it? Would Angela be scarred?

After that it had been the most wonderful term of Charlotte's entire school life. She alone saw the irony. *She* had done the deed, got the sympathy, got the part. *She* had played Yum-Yum. *She* had gained everything.

Angela had lost her left eye.

Chapter Ten

Angela never returned to St Margaret's. Her distraught parents had removed her to a school nearer their home, where she had become a 'day' girl. For Charlotte that had been two problems solved – she had got the part of Yum-Yum and would never have to see Angela again.

The phone was ringing inside the house. Grateful for the interruption, Charlotte went in to answer it. The nearest phone was in the kitchen.

Barty's voice bubbled down the line: 'Charlie ... great you're there! I'm at Heathrow. Just back from Paris. The job's finished a day early. Can I crash out with you tonight?'

Delighted, she felt the huge grin on her face reflected in her voice.

'Wonderful! That's marvellous. When will you get here?'

'They've got problems with a new baggage carousel. Meant to cut down terrorism,' Barty said, 'but, of course, it's got teething troubles. Right now, the bloody thing's stuck and I'm waiting for my gear. I'll just pitch up when I can, shall I? You'll be there?'

'I'll be here,' she said. 'I'm not going anywhere. Are you hungry?'

'Yes ... starving, Charlie. I've got some smelly cheese for us.' Barty laughed. 'Hold on, the carousel's moving. See you soon.'

Characteristically, she had slammed down the phone with no goodbyes.

Smiling, Charlotte replaced her receiver. Wonderful. Just what she needed. A real treat – better for being unexpected. She hadn't anticipated seeing Barty until the weekend. She *loved* spoiling her – and Therese, of course. It would take Barty a couple of hours to hack up the M4. What had she got in the fridge? The sun was streaming in. It was a salady day. Barty loved her *Salade Niçoise*. It was such fun cooking – absolutely true that food is love.

Since the phone call her introspective mood had completely evaporated. She was having a lovely time in the present. She checked the fridge. Yes, everything was there. She took out a carton of eggs and put four on to boil. She knew she had the anchovies, olives and tuna. She returned to the fridge and removed the tomatoes and green beans. She would get the salad stuff out nearer the time and cheat with a supermarket dressing. It was as good as homemade.

Everyone had their own version of *Salade Niçoise*, but Barty had always said hers was 'unbeatable'. Herbs were her secret weapon, tossed in at the last minute. Barty had said she was starving. They would have a pudding as well as the cheese.

How many times had she cooked for Barty – and Therese – in this kitchen? All the trips down memory lane, all the problems they had resolved over bottles of wine – and all the grown-up confidences they had shared since leaving school.

She was remembering one day when Barty had been unusually quiet. They had been about nineteen at the time. She had been cooking a prawn risotto. Normally, Barty would have been sitting at the kitchen table wittering on while she religiously stirred the rice and slowly fed in the stock.

'You're very quiet, Barty,' she had said over her shoulder. 'What are you thinking about?'

She recalled the creak of the chair as Barty abruptly stood up and joined her by the cooker.

'There's something I've been wanting to tell you, Charlie,' she had said, leaning against the work surface. 'To be honest, I don't think it's going to come as much of a shock.'

She remembered that, as she continued to stir, she had felt pretty certain about what was coming next. She had been right.

'I'm gay,' Barty had said, 'and I've decided to "come out" with all my friends and the people I work with.' Her eyes had brimmed defiantly. 'And I'm very happy. I've even told my parents.' She paused, suddenly shy. 'It doesn't worry *you*, Charlie, does it? It won't affect our friendship, will it?'

'Nothing in the world could affect our friendship,' she had replied, adding gently, 'I think I've always known, Barty. Nothing's changed between us. But . . . d'you mind me saying this: will it affect your work? I mean, will you lose jobs because of it when people find out?'

'Good God, no,' Barty had said, obviously relieved at how well she had taken her news. No drama. Just acceptance. 'Being gay is a plus in my circles. Many of the girls – and boys – are.'

They had the risotto and shared a lager-and-lime to celebrate.

'So all those times,' Charlotte laughed, 'when I said "Did he ring? Did he take you to the concert? Did he kiss you? . . ."'

'It was a SHE!' Barty had laughed uproariously. 'It's such a relief now I've told you. I don't have to keep covering up to you of all people, Charlie. Hey, it'll be great – you can meet my girlfriends.'

It had seemed strange, but somehow so right for Barty that they could now talk about the women, rather than the non-existent men, in her life. She had looked so at ease across the table – comfortable with herself at last. There would be no more lies. Simple really, just substitute man for woman. Easy.

'Have you got a girlfriend now?' Charlotte had ventured.

'Actually, I've had several recently,' Barty had replied, 'but there's a special one now. Have you got any ciggies?'

They had lit up and had another lager.

'Well, come on,' Charlotte had said, enjoying their new intimacy. 'Tell me about her.'

'She's older than us.'

'How old?'

'Thirty-one. She's a lecturer at the London School of Economics . . . LSE.'

'How did you meet her?'

'At a gay party. I *so* needed an older woman.' Barty had laughed. 'I was pretty green in bed – and Frances has taught me a lot.'

The eggs must be done by now. She put the saucepan under the tap and ran cold water over them. Everything else she could do at the last minute after they had had a drink. Barty would be here in just over an hour, sitting at the same table, probably in the same chair where she had admitted being gay twenty-two years ago. Charlotte started shelling the eggs, reflecting how most teenagers moved from bedsit to bedsit, from town to town, graduating to a tiny flat then a series of houses. Thanks to her family wealth, she had always lived here and had no intention of moving. Her past – and future – were here.

Far from minding that Barty had been gay, she had been *very* pleased. Look at the alternative: a husband and children. A husband could have been permanent, could have been moved anywhere and taken Barty with him. Yes, she remembered thinking at the time, Barty's sexuality was perfect. She would not have a family of her own. She would not be transported away by some man on a boss's whim. She would flit from flower to flower. Their friendship would not be threatened.

Charlotte ferreted in the fridge for a punnet of strawberries. They needed to be room temperature. Later she would douse them in pudding wine – one of Barty's favourites. She husked them first, throwing away the pile of green leaves, then, getting her favourite knife, started to slice them in half. The red hearts piled up in the cut-glass bowl.

Hearts. That last day of term at St Margaret's. *The locket.*

She nicked her finger on the sharp blade. 'Damn!' She turned on the tap and rinsed her finger in the cold water. She had not thought about that gold heart-shaped locket for a long time. A family heirloom, an Elizabethan locket, Therese's godfather had given it to her for her eighteenth birthday during their last summer term. The day they were due to leave school for ever, when all the goodbyes had been said, addresses exchanged, and all their trunks had been packed up, Therese had discovered, to her horror, that the valuable locket was missing. She knew where she had put it, she had staunchly told the headmistress, and it was no longer there. The Head had taken her very seriously, summoning all the girls into the Assembly Hall.

'Has anybody seen Therese Allinson-Smith's locket? It's a very valuable piece of jewellery, with great sentimental value, and Therese is naturally very upset about misplacing it.'

Her questions had been met by silence. Everyone present was champing to go home.

'If the locket isn't found in the next half-hour, girls – I know you'll be disappointed, but I'm afraid you will all be very late leaving because everyone will need to unpack their suitcases for a search. This locket has got to be found.'

The locket had not been found. Parents' cars started to arrive in the drive. The inference of theft had irritated everybody: parents, staff and girls. The younger ones had thought all the suspicion and mayhem was a great lark, a fantastic end to term. Staff had come out of the woodwork to help the housemistresses supervise the unpacking and searching of every trunk and bag.

In their dormitory Therese had looked on as her things had been searched first. She was distraught, and deeply embarrassed about holding everybody up. The searchers had moved systematically down the dormitory, pausing by each iron bed to check trunks on the floor and duffel-bags on the green candlewick bedspreads.

It had been Charlotte's turn next. Miss Gregson, their housemistress, had deftly continued the distasteful task of rooting through her charges' belongings, obviously hating it. Finding nothing, she had said politely: 'Thank you, Charlotte.'

After each search, there had been frantic repacking. If you had been searched you could go. The Head had not wanted parental revolt.

It had been Barty's turn next. Miss Gregson had followed the now familiar procedure and had tipped out Barty's duffel-bag. There, among the comb, the sweet wrappers, the letters and the dog-eared book, was the heavy gold locket.

For years Charlotte had blocked out the memory of the crackling tension in the dormitory that morning. Now, as she covered the strawberries with cling-film, she remembered the blank openmouthed expression on Barty's face.

She was also remembering how, as they grew older, the Triangle had become tiresome: 'Two's company, three's a crowd'. Charlotte had become increasingly fed up with always being at the bottom of the pile. She had been terrified that when they left school, Barty and Therese would gravitate back to each other and she would be left alone again, her carefully nurtured family disintegrated.

Therese had already offered Barty some studio space to practise her photography.

The doorbell rang. Barty.

Of course, Barty had not taken the locket. But she and Therese had never spoken to each other since that day. Charlotte had comforted them both, kept them separately for herself. All these years neither of them had known that she was seeing both of them. Like a spy, she had perfected a double life. She had never given anything away to either of them. Individually, both believed *she*, Charlotte, was their best friend.

Her theft and planting of the locket had worked.

Chapter Eleven

⚜

Charlotte had just made it to Waterloo in time for the 8.40 a.m. to Salisbury. If she had missed it, Uncle Victor, Papa's oldest friend, would have been in a terrible tizz-wozz. Old people hate sudden changes of plan and he didn't have a mobile phone. Normally, she was never late, but today the battery on her alarm must have died because it read 3.20 when the radio said 7.40 a.m. This had resulted in the mad dash to Waterloo – make-up could be done on the train. She just had time to grab a coffee and a cheese croissant and teeter with them down the rocking aisle. Ever since she had once landed in a famous politician's lap, she hated walking down moving trains. He had not seemed to mind, but she had felt very foolish and had gone scarlet.

Settled alone in a first-class carriage, she resisted sucking the froth from the polystyrene lid, took a sip and put the cup on the little shelf. The train was picking up speed. She loved this run and was looking forward to the familiar fields, secretive houses, nestling churches and, at Salisbury, the tweedy figure of Uncle Victor. Propped up by his stick, with his fat black Labrador – in doggy years almost as old as his master – he would be waiting to meet her from the train, in his battered pork-pie hat, with his old Volvo in the station yard. The scene was repeated four times a year. She could 'run' the lunch before it had happened: Uncle Victor giving her financial advice way past its use-by date, more relevant to the time when he had been Senior Partner in a City firm. Charlotte would smile, look interested, concerned, admire his garden, listen, then go back to London.

The cheesy croissant did what all cheesy croissants do – disintegrated. She stood up, shook the crumbs on to the floor, found the ticket for the ticket collector, and relished the thought that the next one-and-a-half hours were just for her. She could have driven down, but she wanted time to think about the Family – Therese in particular.

Saint Teresa of Avila, Saint Teresa of Lisieux, now her very own Saint Therese of Surrey. Charlotte felt her mouth quirking at the corners. They had come a long way since that Saturday afternoon at school when, arm-in-arm, they had confided their angst about the future, Therese saying: 'Do you realize, Charlie, everyone knows what they want to do . . . except us?'

'Abigail – chartered accountant. Mary – vet. Suzie – marriage. Barty – photographer,' they had recited together.

They had then made Joanna a missionary. Today, on the train, that did not seem so funny. She was one of the first women priests to have been ordained.

'You and I aren't very good at anything in particular,' Therese had said miserably. 'What will happen to us when we leave, Charlie? What are *we* going to do? Mother says I've got to do cookery, flowers, fine arts.'

She remembered commiserating: 'Oh, yeah. They're telling me the same thing. I listened at the door last holidays when my Godfather was down – you met him at Speech Day – and Papa said, I didn't catch it all but something about: "Don't know what to do with her." I missed the next bit, but it went along the lines of me eventually getting married . . .'

At fifteen, none of these options had been very exciting. Uncertain of their future, they had felt like misfits.

Charlotte looked out of the train window, registering the signs of approaching summer speeding past. The buffet trolley came and went. She gave a man who got on at Woking a filthy look. She wanted the carriage to herself. Mercifully, it did the trick, and he moved off to find another.

Yes, that afternoon had been a true bonding for her and Therese.

After leaving school, Charlotte had never allowed them to lose touch, had made sure she was Therese's best friend. They had spent hours on the phone, swopped silly postcards, gone out on occasional blind dates and ganged up on men they thought were awful. Parental influence had, of course, prevailed. They had been enrolled for the fine arts course and flowers, but had both dug their heels in at cookery. They had travelled a bit – together and separately – and drifted for longer than they should.

They met whenever possible – usually in London. Therese's shameless elitism throughout her schooldays had started to evaporate, most likely because she had been working 'just for fun' with normal people – people without money, without a 'cushion', without Mummy and Daddy's Coutts' cheque book. Dear Therese, Charlotte thought fondly, it wasn't that she was weak, it was just that – she tried to hook the right word – she was always so easily influenced. That was it.

Basingstoke. The train slowed and stopped. The station had some rather good hanging baskets, and a fine set of train-spotters lurking at the end of the platform. What did they see in their obsession? Winter and summer, flasks and anoraks, chummy notebooks at the ready, they were always there as yet another 125 shot through. After a couple of minutes Charlotte's train pulled out again.

Yes, with her wealthy, pushy, genteel parents, Therese had floundered around, not knowing who she was or what she wanted to be, and eventually came round to rejecting her parents' values and lifestyle. She was certain of one thing: she didn't want to be like them, part of the huntin', shootin', fishin' brigade.

Once Therese *had* found her vocation in life – had found not God, but animals, and set up her animal sanctuary – visiting her had been a nightmare. Charlotte had hated it then and hated it now. She would never, of course, voice such disloyal thoughts out loud to anyone. After all, Therese was her best friend. If she was happy, having found a Cause and a Conscience, then Charlotte was happy for her. Therese, once happy to be 'blooded', now died at the sight of a flattened hedgehog, kept alive cats with no ears and foxes with three legs. She recklessly threw herself in front of juggernauts of sheep and calves, feverishly recycled every scrap of paper to save a tree. She was frequently in tears at the pain of animals in the world.

When Therese remembered to eat, it was rock-hard bread with a vegetable spread. She seemed to exist on carrots; had lost at least three stone, and all personal vanity.

Yes, visiting her at the animal sanctuary had become a nightmare. Before going, Charlotte felt she had to shed all frivolity – leather jackets, conspicuous wealth, leave her sense of humour at home – and become 'politically correct'. Then, when she arrived at the sanctuary, passing through gates sporting donation boxes, she had to share what accommodation there was with blinded barn owls, orphaned fox-cubs, wingless swans and bleeding remnants of badger-baiting.

Then, to top it all, there was Mick.

Chapter Twelve

At the beginning Charlotte had not minded about Mick. She had guessed he would last perhaps two years, and certainly not become a permanent fixture in Therese's life. She had even thought he might be a good idea – save Therese, and the Family, from a more serious threat.

The train was running on time. Her coffee had gone cold. Charlotte was remembering that when Therese first met Mick about seven years ago, she had been working in a vegetarian restaurant – 'just for fun' – and was quite enjoying all the chopping and learning about herbs and spices. Charlotte had teased her about her cooking.

'You see, Therese, Mummy darling knew best after all! What did you say at St Margaret's: "I'll do the fine arts, but she can shove her Cordon Bleu"? Now, look at you – spaghetti à la sprouts with gladioli salsa.'

Ruefully, as the train gathered speed, she recalled how Therese had lost her sense of humour. Before the sanctuary years, peals of laughter had rung around the restaurant kitchen whenever Charlotte had dropped in to see her. But nowadays Therese rarely laughed. It was all tears and suffering – over cows, horses, newts, culled ducks, and puppies left in a box on a train. She had become a martyr, crucified on the Animal Cross, had lost her sense of humour, health and wealth . . . and, Charlotte felt, a little bit of her sanity.

She shook herself, consoled by the thought that at least Therese was happy in her self-sacrifice. Happy with her carrots, her soya milk, and sloshing around in animal manure. Happy with Mick.

With Therese, it seemed, all roads led back to Mick. Since his arrival, nothing had been quite the same.

The train slid out of Andover and then ground to a halt further down the line. Charlotte glanced at her watch, her thoughts returning to Mick. Whenever she was with him, she felt uncomfortable, felt he was laughing at her, sneering inwardly at her lack of principles, lack of militancy, lack of commitment. But she knew something he did not – she was totally committed to Therese and, what's more, had got there first. She had known the girl for thirty-plus years, Mick-come-lately, a piffling seven. Yet she had misjudged him. He had lasted longer than she had predicted. And during that time he had brought Therese down to living like a peasant . . .

But, Charlotte made herself add, Therese loves him, so for her sake I have to put up with him, and pray she doesn't get pregnant. That, at any rate, did not seem to be a problem. Therese appeared to have substituted animals for children. That was probably Mick's influence too.

Sex was very important to him. On a trip to London, to collect a donation Charlotte had offered for a new animal hospital, Therese had confided over lunch: 'He'll do *It* twice a day if I let him . . .'

Instinctively, she had known Therese *did* let him. Charlotte had let her imagination run riot – he probably forced her up against trees, bent her over the horse trough, and did 'It' three times on Bank Holidays.

Sitting there on the train, she was more and more conscious of Mick's increasing hold over Therese, and flinched at the thought of *their* bedroom. The small Mick-influenced room littered with old mugs of tea, roll-your-owns, yellowing newspapers, the greying sheet half on, half off the bed. There were also the jerseys, sweat-stained T-shirts, trainers with dry manure-caked soles, the odd beer bottle next to the dead pot-plant. She had brought this for them on her last visit, but neither of them had bothered to water it because both were so busy saving lives. She had once dared to mention saving human lives, but would never do that again.

Charlotte knew she was frightened of Mick. Working-class, he had been shunted from one foster home to another, never chosen for adoption. He had not had an easy childhood and had carried the damage into adult life. To her, he was like an alien. Other than Therese – whom he called 'T', which irritated Charlotte like nails on a blackboard – she and Mick had nothing in common. Her animals had been sleek gun-dogs, the *de rigueur* Jack Russell, a fat Burmese, plenty of horses and a donkey for company. All these animals had been in peak condition, had known their place.

'Dogs outside. You'll get fed when I'm ready,' Papa had barked at their pleading eyes. 'My whisky comes first.'

He had never acknowledged set feeding times except his own.

Mick's body had always unsettled Charlotte. He wasn't tall, about five foot ten, slight, but with that SAS hardness. He wore the same clothes winter and summer – sweat-stained T-shirts and filthy jeans.

'Not much point in changing them too often, is there?' he would mutter to Therese whenever she attempted to clean him up.

He never seemed to feel the cold, his only nod to winter a woolly hat. He usually walked about with a bucket in hand, a knife at his belt, and looked as if he knew exactly where he was going. Charlotte remembered the sound of his steel-capped industrial boots ringing out across the yard as, with eyes down, he avoided visiting parties of fluffy old ladies and children from local schools.

'We need to educate the young and the old dears,' Therese would say. 'Did I tell you, Charlie, we bought the wood thanks to Mrs Seymour's £70,000?'

Overhearing this, Mick had butted in: 'I clinched *that* by listening to endless gripes about her son not visiting her from London – too much trouble, too busy.'

'Yes, you did,' Therese had agreed submissively.

On her last visit, Charlotte had brought down some special vegan dishes, packed in a box, carefully wedged on the back seat of the car. They had eaten at the kitchen table, and Mick had shovelled most of it down himself. Watching him, she had thought: If his sexual appetite is as wolfish as his appetite for food, God help poor Therese.

The train was slowing down. A 125 shot past on the 'up' line. This was a good opportunity to do something about her hair. Charlotte stood up, looking in the none-too-clean carriage mirror. It was smeary – looked as if one of the cleaners had sprayed on, but not wiped off. She turned to the mirror behind her which was cleaner and combed her hair. As the train juddered into movement, she sat down again, feeling in her bag for her powder compact.

Therese and Mick had met by accident. Her mother had been suffering from depression since her husband's death and Therese, with typical kindness and generosity, had said: 'Come on, Mother. We can stay the night with aunty. Then, with the hovercraft from Folkestone, we can be in Calais and eating oysters in Boulogne by one o'clock. The air will do you good. And Daddy would have loved us to have a day out.' Mother would much rather have sat with her grief, watching racing on Channel 4, but Therese had steam-rollered her into the outing.

According to Therese, they had set off for La Belle France and a harmless plate of *fruits de mer*. Harmless! Charlotte sighed. Neither she nor Therese could have bargained on an innocent away-day culminating in her meeting Mick and his picket-line leaflets.

On the day when Mick and Therese first met, her mother, bored with waiting in the queue to get into the docks, had got out of the car to stretch her legs and have a cigarette. Therese also got out of the car.

Later, during one of her regular telephone calls, to Charlotte she had sounded different on the phone. Then, at their fortnightly lunch, she had mentioned that first meeting with Mick.

'He just came up to me and said: "D'you care about animals?" I thought he was wonderful – so strong, so determined. He's not classically good-looking, Charlie, but he's dynamic, charismatic, different . . .' Therese's voice had trailed off.

'So . . . ? What happened then?'

'Well, I was standing by the car, waiting for Mother, and he just looked at me . . .'

'Then what?' Charlotte had prompted.

'He took out a pen, wrote down a number, thrust the scrap of paper into my hand, and said over his shoulder as he walked off: "Just in case you want me." Then, as I saw Mother coming back, weaving her way between the cars, he paused and said:

"I *certainly* want *you*." Then he walked off, distributing leaflets protesting about live animal transportation.'

After this, Therese had admitted to her, the mother-and-daughter away-day had been a bit of a blur. Her mind had been hi-jacked by Mick.

Back home, she had apparently resisted picking up the telephone for four days. The rest was history. Mick was *In*, spending Therese's money on his causes, having her over the water-butt, seducing her mind and body.

Mick had proved he was very effective at distributing leaflets . . .

'The next station stop will be Salisbury. Please remember to take all your personal belongings with you when you leave the train.'

Charlotte only had her handbag to remember.

Once she had met Mick, she sensed he had his fingers in many pies, and could always be relied on to find something to protest about. She had no proof but also suspected he was the brains behind endless militant demonstrations, from motorway protests to the movement of nuclear waste. Therese had let slip a few famous names in conservation – all seemingly friends of Mick's. He had remained what he had always been – a bit of an enigma – and Charlotte had remained convinced – as she had always been – that somewhere down the line the police were involved and only too aware of his activities. If not, why on the rare occasions that she stayed for supper did the phone ring constantly, always for him? Why did he return to the table hard-faced, all pumped up, and take at least ten minutes to get back to Charlotte-baiting? In Belgravia, she was not used to being attacked at the dinner table – it was *not* the 'done' thing. Mick's abruptness, his ignorance of the usual courtesies, his lack of table manners – he never passed anything – left her breathless. He was only interested in issues. Certainly, those calls had not been invitations to whist drives.

'Salisbury . . . This is Salisbury . . .'

Predictably the train, as if hearing the announcement, had decided to take a short siesta before gathering speed for the final push into the station. Charlotte sighed. What did all this Therese and Mick stuff add up to? Privileged wealthy Therese meets determined secretive East End boy. The result: Therese has a cause and seems to relish her bit of rough. But was Mick a threat to the Family?

Every instinct and nerve told Charlotte he was, but she did not yet understand why.

As the train drew into Salisbury, she caught sight of the black Labrador and the old pork-pie hat looking more battered than ever. Dear Victor. He and Papa had been prisoners-of-war together. She picked up her handbag.

As she stepped off the train, Mick's foxy face was still imprinted on her mind. She must stay on the alert. At the moment she felt she was on standby, sensing something was about to happen. On the platform, she remonstrated with herself. How stupid. What would actually happen was Uncle Victor, coffee, a trip around the garden with a glass of dry sherry, followed by an early scampi and chips at the local pub. They would both insist on paying. The smiling figure moved down the platform towards her, waving his stick. She felt relieved – and cheered at the prospect of this avuncular diversion.

Inside, though, deep inside, she knew as she walked towards him that this was only a momentary interruption. Something *was* going to happen. It might not be next week, next month, next year, but something *was* going to happen to threaten her friendship with Therese. Charlotte was certain of that.

And she would be ready . . .

Chapter Thirteen

Charlotte had dreaded waking up this morning. Her life at the BBC had been decidedly bumpy lately. She had hit a sticky patch, been easily distracted while on air and had made a few gaffes. They had only been small ones to begin with, but then she had dropped a real clanger. She could not think of it without going first hot, then cold, then hot again. After the last mishap, Felicity, her BBC Producer, had done away with the usual 'Well done, Charlotte', and gone for her. Today, at Charlotte's invitation, she was coming for what the spin doctors called a damage-limitation lunch.

Standing in the drawing-room, nervously anticipating Felicity's arrival, Charlotte was reminding herself this lunch was serious business, that for the next few hours she would have to keep her wits about her. She might be thinking one thing, but knew she would have to mouth another. She checked her immaculate dining-room, appreciating the lavender polish, the fresh white lilies and the hoovered carpet. Josefina, from the Philippines, had been with her for ten dust-free years.

Waiting in the kitchen was the poached salmon, the mayonnaise and potato salad. The raspberry mousse was in the fridge. She checked herself in the large gilt mirror and sprayed her wrists with scent. Yes, she was ready for battle. Her opponent was Felicity, who had seen through her. Outwardly, from her reflection,

Charlotte knew she looked composed and sophisticated; inwardly, she was feeling exposed and threatened.

That woman. She felt their row rampaging through her head. Felicity – bristling with anger – spitting out the words: 'We're never going to do *that* again, Charlotte, are we?'

At the memory of that unscripted phone-in eight days ago, she shuddered. The Team had dropped in an unscheduled question because the programme needed a 'filler'. Charlotte had dried. There had been a gut-wrenching embarrassing silence; an uncomfortable clawing for sense and words that wouldn't come; then bumbling nothingness. Charlotte had felt hot with shame. She still felt hot with shame. She had delivered nothing.

After the programme, Felicity had said viciously: 'Well, you really fucked that one up, didn't you? You were deadful. What happened to you? It was a simple enough question – she only asked you about nightmares.'

Charlotte remembered how she had been struck dumb by her vision of the duckling necklace. Five years old, skipping by the pond, she had trodden on one of the tiny ducklings. Her mother had been furious. Seconds later that duckling had been strung around her neck and she had been forced to wear it as a necklace *all* day.

'That will teach you to be more careful, Charlotte,' her mother had said, cruelly.

She had known, as she slunk away, she would never forget the thudding of the duckling's warm body against her chest. By teatime, it had been cold and stiff when Cook, her only friend, removed it. After that, even at five, she knew she had grown inwards rather than outwards.

Yes, remembering that awful day she had frozen. Pauses on radio do not work. *Dumb. Dumb. Dumb.* She had been dumb. Images of her own childhood nightmares had triggered off a frozen nothingness. Dead air. She could still feel the atmosphere in the studio; hear Felicity's voice in her headphones: 'Charlotte . . . respond! Say something.'

But she had her own voices in her head. There had been no one to rescue her. Drowning, she had heard the whinging Essex voice saying: 'Nightmares . . . 'e's havin' nightmares. 'E's only four . . . I've got a new lover, but 'e won't accept 'im as his new dad. That's how 'e sees it. 'E's runnin' round like a nightmare durin' the day. Then, at night, 'e won't sleep. What d'you ... what d'you advise?'

They had come back to Charlotte. Then had come her deadly pause. The word 'nightmare' had sent her reeling back to the big house, the long passages, that dead duckling, the unwieldy shape of Cook sleeping. *Dumb. Dumb. Dumb.* She had fucked up and dried.

Had Josefina got the butter out of the fridge? Of course she had. Charlotte checked the Chablis. Yes, it was cold. Corkscrew? Yes. Glasses? Yes. She had ten minutes to wait. The bitch was coming to lunch.

After the phone-in, Felicity had called her a 'waste of space'; had finally come out in the open and accused Charlotte of getting the job through her brother.

'People like you are foisted on us,' she had snarled, 'and can't do the job without a support network. How many people does it take to keep the Honourable Charlotte Pierce on the air? Because that's how people think of you, Charlotte. Look at you – all designer suit and handbag. What you didn't know is that today's programme is up for Review Board. This reflects badly on me. I'm the fucking producer, and my fucking Agony Aunt can't speak!'

Anger had propelled Felicity on and she had stuck in the stiletto.

'You can talk, but only with a script in your hand – written by other people. Sally, Chrissie, Derek, Karen ... they do your work and you take the glory.' She breathed heavily and spat out: 'Ah, connections. But, of course, brother Henry, much loved by us at the BBC, will keep you in place ...' She had paced around the studio, white with anger. 'You're probably dining with him and the Chairman tonight, aren't you? I can hear you now. "I had a *terrible* day. That Felicity Grantham is impossible to work with."' She slammed down her polystyrene cup of coffee. The viciousness of the action splattered the Thames-like liquid on to the studio consul – a cardinal sin.

Now the bitch was coming to lunch. Charlotte had invited her. Bridges had to be mended. Felicity was very experienced and highly thought of. Felicity was in her mid-forties. Felicity was an opponent. A career woman, she had done everything from drama to current affairs, and was greatly appreciated as a 'safe pair of BBC hands'. She would never make head of anything, but she had an excellent track-record. A first in English, Charlotte thought bitchily, but a fourth in life. Health-wise, she had a history of high blood pressure – and a heart murmur.

Charlotte looked down at her immaculate nails. Felicity was very overweight – not ugly, but saggy. She had no clothes sense – no style. Sex appeal? Charlotte dismissed the idea – laughable. She actually laughed out loud. The thought of Felicity in bed with somebody was a hoot. Rumour had it she was shacked up with some rhythm-and-blues presenter though it seemed highly implausible.

She would put on some lipstick. The bitch had a vicious tongue. The bitch could bring her down. If Felicity succeeded in ousting her, what would Charlotte say at parties when people politely enquired: 'What do you do?' It was so gratifying to be able to say: 'I work for the BBC. My name is Charlotte Pierce.' The immediate recognition was so flattering. 'Oh, I thought your voice was familiar. I've heard you on the radio.'

Oh, yes, she was determined to hang on to the job.

The doorbell rang. Charlotte braced herself. This was the moment to put things right. She would be apologetic, ameliorating, would stroke Felicity's ego, tell her what a marvellous producer she was. She had her excuses ready. She settled a smile on her face and opened the door. Felicity entered. They exchanged air-kisses and moved towards the chilled white wine. The mending and patching began; the arbitration, conciliation . . . was under way.

At the table, the salmon remained untouched. The wine was going down very fast. Charlotte refilled Felicity's glass again. She had looked flushed and flustered when she came in and looked even more flushed now. Victory was in sight. If Charlotte grovelled enough, she knew she could win.

Henry might be a pain in the neck, but at this moment she acknowledged it was very useful having a brother who had become a Governor of the BBC. He had influence. She replayed images of last night's Chairman's 'do' in the Council Chamber. Around a hundred or so people: 'talent', journalists, writers and producers – and Felicity, across the room, watching. Charlotte knew Felicity had 'clocked' her last night, had witnessed the kiss from the

Director General, the kiss and familiar squeeze from the Chairman. She was pretty certain Felicity would be the loser on this one. She looked across the table. Felicity, having taken in her opulent surroundings, had visibly dwindled in confidence. She was obviously realizing she was a mere producer, an employee who could soon be dispensed with. Cuts were in the air and it would not be a clever move to upset one of the Governors. If Charlotte herself wanted to keep her job, Felicity desperately needed to keep hers. Unmarried, childless, a career woman, it was all she had.

This was the moment to put on the screws.

'Sorry I didn't get to talk to you last night,' she said, 'but I'm sure you and the Team would like to know that the Chairman said his wife listens every day and particularly enjoys *my* slot.'

Felicity visibly squirmed.

Inwardly Charlotte knew, with a soft secret comforting feeling, that Felicity had lost and she had won. Oh, yes, Felicity *would* eat her words: 'The Honourable Charlotte Pierce – a waste of space—'

She poured her guest a third glass of wine. Felicity was certainly knocking it back and her face was becoming very red. Obviously embarrassed and uncomfortable, she suddenly excused herself and retreated to the bathroom.

Charlotte sat back in the Queen Anne chair. When Felicity returned, there would be a truce. She didn't want a confrontation. It could go: 'Look, I'm sorry I let you down last week. It won't happen again.' She would pause, then add: 'I know you're cross. You could damage me, but I can damage you more . . .' That should do it.

At the coffee stage, it would end up with a mutual white flag. Life would carry on as normal. Felicity would keep *her* job, would keep quiet, protect her. Charlotte would keep *her* job – and her position. Aggression forgotten, they could both look back on a very successful lunch.

She took her first sip of wine. Yes, nothing had been eaten yet, but it was turning into a most satisfactory lunch.

Chapter Fourteen

THUD! With the wine still held in her mouth, Charlotte registered the noise. Christ, what was that? Silence. She stood up, forcing herself to swallow. She had not imagined the thud. Had Felicity slipped on the marble floor? Did Charlotte care?

Slowly, she moved upstairs, pausing to realign a painting, moving it a couple of centimetres to the left. What was she going to find? There was no sound. Holding on to the banisters, she moved across the landing. Was she becoming a drama queen, anticipating problems that were not there? She shook herself. Maybe she had imagined the thud.

She looked at the bathroom door. Should she call out? Was Felicity okay? It was always rather embarrassing interrupting people in the loo, but she had heard that THUD.

It would be one of two things. Felicity was known around the BBC as a bit of a soak. Maybe she had had a few, for Dutch courage, before she had arrived. Perhaps the tension, the prospect of a mega-row, exacerbated by the wine, had caused her to collapse. Alternatively, she could have slipped – had an accident. A cracked head, a broken bone? Oh, God, she would have to take her to Casualty. That would be the afternoon wasted, and was certainly not part of the plan.

Tentatively, she knocked on the door.

'Felicity? Are you all right?'
No response.
Slowly, she opened the door.

The guest bathroom was grey and white. Charlotte had chosen the tiles with enormous care. It flickered through her mind that the body on the floor was a perfect match for the décor. Grey-faced, blue-lipped, Felicity was lying on the marble tiles, gasping for air and clutching her chest. Charlotte could not help noticing her legs. They were like a rag-doll's splayed out in opposite directions. She had cracked her head on the side of the bath. There was a small trickle of blood slowly making a red trail down her left cheek. Her eyes were screwed up, tightly shut, as if she were in terrible pain; a tortoiseshell comb had fallen from her hair and landed by the basin pedestal. She was making odd guttural noises and was totally oblivious of being watched.

Charlotte quietly backed away from the scene in front of her – the stark clinical whiteness of the bath and basin were host to horror. Gently, she closed the bathroom door on Felicity's heart attack. She knew only too well what she should do. She should have made her comfortable, sat her up in a half-sitting position, given her an Aspirin, told her to chew it slowly, and then dialled 999.

She did none of these things.

She didn't wish Felicity harm, but if fate had decided to interfere, she would allow destiny to take its course. There were always other producers. Felicity had seen through her. Felicity had uttered the words 'waste of space'. Felicity had witnessed her on-air trauma.

Mentally, she was shrugging her shoulders, shutting out the scene in her bathroom. Bustling, capable, efficient Felicity, from the BBC, could never cope with the aftermath of a heart attack or stroke. Felicity in a wheelchair? No, she herself would not want that. Who would look after her? Fully justified, she closed the door on the contorted body.

With a few swift excuses, she had batted away all self-doubt. This heart attack was a gift. For one brief moment her eyes focused on the cream telephone, resting on the figure 9, but she paused only a second.

Her handbag was lying on the sofa. She rattled it, checking for the jingle-jangle of her house keys. They were there. She could go out and do some shopping – excuse shopping. Yes, she had always been good at decision-making. She moved to the front door. She would go out for five minutes. Closing the door behind her, she blanked out what she might find when she returned.

Charlotte would need a water-tight excuse, of course, for going out. As she walked down the street, she considered the situation. Untouched, the lunch was still on the table. What if Felicity was unconscious when she got back – or, alternatively, recovered and slumped in a chair?

She was convinced – ninety per cent certain – Felicity would be where she had left her: grey-faced and blue-lipped, and still in the bathroom. Perhaps the trickle would have turned into a pool of blood. Yes, as she walked, Charlotte became convinced that her lunch guest would be leaving her house on a stretcher.

A summer shower was splashing the pavements. She wished she had put on a scarf. Her mind was racing. *Concentrate.* She had to be opportunistic. How could she justify popping out? She could say she had written Felicity a quick note, saying: '*Back in five minutes. Forgot you were a chocoholic and I need some cigarettes!*'

It was only a five-minute walk round the corner to the Royal Court Tavern for her cigarettes and to Partridge's for the chocolate. This would give her the perfect alibi for not being in the house when Felicity collapsed. After all, she had not been there to *hear* the THUD. What Thud? They would believe her story that she was beautifully, perfectly, blissfully ignorant of Felicity's seizure in the bathroom.

Partridge's – *Providers of Good Things for the Larder* – was usually a silky-smooth shopping experience. But today its plump bowls of pâté, fine wines, spirits and rows of Gentleman's Relish irritated her. Whoever bought those little white pots nowadays? She had always hated the pungent sting of anchovy on her childhood toast – its ghastly salty fishiness. Henry had always golloped it down. She shuddered at the memory, bought the chocolates, by-passed the Sloanes taking all day to buy a tin of up-market toffee, and exited from the shop.

She was not relishing the thought of getting home and having to open the bathroom door.

'Felicity, are you all right?' she would make herself call. 'You've been in there for hours.'

Deep in thought, she had not bargained on Marina – a near-neighbour – who suddenly loomed up in front of her. They had met three weeks ago at a dinner party. Charlotte had been paired off with the dullest man in London, and the food was cold. Marina had been good fun, a gossip, an admirer – she listened to the show.

Charlotte registered her new friend's smiling features, her blue jeans, white shirt, maroon designer belt.

'Charlie, I've been meaning to give you a ring,' Marina said, delighted to see her. 'Wasn't Anthea's cooking dreadful! That second course – the chickeny thing – was stone cold. Andrew's only just recovered from it.'

On the pavement, Charlotte went through the motions of listening to Marina and bitching back. Secretly, her mind was in overdrive. Was this another heavensent opportunity? Marina could be her accomplice – a witness to the lunch and, hopefully, the body in the bathroom. They could be shocked together. Perfect. She led Marina by the nose.

'Have you had lunch?' she asked, innocently.

Marina looked momentarily surprised. 'No . . . why?'

'Well, there's someone I'd love you to meet,' she said. 'Have you got time?'

The prospect of girlie gossip, a glass of wine, meeting somebody new, obviously appealed to Marina.

'Are you sure I'm not gate-crashing?' she asked.

'Of course not. She's my producer at the BBC. I've just popped out for some chocolates for her. She's a chocoholic. Oh, come on . . . do come.'

'Okay, why not?' Marina checked her watch. 'I'll pop in for just half an hour – I've left the dog in the car.'

It was done. She and Marina walked chummily back towards the house. Charlotte's hands felt sweaty. What were they going to find? Marina was anticipating a comforting glass of wine and some nibbles; Charlotte was expecting – and *hoping* for – a dead producer.

They walked on past the shops, and rounded the corner into Eaton Square. She forced herself to make small-talk. Outside the cream-faced six-storeyed house, she said in answer to Marina's question: 'My family have always had this place – been here for ever. It's a great luxury, but so handy.' They commiserated about the parking.

In her mind, she could hear Felicity saying: 'How can you whinge about minor inconveniences like parking when you have so much?'

For Felicity, with her flat in Leytonstone and her Central Line commuting, such jibes would be natural.

But would Felicity be commenting on anything anymore? Soon, she . . . Charlotte corrected herself . . . soon *they* would know.

'Waste of space . . .' Felicity's words ricocheted around her brain. Dead, she thought. *Dead.* Felicity, please be dead.

They entered the house.

'It's lovely,' Marina gushed, looking around. 'Aren't those lilies gorgeous!'

Marie Celeste-like, the untouched lunch sat there.

'Felicity,' Charlotte shouted upstairs. 'Felicity, where are you? I've bumped into a friend.'

She turned to Marina.

'Hang on, I'll get you a glass of wine and a plate.'

Outwardly, she moved smoothly to the kitchen. Inwardly, she was fizzing with excitement. There had been no response to her call.

Carrying the wine bottle, she said to Marina: 'I think Felicity must be in the loo.'

Now she would have to play for time. She couldn't discover what had happened for at least five minutes. Manners. Manners. Echoes of the nursery and Nanny's words: 'Charlotte, always wait at least one hour before going to the lavatory in somebody else's house. It is most impolite to do such things on arrival.'

Acutely shy, she had *always* wanted to 'go', but had wriggled in torment. Impeccably behaved, she had watched the clock and done as asked. She recognized the childhood resentment which had fermented compost-like inside her for so long. Stupid. Stupid. Stupid rules. But she must not be seen to be intruding on Felicity's bathroom privacy too soon.

A bit more small talk. Then, lightly, she said to Marina: 'Bring your wine . . . I'll show you around. I'm a tiny bit worried about Felicity . . .' she added ingenuously. 'She might have got herself locked in the bathroom. While we are up there, let me show you that painting we were talking about at the party.'

Marina stood up eagerly.

'Oh, yes, I'd love to see that – Andrew was incredibly jealous when I told him on the way home you had a Lowry.'

Together they went upstairs. Marina, the dupe, was now with her to witness Felicity's body – alive or dead?

On the bathroom landing, they paused and Charlotte gently tapped at the door. There was no answer.

They looked at each other.

'She must be in there,' Charlotte whispered to Marina, calling again: 'Felicity, are you okay?' She called again louder. 'Felicity . . . are you okay?'

She turned to Marina, switching on a baffled face. Marina was picking up on her nervousness and giggled: 'Echoes of "Three Old Ladies Locked in the Lavatory" . . .'

Charlotte ignored the flip remark and said anxiously: 'I think we had better open the door. I'm really worried.'

She gently pushed it open.

Exactly as she had hoped, Felicity lay where Charlotte had left her.

She was dead. That was obvious to both of them the moment they opened the door. Marina gave a half-scream. Shock cut off the rest of her cry. They looked at each other.

'Oh, my God!' said Charlotte as Marina took a step backwards. She knelt down, forcing herself to search for the non-existent pulse.

'Oh, my God . . .' Marina was repeating. 'Is she . . . ? She's dead, isn't she?'

'Yes,' Charlotte replied, bursting into tears of relief. 'She's dead.'

The afternoon passed in a blur of ambulance sirens and insincere calls to BBC colleagues. Charlotte had cried for her ex-producer, mouthing: 'Poor Felicity. Of course, she always had heart troubles.'

They had comforted each other, the PA revealing down the phone: 'She had tests only last week, but didn't want anyone to be told. You know what the BBC's like. She was paranoid about being side-lined.'

'Yes,' Charlotte sympathized, 'but I don't think any of us could have expected this. It's been such a shock – especially for me. She was just here for lunch. Finding her in the bathroom . . .'

Marina had forgotten the dog in the car and stayed to commiserate.

'Were you close?' she kept asking. 'How long had you worked together? How old was she?'

Charlotte had bathed in all the sympathy. Her bathroom had become the focus of attention – and so had *she*. Her life's ambition had been trying to lure the spotlight on to *her* when its glow always seemed to light up other people. It was all so reminiscent of St Margaret's – that afternoon when she had blinded Angela.

There are moments in life, she thought, when, whether we want to or not, we need to give destiny a nudge. There are other moments when life gives *us* a nudge, when we need hardly lift a finger to make something happen. The lunch with Felicity was one of *these* occasions – the gods had chuckled, presenting opportunities not to be missed. All that had been necessary was to 'go with the flow'. She had seized the moment.

Yes, this afternoon the gods had smiled on her. A fitting finish to Felicity who had dared call her 'A rich bitch . . . a waste of space . . .'

When Marina and the uniforms had all gone, Charlotte picked up the untouched salmon and chucked it in the bin.

Yes, it had been a most satisfactory lunch – most satisfactory.

Chapter Fifteen

❦

Summer holidays, Christmasses, Easters, Bank Holidays, came and went. But the best days always began with phone calls, letters and postcards from Barty or Therese. Barty was particularly good at writing silly postcards in her bold black ink. Charlotte kept them all in a pile. They were well fingered, dog-eared and often re-read. They were from all around the world. One read:

> *I've been to Hell and back! It's bloody cold here – I thought Hell was meant to be hot.*

It was only when she turned over the card, she realized Hell was a real place in Norway. The PS had said:

> *Reindeer balls are exquisite. You'd love them!*

What a job that girl had! She bloody deserved it. Barty worked jolly hard and was now in a position to pick the cream of the photographic assignments. She was so proud of Barty's success. Last month she had been in the Seychelles.

> *The ship I have been on is called the* Foghorn *with a right Captain Ahab as the skipper. I don't think he likes*

women. Coral reef brilliant. No sharks as yet – except for the honeymooning, hairy-arsed footballer I'm supposed to be snapping for the colour supplement. Still better than being in an office, eh?

Bare-footed and bath-robed Charlotte padded to the door to pick up today's post. *Yes*, there was one in that familiar black ink – this time from Colorado. She knew Barty had been back for four days, but, however late the postcards arrived, it was always lovely to have been remembered in the middle of a shoot.

Howdy, partner. God, the Americans can eat! I've put on six pounds. Had to let out my belt a notch. Can't resist the maple-syrup waffles. Colorado is fantastic. At the weekend, I'm going fly-fishing. Monday, I'm seeing Robert Redford. Tough on you. All that masculinity, testosterone, will be wasted on me – but maybe his girlfriend will fancy me!!!

Pouring out her coffee, Charlotte smiled to herself. Barty had been such a 'naughty' girl over the years. She really had flitted from flower to flower, exploring and developing her sexuality. Those had been the fun times – for Charlotte as well as Barty. Her friend really had lived life to the full and so had Charlotte, by proxy, sharing each vicarious thrill.

There had also been the jobs, the famous names, the exotic locations. Barty always came back with some scurrilous gossip – only half of which ever hit the tabloids. Charlotte herself only took *The Times*, but thanks to Barty's influence she now read the *News of the World* on Sunday! In the last ten years Barty must have been around the entire globe. Now, at nearly forty-two, she had a formidable portfolio and was an award-winning photojournalist.

Sitting at the kitchen table, nursing her coffee, Charlotte fingered and re-read the card from America. Barty fat? *Never.* She focused on the stamp – the Statue of Liberty. It was not one of her favourite landmarks. It always reminded her of Barty's first meeting with Jules that Sunday morning on the Manhattan Ferry. Jules, originally from San Francisco, had been living in Greenwich Village, throwing pots and being professionally Bohemian. The British bulldog, Charlotte thought wryly, had met the American bald eagle.

It had been love at first sight. They had dismissed all problems concerning different countries, cultures and traditions. Within a month Jules had moved, lock-stock-and-pottery-kiln, across the pond to Midhurst, Sussex, England.

'This one's for real, Charlie,' Barty had spilled out. 'I *love* her. I absolutely *adore* her.'

She remembered *that* bit *very* clearly, remembered the Pang – the sense of loss, of being suddenly shoved out. Once again: 'Two's company, three's a crowd.' She was used to Barty messing around, but this girl was *very* different. This time Barty was *in love*.

'I can't live without her,' Barty had said, touching Charlotte's hand.

She had known that her Pang must not show; that she must keep her feeling of being threatened under wraps; *must* look happy for Barty; must never ever risk their friendship – and Barty's confidences – by being churlish, petty, jealous. That *would* threaten them.

She had never wanted to be one of Barty's 'flings'; had always known that the way to hang on to her, while others came and went, was simply to be there for her, to know when to look happy, sad, bewildered, confused – whatever colour of the emotional rainbow Barty required.

'Gosh, Barty,' she had pretended to enthuse, 'you *lucky* old soddo.' She had picked up some of Barty's gay vernacular. 'You've found the love of your life. It's *great* to see you so happy, so . . .' Her voice had trailed off. 'I can't *wait* to meet her.'

Barty's beam back had confirmed she was on the right track.

'You're *such* a good mate, Charlie,' she had said. 'You *do* know that whatever happens to me, you'll always be the first to know?'

Yes, she had thought, but I'm number two now in the emotional pecking order. Barty had squeezed her hand. That sudden tenderness had nearly undone Charlotte's pretence.

'That's what's so bloody marvellous about our relationship,' she had lied. 'Whatever happens, you and I, Barty, will go on for ever.'

They had drawn closer together at the table. She remembered panicking at the threat of Jules – this foreigner who was about to become a permanent fixture. Barty, propelled by love, had not noticed what was happening to the person opposite her.

Since childhood, Charlotte had learned how to block out threats and anything nasty and disturbing. This news of Jules had been devastating. As Barty rambled on about all aspects of her lover's life, Charlotte had coped, as she always had, by going ostrich-like, submarining away from reality into her perfect world of the Family, all together, no outsiders. Barty, she had cried miserably within. Barty . . . Barty . . . Why do you need another permanent fixture when there's me, the Family?

In her subterranean world, she had not heard a word that Barty was saying. Surfacing back to reality, all she had been aware of was that Barty had moved on, this new girl filling her thoughts, her emotions – her eyes.

'And she lives . . .

'And she's a wonderful potter . . .

'So sensitive . . . So loving . . . So clever . . .'

Charlotte only caught snatches of all this 'embroidery'.

She had felt empty, sick – *and jealous.*

What *was* it about people in love? She poured herself another cup of coffee and returned to the table. Why were they always so devastatingly attractive suddenly? It was a kind of contagion – *you* wanted to experience the *frisson* of excitement that punctuated the boredom of everyday life. You, too, wanted to be on Cloud Nine. It was something to do with their eyes, a kind of fanaticism – a one-track *gleam* – that sucked and suctioned everyone in its path. Their love and lust leaped from them to you, but then you were left isolated – totally alone.

'*Jeeee-sus!* I can't wait to see her again,' Barty had rattled on. 'I *hurt*, Charlie – I *bloody* hurt. I miss her physically and mentally. I *ache* for her.' She had grinned her lovable rascally grin. 'She's just wonderful in bed.'

Women in love: women in bed.

They had both blushed and squeezed hands again. Strong hands, Barty's. Man's hands on a young woman's arms. She could have been a sculptress, but had chosen to be a photographer.

Charlotte thought back to school. There had been a lot of passionate crushes in those days. Even in daylight, Barty and some of the other girls had escaped from the ever-watchful eyes of the teachers and slid into the bottom of the rowing boats on the school lakes to hold hands and sneak a kiss.

Why *hadn't* she and Barty – or Therese – ever played around with each other? she asked herself now. Instead, she had confined herself to observing others. After lights-out, lying alone in the dark in her own bed, she had been embarrassed by other thirteen and fourteen year olds' sexual experiments.

Looking back on it, all she had were images of girls in their nighties returning to their own beds with tired fingers. Drained and frustrated, they had fallen instantly asleep.

Charlotte heard the sound of the milk-float in the street outside. She had finished her coffee and now felt ready for some toast. Damn, she should have taken the butter out of the fridge beforehand. Waiting for the browned bread to pop up, she was remembering the angst she had felt when Barty had first got her crush on red-headed Angela. It had been the *Mikado* term, of course. Barty had relished her part. As Nanki-Poo, in male attire, every girl in the school seemed to have a pash on her. Girls at St Margaret's rarely saw a boy during term.

After one of the first Dress Rehearsals, Barty had told Charlotte a secret.

At the finale, when Angela had sunk into Barty's waiting arms, she had abandoned the carefully rehearsed tight-lipped kiss. Miss Kenny, the notoriously short-sighted drama teacher, had called up excitedly: '*Well done*, girls. *Well done!* Most professional. Right on the X-mark. The lighting was perfect.'

Miss Kenny had missed the moment when Barty, shielding Angela's mouth with a delicate Japanese hand-movement, had parted Angela's lips and given her a 'real kiss'.

Chapter Sixteen

꩜

She must have been mad to go shopping in Bond Street on a Saturday afternoon, with all those crowds. After all she could have done it mid-week, but had gone out on impulse, having seen a cashmere coat in *Vogue*. It had been a 'must-have' purchase, and she needed something for that wedding in October.

Back home, she flung down all the glossy bags. As usual she had been seduced into impulse buys – another little suit, a lovely ring, and a pair of shoes that would do for the wedding, too. She needed a cup of tea and switched on the kettle. It was Barty's birthday next Wednesday. Charlotte had already bought her a present – a hurricane oil lamp for the cottage at Midhurst – but that would be shared by Barty and Jules. In her heart of hearts, she knew that shopping for the coat today had been an excuse. Really, she had wanted to buy something more personal for Barty – something she wouldn't have to share. Charlotte's hand twitched. She was longing to write the tag:

Darling Barty. Happy birthday. This is to keep you warm on your Icelandic shoot. You can think of me when you are on the ice-floes. All my love, Charlie. XXXXX

Waiting for the kettle to boil, she rummaged in the bag. Oh, God, she thought, I haven't left it in the taxi? No. It was there. She could feel the wonderful, soft, reassuring cashmere. It really was a beautiful Dr Who scarf with tassels – a lovely aquamarine colour. Barty could wrap it round and round her neck and tuck it into the battered knee-length anorak she used for cold-weather shoots. Charlotte so loved spoiling her.

She sat down with the tea. Jules had given Barty that anorak.

Last year, for Barty's birthday, Charlotte had scoured London and found a superb replacement outdoor coat, but to her knowledge Barty had never worn it. She had continued to wear that old coat; had refused to be weaned from Jules's gift – sentiment triumphing over practicality. Charlotte had been hurt by that. Barty had not even pretended to wear it – not even when Charlotte visited her in the country. Charlotte had never seen her in the coat and it had cost £500.

There was a real autumnal chill in the air. She went into the living-room and lit the log fire. It was gas, of course, but some nincompoops still believed it was the real thing and tossed their cigarette butts at it.

In the beginning, she had truly never believed that Jules would endure in Barty's ephemeral affections. Barty and Charlotte had been in constant touch, of course, but she had had to wait six months before Barty had phoned and said what she had been waiting to hear: 'I want you to meet Jules.'

She remembered her mixed feelings of pleasure, curiosity and, she admitted to herself, massive nerves. She had then consoled herself, thinking Barty had a mixed track-record when picking women. Some of them had been quite nice, others had obviously lived in the shadow of her success and her cheque-book. A couple had been downright 'flaky'. The New Zealander had clung on past her sell-by date. That really had been a drama – anguished phone calls from Barty with yet another plan to shoe-horn the girl out of her life. She had gone eventually.

Which category would Jules – this paragon – fit into?

The moment she met Jules, Charlotte instantly recognized that she was what Barty had always said: special. Over the drinks and the lunch, she had to admit Jules was 'caring', 'loving', 'intelligent', 'sexy', and was obviously making Barty happier than Charlotte had ever seen her before.

The getting-to-know-you conversation had ranged from what it was like for Jules to leave the States – her family and her friends – and settle into English life. They had then cantered on through politics, comparing the National Health Service with America's health provisions, and Jules had mentioned she was hypersensitive.

'She's so allergic,' Barty had laughed, 'we can't even have a plastic washing-up bowl.'

Jules had also complained about a bad back from leaning over her kiln, and Barty had chipped in: 'What about *my* back – lugging around all those camera cases?'

Charlotte remembered how she had concealed her own psoriasis and her migraines. They had laughingly concluded they were all turning into old crocks and had opened another bottle of wine.

'Red wine – good for the heart,' Barty had said.

They had all drunk to that.

Begrudgingly Charlotte had admitted to herself that she *really* liked Jules who was a smashing girl. But before Jules, it had been she and Barty who had met up on Sundays with the papers, had the curry and gone for walks in Battersea Park or Kensington Gardens. Echoes of 'Two's company, three's a crowd'. The arrival of Jules had highlighted her own single state. Now, Charlotte had to wait for an invitation to join them.

They had become a Family – she had become a visitor.

Warming herself by the fire, now she was remembering a day one year later.

'Fuck Jules! Damn her,' she had sobbed.

Barty's news over cucumber sandwiches at the Ritz had reduced Charlotte to tears in the Ladies' Cloakroom. They were having afternoon tea, perched on the hotel's tiny gilt chairs, and the female harpist was a little too close to their table. She remembered the twanging bars from the *Narnia Suite*. Barty had some news, but was taking her time getting to the point.

In contrast to the music, there was a peace, a tranquillity, a quiet dignity about the way Barty was talking about Jules. This relationship was becoming *totally exclusive*. Charlotte had somehow known that she was about to be told something she did not want to hear. Barty usually had the courtesy to ask her about her own life. That afternoon the conversation had been totally dominated by Barty's obsession with Jules. The subject was becoming a bit of a bore.

Irritably, Charlotte had waved away the waiter with his tiered stand of exquisite cakes.

'You've got it bad, Barty!' she had said.

'No, not bad. *Good*, Charlie!' she had replied. 'After a year, the cracks are usually beginning to appear, but with Jules it's getting better and better.'

She had sipped her tea, and spoken with a rare feminine softness. Usually, she was rather masculine, matter-of-fact, about the women in her life. She *liked* the girls on her arm to be exceptionally attractive, to turn heads. She herself liked to turn heads. She loathed the commonly held theory that all lesbians were only gay because they couldn't pull a man. After a glass or two of wine, she would accuse television of always portraying lesbians as overweight and unattractive, and gay men as limp-wristed pink poofters.

'Jules and I are going to exchange vows,' Barty finally announced.

Instantly Charlotte had gone into panic-mode.

'Vows! What do you *mean*, Barty?' she had stuttered. 'Vows? You've always *hated* all that gay weddings crap – pseudo, you called it. You're not going down what you've always called the "clowns cloning heteros" path. You've told me a million times you're not a card-carrying, banner-waving, protest-marching lesbian . . . What's happened to all your principles?'

'I've not changed my mind about any of that,' Barty had replied coolly, adding tersely, 'but Jules and I are different. Good God, Charlie, don't look quite so horrified. You might get married yourself one day. Why shouldn't we? After all, she's certainly not going to wear white and I'm definitely not wearing a tuxedo.'

There had been a horrible pause while the harpist harped on.

'You are pleased for us, aren't you?' Barty had said, staring at her with a wariness Charlotte had never seen before.

She had known she had wrong-footed herself, that everything was going wrong in this tea-time exchange. She had somehow lost her way. She had been guileless. She had better be careful, *very* careful. But her head, heart, stomach, legs . . . She had felt breathless, unearthed, felt herself drifting, floating . . . deaf, dumb, blind. Oh, God, not a public wobble, she had thought.

'Charlie? *Charlie?* What's the matter?'

She had recognized this state of mind, had experienced it often enough in childhood when threatened. She *could* get back to reality. *She could, if she concentrated . . .*

'Charlie? Are you feeling faint? *Charlie!*'

Barty? She had heard the dear voice from afar, had thought she heard her friend calling the waiter for a glass of water. She had come round as Barty dabbed her forehead and neck with ice-cold water, and then sat her with her head between her knees.

Thank you, Barty. *Thank you*. The thank yous had run like a silent litany through her mind. She had not 'lost' it. This time she was back to reality . . . had touched the surface.

'Charlie,' Barty was saying. '*Bloody hell*, you nearly fainted.'

'I'm all right.'

She was. Thanks to Barty's intervention, she had somehow made the return journey. Barty had thought her trance-like state was physical, she had known it was mental.

'You fucking nearly fell off your chair.'

Charlotte had returned to reality sufficiently to register Barty was rattled.

'I'm okay, Barty. Really I am.'

'What happened? Did you feel faint?'

'Yes, it's hot in here,' she had lied. 'That bloody harpist is twanging my brain.' She had searched for another excuse. 'Sorry to give you a shock. I'm a bit pre-menstrual.'

'Oh! Well!' Barty had said dismissively, relieved. 'I must say it would have been *bloody* embarrassing if you fell off your chair in the Ritz . . .'

That was Barty. With her working-class origins, she was easily embarrassed, especially in somewhere as smart as this place. Not in front of the waiters, horses, children, other people . . . If anything untoward was going to happen, keep up appearances, don't do it in public. That was what Barty's parents had drilled into her. Laconically, she had always compared this with the appalling 'don't-give-a-damn' behaviour of the upper classes.

'I want to go to the loo,' Charlotte had lied.

Barty had looked doubtful, then alarmed that she might draw more attention to them.

'Are you sure, Charlie? Do you want me to come with you? I mean . . . you won't stand up and fall down on the carpet?'

'No.' She had managed her first fleeting smile of the meeting. 'But if I do fall over, Barty,' she had added, concealing her hurt, 'I *promise* I won't let anybody know I'm with you.'

She had stood up, squeezing Barty's shoulder as she passed her, and wended her way through the fragrant tea-drinkers to the cloakroom. Barty need not have worried, nobody at the other tables even looked up. Nobody ever noticed anything in the Ritz, except possibly jewellery, dress sense, shoes, celebrities and film stars.

Safe in the cloakroom, she had lowered her head into her hands and muttered: 'Fuck Jules! Damn her!' Knowing she was being unfair, she had added: '*Fuck all Americans . . .*'

She had known in the cloakroom that she could not – *should not* – take any more Jules-talk-punishment that day, had known she was too overwrought. This news of the permanency of their relationship had made her feel vulnerable. She must make a quick exit. She *had* to concentrate on getting safely home. She needed privacy and time to think.

She had returned briefly to the table, but not sat down again. To the strumming of the harpist's *Timeless Narnia*, she had plonked a kiss on top of Barty's head.

Mustering up a normal tone of voice, she had said: 'Eat the cucumber sandwiches, for God's sake. My treat, Barty!' She had gently placed a fifty-pound note on the table. 'I'm getting one of my headaches. Nothing to worry about, but I'd better take it home.'

Smiling her sweetest smile, she had added: 'So sorry, darling. Give Jules my love.' She had paused for effect. 'I was a bit clumsy when you told me about the vows. Forget what I said. Don't you dare do it without me!' She had bent down, kissing Barty on the cheek. Then, on the wing, turned and said: 'Love you, Barty. 'Bye.'

With her back to her friend, she had weaved her way through the tables, only too aware of her falling tears.

Outside, quivering from head to foot, her brain buzzing like a beehive, she had all but fallen into the waiting taxi. Home! A vodka and tonic. She had felt inadequate, rattled. But tomorrow, she had told herself, she would feel stronger. She was beginning to realize she could not let things drift. Jules was becoming *too* permanent.

Perhaps the time was coming when Charlotte might have to do something about her . . .

Chapter Seventeen

It was Thursday, a BBC day. After Barty's birthday celebrations the night before, Charlotte had not felt her best when the alarm had gone off at seven a.m. She had taken a couple of pills for her hangover.

Four hours later – after a particularly smooth programme – it was a relief to be back home in the kitchen with the prospect of lunch. Bev, the producer who had replaced Felicity, was considerably younger and less sure of herself.

As Charlotte heated mushroom soup and buttered a roll, she thought what a relief it was to have somebody who deferred to her. Bev had once said in the early days: 'Charlotte, you know what you're doing. You've been doing the programme much longer than me and I really value your opinion. After all, you know the BBC – I've just come over from commercial radio.'

Yes, she had liked that compliment and the accolade. Bev had continued as she had started: efficient, no-frills and respectful to her agony aunt. Charlotte poured the soup into a mug.

Sitting at the kitchen table, waiting for the soup to cool, she thought back to last night's celebration. God, that restaurant had been noisy. It had been Barty's choice – a trendy place in the Fulham Road, full of real tree-trunk columns and steel girders. The stainless steel tables, combined with the bare wood of the floor – and then the music – had made any conversation between Barty, Jules and the other two couples practically impossible. Charlotte had wanted to do a special dinner party here at the house, in her own dining-room. That would have been so much more intimate and civilized. She had been disappointed to be refused – felt strangely cheated – but supposed Barty had enjoyed it. She had certainly laughed and smoked enough.

Charlotte took a sip of the soup. She had made it yesterday and frozen most of it. It really wasn't bad. The strange thing about celebrations, she thought, was that the ones you really looked forward to so often went off like a damp squib; the ones you dreaded invariably turned out much better than you expected.

How she had dreaded that particular weekend – the one when Barty and Jules had celebrated their infamous vows. Years had passed since then – for them blissful years, for her agonizing years of being sidelined.

She vividly remembered how she had felt driving down to Burford, in the Cotswolds, that weekend. She had been touched to find that apart from her the only other person present in the tiny church in the middle of a field was a priest, Father Conrad Hennessy. He had crossed his hands over the two girls, then resting his palms on their heads, had blessed their partnership for life. Charlotte had dreaded this moment throughout the long journey – the moment that would officially seal Jules taking Barty away from her. She had not, in her wildest dreams, expected to cry, and when she had it had been for the wrong reason. Barty, Jules and Father Conrad had thought she was simply very moved.

Afterwards, all four of them had gone for lunch at the Burford Arms. In the bar, one of the locals had been boasting to the tourists that Princess Margaret and Tony Armstrong-Jones had done their courting in Burford.

They had giggled about this as Barty, with her arm around Jules, led them into the restaurant.

'I've got it all organized and they're sending me the bill,' she had said, delighted with her forward planning. 'Champagne for us girls – and don't worry, Father C, I know you'd rather stick with your whisky.'

'Oh, yes, a priest's work is never done. I've got a christening and another wedding this afternoon,' he had replied.

'But you can at least enjoy the lunch – it's Jules's favourite. The chef's done it especially for us. We've got our own menu: Caesar salad, grilled chicken, steamed vegetables and rice and prawns. All very Californian and low-fat.'

Father Conrad's face had dropped. He had been unable to conceal his disappointment at this health-food feast – obviously not his idea of a good lunch.

'Father, I've known you for so long,' Barty had chuckled then. 'I couldn't give *you* grilled chicken.'

He had beamed: 'Oh, good. What's my treat, then? A cheese ploughman with pickle?'

'No, your favourite. Rack of lamb, roast potatoes, lots of gravy, cauliflower cheese – and trifle. And there's cheese for all of us.' Looking at Jules, she had added: 'And for you, darling, pecan pie with ice cream.'

'Phew!' Father Conrad had said. 'That's a relief.'

At fifty – and celibate – food was his harmless indulgence – and over the years he had become nicely plump.

Sitting at the best table in the restaurant, Barty had beamed at Jules. 'Happy?'

'Everything's fantastic, honey,' she had drawled back, looking up into Barty's eyes. 'I'm so happy – I'm going to remember this day for ever.'

The two girls were seeing only each other. Charlotte and Father Conrad had exchanged glances, knowing that at that particular moment they were surplus to requirements.

'Married then,' Barty had joked, raising her Champagne glass and winking at Jules across the table.

'Hitched!' she replied, raising her glass.

'Blessed,' Father Conrad had gently interceded. 'And I really hope you'll remember *this* . . .' he had paused, putting particular emphasis on the word, '. . . *blessed* day for ever.'

In the kitchen, having finished her soup, Charlotte decided to polish off the remains of a bottle of white wine in the fridge.

Once the priest had gone off to the two-o'clock christening, Barty and Jules had visibly relaxed, their conversation and intimacy making her wish she had left, too.

'No more clubbing for you, my girl . . .' Jules had cracked. 'You heard the good Father. You go party, I go party. *We* go party.'

Charlotte had not been mentioned, of course.

'After our vows in that beautiful church, how could I ever want to do anything else? You know, I just want to be with you for the rest of my life,' Barty had said, holding Jules's hand.

She had noticed two of the young waitresses giggling in the corner at this intimate scene between two women.

Perfect. There was just one glass of wine left. She poured it out and binned the bottle, realizing she was still peckish. She removed the cling-film from last night's six remaining olives, and took them out on to the terrace.

This autumn was turning into an Indian summer, a brief respite from the approaching five months of winter dark, probably followed by a dodgy spring. Sitting on the terrace, her mind went back to Barty. She was a such a funny mixture of a girl. Good at dishing it out, but would be crucified if it came back. In the past, flitting from female flower to flower, she had been massively unfaithful to her partners but had expected total fidelity from them. Even at school, she had been seamed through with jealousy. God help Jules if she were ever unfaithful to her!

Charlotte was remembering how amazed she had been when, at one of their lunches, Barty had unexpectedly declared: 'Charlie, I'm sick of deceiving and betraying. Sometimes when I was younger I couldn't even remember the name of the woman I was waking up with.'

She remembered how shocked she had been at that confession. The thought of a nameless stranger in one's bed was unthinkable. How could people get themselves into such an unsavoury mess? How could they? What did they say to each other in the morning? They would want to use your bathroom. Did Barty have to give them breakfast and then bundle them out of the house? Awful. How could she have done that? But at least, Charlotte had comforted herself, those girls of Barty's were temporary – mere one-night stands.

She knew there had been a sea-change when Barty had casually dropped the name Jules into the conversation, and blurted out over coffee: 'Like the swans in that pic I took last week in Belgrade, Charlie, I'm ready to mate for life.'

She remembered her shock.

'Thank the lord for that,' she had lied over the table, her hands folded knuckle-white on her lap. 'I won't have to keep listening to all your messes. You've got into enough of them over the years and, God knows, I get enough of them in my job: Ms Wildly Promiscuous – "I've had the Father and at the weekend I had the son".'

She felt a sudden chill. Now, after Jules, she would happily settle for Barty rampaging through life with one-night stands in her bed.

For once, at that long-ago lunch when Barty was talking about 'mating for life', she had not been expecting to receive a compliment herself.

'Have I ever told you,' Barty had said, 'that you are a *very lovely, lovable* person.' She had wagged a finger to quash any disclaimers. 'No, Charlie! Let me say it – just this once – because I so often think it but find it difficult to say. You're just so . . . understanding, never judgemental about my life. I'm sure some of the things I've told you over the years must have shocked you. But you've never let on. You're always there when I need you. I'm always amazed at how much you care . . .' Barty's eyes had filled with tears.

'We're Family, Barty,' she remembered replying softly. She had been slightly unhinged by the unexpected gentleness. 'We're Family . . .' she had repeated, her voice trailing off.

'Yes, and families stick together,' Barty had confirmed, adding: 'I really don't know what I'd do without you, Charlie. I tell you everything. I don't tell anybody else what I tell you.'

Typically, she had then returned to her usual equilibrium.

After that lunch, Charlotte remembered nestling back in a taxi, thinking about Barty's exhilarating and unexpectedly tender words.

I couldn't stop being there for you, Barty, if I tried, she had thought to herself. You – and Therese – will always be the most important people in my life.

That was *her* secret.

Chapter Eighteen

꧁

Why did she always pack so much? It was nerves on this occasion. Henry always had that effect on her. Having to visit her brother, in what she laughingly had to call home, was a regular, if infrequent, duty. The reason, this time, was the need for her signature on some family trust papers.

Back in her old room, in the family pile, she realized how many awful memories this place contained. She hated the carpet, the curtains, even her cross-eyed teddy bear, losing its stuffing, propped on a fading velvet chair.

Above all, she hated the bed. Her suitcase was lying open on the floor. God, what a farce! Tissue-paper separating the painstakingly chosen clothes. There was a Barbour, if it rained, a cocktail dress if there was a party – you never knew with Henry. It could be hot, it could be cold. She looked down at the suitcase. She had packed the lot and had to cart it from Paddington to Taunton where Henry's chauffeur had picked her up. It would never occur to Henry that she might like to be greeted personally by her only brother. He hadn't even been in the house when she arrived. He had been out fishing with the other weekend house-party guests.

Charlotte looked at her watch. It was that horrible time between tea and drinks. She would stay in her room, much as she hated it, until she absolutely had to go down.

At least when Henry had been married to Jane, she'd had another woman to talk to. Charlotte had rather liked her, but the childless marriage had only lasted for eighteen months. Like father, like son, Henry had never been sympathetic to his wife's problems. Jane had been highly strung, artistic, but Henry's congenital coldness had triggered off an eating disorder. She had obviously felt marooned in Somerset where he was prone to dumping her. Since the divorce, he had returned to 'playing the field'. Who would be in the drawing-room tonight, hoping to be the next lady of the manor? Thinking about Henry was a waste of time.

Charlotte glanced down again at the suitcase – shoe-trees always looked like dead men's feet. She lined up the shoes on the mahogany shoe rack and hung up her ridiculous array of clothes in the walnut wardrobe. Stupid. Tomorrow she would have to re-pack and cart them all back to London. Why on earth had she bothered with a hat?

She threw herself on the four-poster bed, not bothering to take off her shoes. Why did she never feel at home here? She felt much more at home in the cottage Barty and Jules had moved to a few years ago in Midhurst. When she went there, she could shed the suits and court shoes, and sport casual designer jeans and crisp white shirts. She felt *avant garde* in those. She was never quite as casual as the two girls – could not let herself go as far as Barty. When Barty wasn't working she looked like an unmade bed, dressed in her favourite, grubby, blue-denim 'babygrows'. Jules, on the other hand, always managed to look stunning, even when splattered with clay. How did she do it? It always took Charlotte hours with the hair-tongs and the make-up bag before she felt able to face the world.

Jules had a perfect ivory skin – never wore make-up – and her copper-coloured hair was usually pulled back off her face and tied in a pony tail. After a heavy potting session, she would emerge with wisps of it clay-covered. She was quite tall, about five foot seven, somewhat androgynous-looking, with enviable coat-hanger shoulders. Her best feature was her Caribbean blue eyes, smiling above her Cornish smock and long flowing cotton skirts. When she wasn't potting, she always draped herself with a long scarf, and was never seen without her granny glasses hanging from her neck on an amber chain.

One afternoon when Barty and Jules had been renovating the cottage and re-landscaping the garden, Charlotte had happily mucked in on what Barty had called an 'all hands to the pump' weekend. What a mess that cottage had been! The three of them had worked from morning to night. Barty had enjoyed her role as foreman and dished out chores.

'I'll be manly and put back the bookshelves. You two can start making a bonfire down the garden. And, if you've time, you can start creosoting the fence.'

Lying on the bed, Charlotte laughed at the memory of Jules and herself simultaneously clicking their heels and giving a West Point salute.

'Yes, ma'am,' Jules had said.

They had worked their socks off that day. About four o'clock, Barty, hammer in hand, had emerged into the garden, saying: 'I don't know about you two, but I'm starving. Shall I make spaghetti bolognese?'

'You bet,' Jules had called back. 'Your chain-gang is beginning to flag.'

As Charlotte and Jules were finishing off planting grape hyacinth bulbs, Jules had suddenly come out with: 'I've never really worked out why you and Barty were never an item. How come, Charlie?'

She had been momentarily embarrassed and had continued random-scattering the bulbs under shrubs and trees. That had been a good excuse for not looking up.

'Well,' she had said slowly, 'two reasons really. First, Jules, I'm heterosexual – always have been. Second, Barty and I are ... *Family.*' She had been unable to resist the special note that had crept into her voice when she said: 'We've known each other for donkey's years.' She had known that time-span would make Jules jealous. 'Even if I were gay,' she had added, straightening up and stretching her back, 'it would have been like having an affair with ... well, my sister.'

'But you're *damned* close, the pair of you,' Jules had replied, leaning against a tree and looking at her. 'I'd heard so much about you from Barty, I'd decided to keep a very beady eye on you, honey.' She had paused and added: 'I tell you something else – I sure was relieved you weren't bi-sexual.'

Jules had given up the gardening for a bit of a gossip. Charlotte remembered her sitting on the rickety garden swing, her mouth ever-busy with the inevitable gum.

'But . . . come on, as fellow gardeners, Charlie, spill the beans,' she had joked. 'Have you never been tempted to try a girl?' As Jules swung gently to and fro, skirt billowing, revealing her tanned giraffe-like legs, Charlotte had felt acutely embarrassed by the sexual probing, and had even sensed that Jules was teasing her – flirting with her. Old gay habits, she had thought, die hard.

Jules had laughed at her embarrassment, jumping skittishly off the swing.

'Hey, ease up, Charlie. Chill out. You're all right, honey,' she had said, draping a languid arm around her shoulder. 'I can see why Barty loves you! And I'm really glad you've gotten to be my friend now, too. It's important to get your sexuality sorted out. There are so many screwed-up people, and bi-sexuals are a load of trouble. Don't talk to me about it! As Barty says – bis screw us all up, gays and heteros alike. And she's right. That girl's always right!'

'But, Jules, you said once, didn't you, that you'd swung both ways?'

'Oh, yeah – in my other life.'

'And now?'

'No. That was *before* Barty. This is for real. No more Tom, Dick or Harry for me.'

'What about Sal, Viv or Brenda?' she had teased.

'Jeez! I couldn't shack up with a Priscilla-May, Tom or Shirley,' Jules had laughed. 'No, Charlie, I can't imagine ever risking what I've got with Barty for what you Brits call "a bit on the side".' She had paused, suddenly serious. 'Anyway, you know what that girl feels about infidelity.'

Barty's call for supper had come then.

Why had Charlotte remembered, as they walked wearily back to the cottage, those bible classes at St Margaret's? Why had she thought 'Before the cock crows three times . . .' remembering the betrayal of the faithful friend? Infidelity . . .

Henry's abrupt knock on the door and his peremptory summons to drinks meant she had no more time for herself.

These were crucial questions. She knew they would not go away. They would have to be answered one day.

Chapter Nineteen

It was Christmas Eve at the cottage. Autumn had been much more fun than Charlotte had anticipated. The programme was going well, there had been a super Hallowe'en party at Marina and Andrew's house, and a totally unexpected invitation to a BBC presenter's annual firework party. South London had been lit up by cascading rockets, and even the catherine wheels had worked. Mugs of mulligatawny soup had warmed their gloved hands, and spiced punch had loosened up a particularly interesting new group of people.

Yes, it had been a good autumn.

Since Barty and Jules had lived together in the country, it had become a tradition for Charlotte to spend Christmas with them. She was lucky – Christmas for many singles meant feeling like the little Match Girl with nose pressed up against other people's window-panes. She was *inside*, throbbing with happiness at the thought of tomorrow – the Day.

Once again Barty had doled out the jobs. Jules was in the kitchen sorting out the giblet gravy and worrying about the turkey being too big for the oven. There had been a last-minute dash into Midhurst when Jules had wailed: 'God dammit, I knew I'd forgotten something – the aluminium foil.'

Barty was in the cupboard under the stairs dealing with the usual annual crisis with the Christmas tree lights. They had been all right for three days, but had then blown the main fuse. The air was blue, and her denim bottom was sticking out of the cupboard.

'Bloody things,' the other end was muttering. 'This happens every damn year . . . What do you mean, what am I doing? I'm trying to change the fuse.'

Charlotte was Head of Fires – a very serious job for the three-day celebration. In contrast to her neat, reliable, pseudo gas-fire at Eaton Square, this one was real and had a nasty habit of going out. It was an open fire with an oak-panelled surround that had been salvaged from an old church. It did not help that Barty had not got round to replacing the cracked iron basket. Every time Charlotte put the coals on to get it started, they fell through. It was exasperating, and she had complained about it at Easter. Once it was up and running with logs it was fine, except when the wind changed direction and everybody choked in the smoke and had to leave the room.

There was a cry of delight from the cupboard under the stairs.

'Has that done it?' Barty shrieked. 'Charlie, can you tell me? Are they on?'

Putting down the poker, she turned round and looked.

'Yes. You've done it.'

'Brilliant!' came back the reply.

'What's on the box?' Jules yelled, misunderstanding. 'Delia here is stuck in the kitchen. Am I missing any of the action?'

Barty, triumphantly wriggling out backwards, screwdriver in hand, yelled: 'I've fixed it. Lights are back on. Time for a Christmas Eve glass of shampoo.'

No one said no.

The fire was now behaving. There was a reassuring crackling from the logs. Charlotte drew the curtains. It was all so cosy, friendly and welcoming, such a contrast to her family-pile Christmasses where ice clung to the inside of windows as well as outside. Icy people in icy houses, she thought.

In a few minutes time they would all be sitting on the carpet by *her* fire, with glasses of Champagne, planning the next day's feast and activities. She heard Barty popping the cork in the kitchen and looked around the room. The cottage really had come on. It had been a labour of love. They had oiled the beams, beeswaxed the oak panelling and scoured antique shops for the right cottagey furniture. They were particularly proud of the dining-room table which they had found locally. Jules had already laid it with tartan napkins, crackers, red candles – and the gorgeous pine-cone arrangement Charlotte had found in Harrods and brought down for them. It was one of the many Christmas gifts she had had such fun choosing for them. She had been planning their Christmas stockings and treats since October.

Sitting on her haunches, custodian of the fire, she admired the rugs on the coir-matting. She had bought them four faded red kelims, and passed them off as 'very cheap', on Jules's birthday. They would have died if they had known they had cost nearly £4,000.

She could hear Jules and Barty bantering in the kitchen. Soon it would be time for the Twelve Lessons and Carols from King's. The radio was all set up – on the right station for once. Charlotte had seen to that. She was imagining the tension in the vestry at King's College, Cambridge, while those small choristers waited to hear – after all their rehearsals – which one of them would be chosen to sing solo, unaccompanied by music, 'Once In Royal David's City'. This would go out around the world and sometimes the boy's pure virginal treble voice would tremble with nerves. You almost died for him, willing him to hit his notes. For her, as for millions, that candlelit procession and service was the true beginning of Christmas.

Charlotte went into the kitchen to collect her Champagne. Jules was taking off her apron – she had done her bit. There were wonderful seasonal smells in there. She caught Barty sneaking a mincepie from the tray.

'It'll spoil your Champagne,' she said.

Barty pulled a face and put it back again on the baking tray.

'And anyway, honey,' Jules had added in reproving tone, 'I haven't shaken on the icing sugar yet.'

It wasn't just the three of them this Christmas – they had been joined by Peanuts the beagle. It was rather nice having a dog. 'A dog is for life – not just for Christmas,' went the slogan. But, in Peanuts's case, he really was theirs just for Christmas. There would be an emotional reunion with his master and mistress on New Year's Eve.

He was a mixture of apricot and tan, the epitome of beagle characteristics – a bustling, eager, merry hound, alert, intelligent, bold and, above all, determined. 'Walkies' were a nightmare. He was off, head down, and they were left with lead in hand and no dog in sight.

Right now, Peanuts was going nowhere. He knew exactly where the turkey was, especially the giblets. Jules had shredded them into his bowl.

'I think I'll feed Peanuts now,' she said, adding his biscuits to the giblets. 'I know it's an hour early, but I don't want to get up in the middle of the service.'

Peanuts, hearing his name, thought this was a brilliant idea. Bouncing up and down, nose quivering, eyes fixed, his rear wagging for Britain, he could hardly wait for her to put the bowl on the kitchen floor.

He scoffed the lot in one, chased his bowl around the kitchen with a clink of stainless steel, then, pinning it down with one paw, licked it clean. Leaving him to sniff around and do the hoovering up, they took their Champagne into the sitting-room and snuggled down by the fire. Peanuts would join them in his own time.

After the service, they would have a light supper, some mincepies, and watch a film they had already 'ringed' for their evening's TV viewing.

It really was a perfect Christmas Eve.

The cold woke Charlotte on Christmas Day. It was only five-thirty. She got out of bed and looked out of the window. It was pitch-black outside; the tree beyond her window, lit up by the porch light, was ghostly white with frost. She shivered and touched the radiator. It had not come on yet.

Quickly, she retreated into the bed, groping for the electric-blanket switch. She huddled down under the duvet. Peanuts stirred in his basket and leaped up on the bed. He had obviously made a midnight foray downstairs and had snuffled around the tree. Barty had promised to close the sitting-room door, but Peanuts had unwrapped somebody's present. There was a piece of red ribbon dribbling from his mouth.

'Bad boy,' she said, confusing this signal with a pat on the head. 'Happy Christmas.'

She removed the ribbon from his mouth, adding: 'Go to sleep, Peanuts.' He snuggled down.

Barty and Jules loved dogs but if he had chewed open and demolished a special present, he would be truly in the dog-house when they woke up.

'If you've done that,' Charlotte warned, 'they won't be sad to see the back of you, matey.'

Peanuts, oblivious of all threats, snuffled away happily.

On New Year's Eve, of course, Charlotte would be taking Therese – and the dreadful Mick – out for a celebratory lunch. She had done this for as long as she had been coming to the cottage. Christmas with Barty and Jules, New Year with Therese and Mick. Of course, neither couple knew about her deceitful pantomime. She had planted into Therese's mind that she spent Christmas at the family pile, and into Barty's mind that she spent the New Year celebrations there. In truth, the last time she had spent either of these festivities at her so-called home had been fifteen years ago.

The bed was beginning to warm up. Would Therese like her Christmas present – the eccentric, sheepskin-lined, calf-length slippers? Charlotte had not been able to bear buying something personal for Mick. She didn't want to know his shape, or any of his intimate measurements. She had got round this by buying other presents for the two of them – a water-butt and a wheelbarrow.

Their present to her was sitting in Eaton Square, wrapped in brown paper. She certainly could not bring *that* down here. It would be a 'token' present. She knew that money was very tight at the moment and that Therese had had a recent ruck with her mother, who was despairing about her daughter and how much money she was pouring into the animal sanctuary.

Did she want a cup of coffee now? No. It was too cold to bother, and the creaking floorboards might wake up Barty and Jules.

Therese, she thought, really was in a financial mess. She was selling everything of value, including precious family heirlooms and a silver tray that dated back to 1650, all to secure a couple of extra acres for the animals. Therese told her everything, perpetually asking: 'What do you think Sotheby's would get for this?'

Charlotte always telephoned Barty and Jules on New Year's Eve to prevent them ringing her.

'Life's so unpredictable there,' she said. 'We're always out –

cocktailing, meeting Henry's same boring old set. We never seem to be in. Much easier if I ring you.'

One New Year's Eve, fuelled by a bottle of Champagne, Barty had taken the initiative and telephoned her in Somerset. Henry had dismissed the 'Happy New Year' call with: 'Oh, Charlotte's not here. Don't tell me my sister's gone missing?'

That had taken some unscrambling. Luckily, she had phoned Henry with her usual midnight duty greeting and had been fore-warned before she spoke to Barty.

By the time the girls came downstairs in their dressing-gowns, saying, 'Happy Christmas, Charlie,' she had let Peanuts out for his constitutional and put back the holly wreath that had mysteriously fallen from the door. She had done her fire, emptied the ashes, relaid and relit it. She had put on the Christmas tree lights, brewed up some fresh coffee, warmed up the oven ready for the croissants, and got the butter out. Christmas Day was ready to go. Peanuts was bragging around in a tartan bow.

'Bird in at noon,' Jules said with military precision, looking at her notepad of timings.

'An hour's walk with Peanuts,' Barty added.

'Queen's speech at three,' Charlotte tossed in.

'Lunch at four,' Jules, as Head Chef, said, adding: 'Which of you two is going to be commis-chef and do the vegetables?'

It was the same every year – Barty ducked the prospect of dealing with the sprouts and volunteered, as usual, to be 'Head of Booze'.

On the walk, Peanuts had long since disappeared, following his instinct to chase hares. The winter stillness of the woods was so enchanting they did not speak much. Their boots crunched over the frozen grass, and they met the occasional fellow walker with the greeting: 'Good morning,' followed by the seasonal rejoinder: 'Happy Christmas.'

Forty minutes later, Jules was wanting to be reunited, hands-on, with her oven. As they strode along the tow-path by the river, she was muttering: 'Okay, the bird went in at noon. We've walked for nearly an hour.' Mentally, she was calculating everything down to the last minute. 'Okay. Okay, the bread sauce is done. Stick that in the microwave, throw the sausages in, roast the potatoes. Okay. Okay. We'll be eating right after the Queen's Speech.'

'Do we have to see the Queen's Speech?' Barty complained.

'Yes,' Jules retorted, admonishing her: 'I've built that into the cooking schedule. And it's *your* Queen after all.'

'A lot of us think we'd be better off with a President,' Barty muttered.

'Perhaps,' Jules replied. 'But Presidents don't look so good in tiaras. Anyway, my turkey's got to rest.'

They trudged back to the cottage, where Peanuts miraculously reappeared. That was a relief. Another person's dog was a tremendous responsibility. Chilled, they took off their coats.

'God, it smells wonderful in here,' Charlotte and Barty said in unison as they entered.

Jules looked pleased.

'Time for a Christmas Day Bloody Mary,' Barty said, rubbing her hands.

This, for Charlotte, was bliss. She *had* to share Barty with Jules, but at least they were together. She loved watching her bustling around the kitchen, mixing the tomato juice with vodka, celery salt and all the spices; loved watching her swearing at the stubborn unyielding ice-tray and the errant lemon pips. She just loved her.

Everything was going to be perfect. Nothing could go wrong. It would be, as always, a true holly-and-ivy country Christmas.

Soon, cocktails in hand, in front of her restoked fire, they were sitting cosily together on the sofa to watch the Queen's Speech.

The trumpeter's fanfare, cut to the rippling royal flag, filled the screen bang on the dot of three. This year the Monarch was in pink and they simultaneously commented on her bust, brooch and immovable hair. Ever fair, Jules said: 'But, hey, look at that skin. That's some perfection for a lady that age. Don't knock her.'

'It's the nation's favourite sport, rubbishing the Monarch,' Barty laughed. 'Wait for the Maundy money, and the endless record of the year's good works, then the Commonwealth bit, and that final plonked-on insincere smile.'

It happened exactly as she forecast.

As the Speech finished, Jules, somewhat miffed at Barty's constant interjections, got up with a mock flounce, saying: 'Honestly, you two! I'm going to finish off my gravy.'

She crossed the room, her exit barred by the ever-sticking door from the sitting-room into the hall-dining-room.

Still on the sofa, Barty winked at Charlotte. They always felt particularly British and close to each other at such moments. About ten minutes later, there was the expected summons from the kitchen: 'Get your butts out here. I need some help. I've dished up. Let's get it on the table.'

In the kitchen, Jules's face was uncharacteristically flushed as she handed Barty the huge platter with the turkey and all its trimmings.

While Charlotte and Barty skivvied to and fro across the eight paces from the kitchen to the dining-room, Jules washed her hands and face and stood ticking off her checklist: 'Roast potatoes, sweet potatoes, sprouts for Barty, peas for Charlie, corn for me . . . gravy . . . cranberry . . .'

'Anybody thought about plates?' Barty called back from the dining-room table.

Jules duly arrived with them, the candles were lit, the claret was in the glasses. As Barty handed around the plates of brown-and-white meat – after all these years she knew what everybody preferred – she suddenly noticed the answer-machine blinking in the corner.

'Hey, Jules. We missed your dad's call. He's done it again, like last year, rung during Queenie's speech. We never heard a thing with the telly on and the door shut.'

Jules leaped up and rushed to the machine, pressing the New-Message button. The deep Californian voice said: 'Hi, Jules. Hi, Barty. Merry Christmas. Daddy here is anticipating his Christmas egg-nog and opening your Christmas presents. They got here safely, but a bit torn up around the edges. Have you eaten yet? Have you opened my present? I sent you the usual cheque, so that you can go out and buy some cute piece for your cottage.' There was a pause, then his voice became suddenly emotional and serious. 'I'm missing you. It's been nearly ten years . . . I'm not getting any younger . . . And, being Christmas, I'm getting sentimental, honey.

'I hope you girls remember saying you'd spend some time living back here in the States? Jules, I'm sending you some details in the mail. A neat little job has come up, near to home, Head of Pottery for an Arts Foundation. You remember my fishing pal, Harry, the one with the moustache? He's a Trustee, and told me about the job over a Bud last night. He asked me to mention it to you when I next called. Anyway, sweetheart, I'll call you again over the New Year. Bye, and love from Daddy.'

There was a strange crackling and the line went dead. Jules whooped on hearing her father's voice, Barty paused from tucking in and smiled at her lover's delight.

Alone at the end of the table, Charlotte gripped and steadied her claret glass. *America*, she thought, dismayed.

'Hey, Barty, didn't Pops sound great,' Jules was saying. 'He seems to have gotten over that hernia thing.' She sat down at the table and started eating and talking at the same time. 'Hey, what about that job? What do you think?'

'Well, it's certainly something we can talk about when we get the letter and know all the facts,' Barty said, getting back to her turkey. 'Hey, Jules, this is even better than last year. You've excelled yourself. It tastes fabulous – the turkey's beautifully moist.'

Everybody was eating except Charlotte.

'C'mon, Charlie,' Barty said, indicating her untouched plate. 'Yours will get cold.'

'Charlie,' Jules said, 'Barty *must* have told you about our plans to spend some part of our lives in the States? Gee,' she added, 'I can see from your face she never mentioned it.'

'If we go, Charlie,' Barty said gently, 'think of the fun we can all have. You can come out for visits. We can have Christmas over there.'

Totally unconvinced, she felt herself nodding. To cover up, she picked up her knife and fork.

'Could you pass the cranberry sauce, please?' she said, knowing she had to conceal her feelings.

It was the *last* thing she wanted. The phone call had tainted the day and poisoned the lunch. She didn't want the sauce, the dead meat, the vegetables. She just wanted to crawl away and die. Barty ... *in America?*

This was the last thing she had expected – the *last* Christmas present she had wanted.

Chapter Twenty

Hyde Park burgeoned with life in May. Lazarus-like, it came alive again. Cherry blossom, late tulips, new green buds – even the ducks looked especially glossy as they spring-preened themselves by the lakes. Charlotte was slowly walking along the path with the lunch-break office-workers looking for deckchairs to eat their sandwiches. London was beginning to fill up with tourists, enjoying the spring sunshine.

Despite the renaissance of the park, she was not feeling happy. The Big Problem would not go away. After the Christmas call dangling a job for Jules in America, things had moved very fast. In March, she had flown to the States to see Pops, and be interviewed at the Foundation. It had not, by any means, been a foregone conclusion that she would get the job. The post had been advertised and there were lots of other applicants. But the discreet personal approach, via her father, had raised her hopes.

Charlotte found herself a deckchair and paid the park attendant. How did the uniformed figures miraculously appear from nowhere the moment a bottom sat on striped canvas? The last months of winter and early-spring had been nerve-wracking. She sat with her eyes closed, thinking back. Jules had been offered the job in April. Charlotte knew quite well there would be no mileage in trying to change their minds. Barty was as thrilled and enthusiastic as her partner.

'Charlie,' she had screamed down the phone, 'the clever girl's got it! She's got it. She's got it. We're off in September – and you're coming over for a Californian Christmas.'

That phone call had made her insides curdle. Charlotte had mustered the right noises, but then, having put down the phone, she had been sick where she stood, hands over her mouth. Life without Barty – the daily call, the weekly lunch, the spontaneous visits to Eaton Square between flights, the country weekends, the bailing her out of constant 'pickles' – this would all stop if she were in America. They would grow apart without the minutiae of daily life. No transatlantic call would compensate for the loss of shared cups of coffee, daily intimacies and being face-to-face. No Christmas and holidays in America could compensate for Barty's physical presence being permanently removed from England. The outlook for Charlotte was bleak and devastating.

Now, she was sitting in a deckchair in Hyde Park, with the prospect of summer, already mourning the loss of one of her Family.

There had been moments when her hopes had been raised. Jules had gone through a bad patch. Maybe, Charlotte had prayed, life itself would intervene and scupper their American plans. She had really hoped that the mosquito bite on Jules's eye that had completely closed it and caused extensive swelling of her face would have 'grounded' her in England. For Jules, hypersensitivity meant she was always on red-alert for any insect buzzing around, but this time she had been asleep and bitten in the night. It was an hereditary problem passed on to her by a hypersensitive mother. Experts at Moorfields eye hospital had unfortunately sorted that one out.

Then Charlotte's hopes had been raised again. There had been a more serious health scare – Jules had discovered a lump in her left breast. Charlotte herself had not really wanted it to be malignant – she liked Jules – but Jules couldn't go to America and start a new job while battling with a life-threatening disease, could she? It had turned out to be benign. There had then been a near-miss when, out driving, a riderless horse had bolted across the road and skimmed her car bonnet, forcing Jules to swerve and nearly wrap the car around a tree.

'My God, Charlie,' a shaken Barty had said illogically on the phone, 'she was only five minutes from home and could have been killed.'

That, she had thought, would have been convenient. Barty certainly would not have gone to America without Jules.

Frustrated she got up and continued her walk around the Serpentine. After those accidents she had often lain sleepless in bed, wondering if there was anything positive she could do to stop the intended emigration. Time was running out. In three months the 'birds' would have flown. Literally.

In April, she had come up with a piece of bribery.

Unknown to Jules, she had shown some of the tremendous pieces of Jules's pottery she had been given as gifts to a buyer at a top London store. The man had been a personal friend and, over dinner, Charlotte had drawn his attention to the pots and slid the idea of an order into his mind. He had come up trumps and thought one of the designs would be a great idea for a Christmas line. The offer he had phoned through to Jules was worth a considerable sum of money. Charlotte knew from Barty's phone call that Jules had been deeply flattered, tempted and temporarily unsettled by such a big unexpected break that would have given her months of lucrative work, with the prospect of more. Just as Charlotte was about to rejoice that her ploy had worked, the recognition, the money, the tempting bait, had all been rejected in favour of teaching in America.

It was beginning to cloud over – suddenly looked more April than May. Was she going to be caught in a shower? Why hadn't her Barty ruse worked either? It had taken some cunning to persuade an editor – who fortunately admired Barty's work – to offer her the job of picture editor on a national newspaper. Barty, too, had been unsettled and tempted, but had said: 'We talked about it all night, Charlie. And Jules, quite rightly, said she couldn't see me "flying" a desk and doling out the exciting assignments to other people with less talent than me. By the morning we'd decided to stick to Plan A. The thought of being separated and the prospect of commuting every few weeks or so was not on. It just wouldn't work.'

Charlotte gave a swan, resting in the middle of the path, a wide berth. Last night Barty had called in unexpectedly, about seven, at the end of a shoot. As usual she had been complaining about the loss of light, ravenous and hoping for a quick snack before she whizzed back to Jules in Midhurst. Barty had been in tremendous form, bubbling with gossip about a certain celebrity's many layers of make-up and face-lift lines.

Had Barty noticed Charlotte was feeling clingy and sentimental? She really hoped her feelings had not shown. She had rustled up a toasted cheese sandwich and some salad. Barty had coffee because she was driving, Charlotte had a glass of wine. Eaton Square was a useful pit-stop for missing the rush-hour exodus out of London. She had desperately wanted Barty to stay the night and have breakfast in the morning. She had wanted just a few more hours of having her to herself, even though Barty was babbling on about America, Jules and their future life together. Barty had always treated Eaton Square as her own and, after the sandwich, tossing down the napkin and obviously ready for off, had said: 'Charlie, I'm just going to give Jules a quick ring to let her know what time I'll be home.'

With Barty and Jules, she knew there was no such thing as a quick ring. It always took at least fifteen minutes. While Barty had been on the phone, debriefing Jules on the celeb's make-up layers and face-lift, she had taken the supper-tray into the kitchen. She really had not wanted Barty to go, but had no excuse to force her to stay. She couldn't suddenly be ill, and Barty had been determined to get back to her own bed. The kitchen knife had lain by the bread-board. Charlotte would *make* her stay.

She had picked up the knife. Barty had been in the middle of the now-familiar story. Charlotte had known exactly how long it would take her to get to the punch line. Slipping quietly down the stairs, she had opened the door and gone down the steps to Barty's blue Volvo parked in front of the house. It had been dark, and there had been nobody around. Viciously she had stuck the knife into three of the tyres. Then she had closed the door behind her and dropped the knife into the umbrella stand. The sabotage had only taken about three minutes. Remounting the stairs, she had heard Barty still on the phone. Charlotte put her head around the study door, mouthing: 'Another coffee before you go? Send my love . . .' Barty had shaken her head to the coffee and nodded to the second.

About eight minutes later she had come out of the study, jangling her car keys, saying: 'Right, Charlie. Thanks for supper. I'm off. I should be home by eleven.'

They had hugged, confirming next Wednesday's lunch. Barty's boots had thudded down the stairs. The door had banged shut behind her.

Charlotte had sat back on the sofa and waited. Determined to look suitably relaxed and casual, she had poured herself a nightcap and opened the *Tatler*. Barty, being so often in London, had her own key. A few sips later, Charlotte had heard it in the lock. Charging upstairs, she had shouted: 'Some bugger has slashed my tyres. Three of them are flat. Not the kind of vandalism you expect in Eaton Square.'

Charlotte had ready her shocked sympathetic face and her response: 'I'm so sorry. It's happened a few times round here recently. Have they done everybody in the road?'

'I don't know. I didn't look. They've certainly done me.' Barty had flopped into a chair. 'Damn. Damn Damn. At least they didn't break any windows.'

'You'll have to stay the night now,' Charlotte had said, adding: 'We'll sort it out in the morning. I'll get you a whisky. At least I'm not working tomorrow.'

Barty had gone off to phone Jules again. Charlotte had won this round. Kicking off her shoes, she had put her legs up on the sofa. What luxury. She would have another two hours of Barty – and was already looking forward to an intimate breakfast.

She snapped back to life in the present. The shower had not materialized. She noticed a group of Japanese tourists photographing the riders on the sandy track of Rotten Row. They must be mystified, she thought, by its extraordinary name. They wouldn't appreciate the typically British inadequacy with foreign words. *Vin blanc* had become plonk; *Route du Roi* had become Rotten Row. It was so dangerous in William III's time that he had commanded 300 lamps to be hung from the branches of the trees to deter highwaymen from his route from Kensington Palace to St James's. In fact, she remembered reading, it had been the first road in England ever to be lit at night. This had obviously not helped one unfortunate woman who had swallowed her wedding ring to foil a highwayman. He had killed her anyway and had been hanged for the murder in 1687. Now, it was an innocent sandy riding circuit.

Barty's visit – and her own intervention – seemed a long time ago, but it was only last night. When Charlotte got home from the park, she would retrieve the knife from the umbrella stand. She had to get to that before Josefina did.

Leaving the park, she crossed the nightmarish junction by the Scotch House, and started off down Sloane Street. In Sloane Square, she would pick up the *Herald Tribune*, the *New York Times*, the *Washington Post* and the scurrilous *National Enquirer*. Forearmed is forewarned, she thought. Since the news of Jules and Barty going off, she had become obsessed with America and all things American. She might never get the opportunity to slip in all the 'negatives' and 'rubbishings' she had been accumulating over the last two months, but she was putting all the cuttings into a jumbo scrapbook. There were muggings and rapes in the parks, endless homicides, drug-related crimes and racial tension. The statistics for obesity and its health-related problems were absolutely appalling. That last one, given that Jules was a Californian health-freak, could certainly prove useful.

So far all her ploys had failed. But, buying the newspapers, she knew she had not given up by a long chalk. Okay, the cards were stacked against her right now. But she had been there before with Angela and Felicity – and she had won. Holding the heavy bunch of newspapers, she knew their 'poison' might prove to be redundant. She might never get the chance to use her knowledge. But . . . the scrapbook could yet prove to be good hard ammunition to gun down the American Dream.

The cuttings might turn out to be blank bullets. But they might not . . .

Chapter Twenty-One

⌣

Charlotte sat in the chair, plotting. It was now the end of June. Barty and Jules would be going to America in just under two months. Destiny had not stepped in to prevent them. Last weekend, she had faced up to the hideous fact that they *were* going but she could *not* let it happen. Now that she had made a plan, she felt calm and focused – even slightly pleased with herself.

She re-ran the scenario she had planned. It was as easy to fake a post-coital bed as it was to fake an orgasm. She would ruffle up the bed, toss a pillow on the floor and, while Jules lay in the drunken drugged torpor Charlotte had lured her into, would throw aside the duvet as if they really had done *It*, and spent the night together. She would then risk three hours in the spare room. At dawn, she would slip into the bed and Jules would wake up to find her 'lover' of the night before stirring sleepily by her side. Even before the girl had opened her eyes, she would make herself put her hand between Jules's legs, faking the non-existent intimacy of the night before. It would work perfectly.

Charlotte rehearsed.

'What have you done to me, Jules?' she would moan in her softest voice. 'I'm throbbing. You've ignited a catherine wheel inside me.'

Gently leaning over her, but aiming the next blow between the eyes, she would add: 'Remember, I told you in the garden, I've always been heterosexual. I've never done it with a woman before – never felt like this . . . so complete. So satisfied.'

She had read these lines often enough in agony aunt letters, and recalled one line in particular, written in turquoise ink: *'After a woman has had a woman, it ruins you for a man.'*

Continuing the scenario: Jules would come awake, her eyes registering shock. Thoughts of Barty would swim instantly into her consciousness.

'Charlie, we *didn't*! For God sake, say we *didn't*?'

Ashen, she would sit up, remembering her vows in the country church – the Jules and Barty for ever vows; the lunch when they had talked about no more infidelities. No more mucking around. She would then, as she registered their two naked bodies, side by side, truly believe she had gone to bed with Barty's best friend. Horror at what she thought they had done would seep into her face. The white bed-linen – a pristine backdrop to the ghastliness of the morning – would reflect her anguished expression. Others had been disloyal to Barty but no way would she tolerate another infidelity – especially when the 'other woman' had sprung straight from her own back yard.

Charlotte shifted uneasily in her chair, lighting a cigarette.

What would happen after that? Jules would sit up on the side of the bed, her head in her hands, sobbing.

'God, Charlie, she must never find out. You know how she feels about betrayal – infidelity. I mean us – the two people she loves most . . . it's like incest. What got into us last night? Oh, hell, my head hurts!' She would turn and look at her: 'Charlie, how much did we drink? You're so cool. Don't you feel guilty? Shit, you were there when we took our vows.' Her long coppery hair would be thrown back, the precursor to a bed-rocking howl.

In the chair, Charlotte realized she was already feeling completely drained. Could she get through this? Could she pull it off? It had to be done. The alternative was too dreadful: Jules and Barty living in America. Where did that leave her? High, dry and alone.

Lying intimately alongside Jules, resting on one elbow, she would go on the defensive.

'What about me, Jules? You *took* me. You made the running.'

Flight would be Jules's first instinct.

Sitting snug and safe in the armchair, Charlotte pictured Jules naked and vulnerable – that triangle of ginger hair. Hands clasped to her head she would shriek: 'I don't remember a damn thing about last night.' Then her tears would come and drown them both.

She, playing the new lover, fresh, still throbbing, would not surrender ground, give in easily.

'How can I . . . How can *we* . . . possibly pretend last night didn't happen?'

Jules would flinch at the *'we'* and fire back: 'Charlie, don't say *"we"*. Please don't say *"we"*. There's only one *"we"* for me and that's with Barty – you know that. *C'mon*, it's been so many years. Damn it, I *love* her. Last night was a god-awful mistake. Let's forget it ever happened and get back to normal.'

Charlotte stood up, walked to the kitchen and poured herself a vodka. Her mind was fizzing. This would be the right time for a little compassion and understanding – her agony aunt trade mark.

Extraordinary, she thought, how in such moments of scheming she could still notice the house plants needed watering.

She would snap back: 'Forget all about it? How *can* I forget all about it? You *knew* I was hetero – Nigel, Hugh, the appalling David. But Jules, you *took* me – you *know* what you did. Don't tell me it was just the drink and you got carried away like some drunken navvy?'

Sipping her drink, Charlotte was relishing her own unravelling drama. She would embroider it with: 'And I *loved* it. I know now I've wasted so much of my life on men.'

Yes, that was the kind of language a girl who had hung out in San Francisco gay bars would understand. What would Jules say to *that*? Probably there would be another plea to her, fired by more guilt – betrayal of Barty would be written all over Jules's naked body.

'Charlie, *don't*. I can't *bear* it. I feel so goddam' awful. I've fucked us all up . . .'

That was almost certainly how she would react. What would they do or say next?

Right now, Charlotte was going to water those dry plants. In the kitchen, she filled the watering can and crossed back into the drawing-room to start with the Rosary plant, its Catholic beads cascading down the side of the bookcase. Damn! The nozzle was loose. Now she had a beautifully sprayed carpet.

'*Don't* go yet,' she would choke out, adding with well-rehearsed hesitation: 'Jules, you've opened me up like an oyster . . .'

Yes, she was rather pleased with that – it had a good sexual connotation. By now, she would have put Jules firmly on the spot – caught between two lovers.

She would make herself the picture of wretchedness and cling – no, better not be *too* clingy. Jules would be struggling into her jeans, and Charlotte would say again, almost in a whisper this time: 'Don't go yet!'

Jules would then need calming down. Comforting. To defuse the situation, Charlotte would add gently: 'C'mon, let's have some breakfast.'

Americans loved their juice – she must remember to get in Jules's favourite apple juice.

Wandering around the room with the watering can, Charlotte vindicated herself. What a shame it had to end like this. Deep down, she *really* liked Jules. But the Family always had to come first. Jules was a real threat. Jules was taking Barty away. That would never do.

When they were dressed and showered, they would lighten up – be friends again. Charlotte would have to back off, but convince Jules she should drive her home to Sussex. For Jules, the prospect of the cottage would be normality restored. She would be lulled into a false sense of security. Home and hearth.

For Charlotte, *that* drive would be crucial. With Barty away on an assignment, she would be alone with the girl.

Her watering can was empty.

There is a time to act for those we love. That time, Charlotte knew, was now. Unwittingly, in swallowing the lie of the night before, Jules would have sealed her lips for ever.

Poor sweet Jules.

Chapter Twenty-Two

The very next week, Charlotte made it happen. The fake seduction, the confusion, tears, recriminations had gone exactly as she had planned. Too simple really. Afterwards she had driven Jules home to Midhurst, through the comforting Sussex Downs. The flinty hills and Radio 3 had calmed their frazzled nerves. With the roadworks, it had turned into a two-hour trip. They had sat separated by silence, seat-belted against each other.

On the drive down, Charlotte thought back on the previous night and how all her plans had come to fruition. Just before Jules had arrived, she had turned on the radio for some music. Prophetically, Neil Sedaka had been singing 'Tonight's the night . . .'

Barty had been away on a shoot in Portugal and Jules had come up to London for a seemingly spontaneously arranged dinner. Charlotte had long 'clocked' how susceptible Jules was to flirting and flirtation. Jules *loved* to play, to trot, to canter. *Yes*, she was faithful to Barty, *yes*, she had no intention of ever being unfaithful, but her gay-bar days had taken their toll. Jules could *not* resist the temptation to flirt – or be flirted with; had to confirm that she was still desirable and attractive, and could still, if she wished, pull the girls. Jules never had any intention of delivering the goods, but occasionally – when she felt safe – loved playing this silly juvenile game.

'Come over,' Charlotte had bubbled to her on the phone. She had known that Jules was completing an order. 'Whatever you're doing, couldn't it wait? I've got a secret.' She had injected a tantalizingly mysterious note into her voice. 'I want to run it past *you* before I talk to Barty about it,' she had said, displacing the usual pecking order. Jules had obviously been flattered, just as she had planned.

'You sound so mysterious, Charlie,' she had drawled. Then, obviously too mystified to refuse, had added: 'Okay ... Barty's back tomorrow, so I'd better come up tonight. I've been stuck here on my own – not talking to a sainted soul for five days. I could do with some company. Yeah, it would be great. I can't get away from here until around five so I'll stay over and catch an early train back in the morning.'

Charlotte had timed her phone call – and invitation – to perfection.

'Sounds good . . .' Jules had added. 'I've had enough clay to last me into the next century. I need a break. That's great. I'll catch a cab from Waterloo – be with you about seven-thirty.'

'Remember, it *is* a secret,' Charlotte had emphasized. 'Don't tell Barty about this. If she calls, *don't* say you're coming up here to see me. Okay?'

'No big deal,' Jules had replied nonchalantly. 'I've already talked to her today. We won't be speaking again. She'll be back Sunday morning.'

Charlotte had counted on their having spoken. The timing of her call had been impeccable. Jules had happily hung up, anticipating their meeting in a few hours' time.

Curiosity, Charlotte had thought, would in this instance kill more than the cat.

Poor Jules.

Chapter Twenty-Three

As the car gently bumped down the unmade road, with its green centre spine concealing the hard ridge which had once ruined her sump, Charlotte was still picking over the details of the night before. She sensed Jules's relief at the prospect of home.

She had got last night absolutely right. The candlelight had been soft and romantic, the right music had been playing and there had, of course, been lots of wine. With perfect timing, at around eleven-thirty, she had dropped the pill into Jules's drink when she was refilling her glass in the kitchen. A week before, she had rehearsed and tried one on herself. It was practically taste-free – a minuscule touch of bitterness. She, of course, had spat the drugged wine out. Jules would surely not spot the Mickey Finn. Charlotte had been right. She hadn't.

In the drawing-room they had lain, head-to-toe, on the carpet, chatting amicably. Throughout the evening, Charlotte had fobbed off any mention of the promised secret, with: 'After dinner . . .' 'After another glass . . .' 'Don't rush me, sweetie . . .'

She knew from observing Barty and Jules, slyly watching their intimate moments, that Jules loved her ankle being stroked – that her breathing would often change and her eyes milk over when this curiously erogenous zone was being stimulated. From her agony-aunt post-bag Charlotte also knew there was a time of the month when women were much more likely to feel sexy and receptive to seduction. Leaving nothing to chance, she had been mapping Jules's menstrual cycle. She knew from Barty's regular wails: 'Oh, God, Jules is pre-menstrual again. She's been biting my head off the whole weekend,' exactly when she was likely to be most receptive to sexual advances. Yes, she had sewn up everything as tightly as possible, had not left anything to chance, and last night had not put a foot wrong.

Totally relaxed and away from her kiln, Jules had swigged happily away at her wine, the secret forgotten. At just the right, perfectly timed moment, Charlotte had moved from girlie talk to flirtation to seduction. She had gently stroked the girl's ankle, then slowly but more boldly slid her fingers inside the bottom hem of her jeans to caress the slim lower leg and calf. With the in-and-out, up-and-down strokes, she had managed to duplicate what she had seen Barty achieve. Jules's breathing had quickened, desire had clouded her eyes. Under the influence of the Mickey Finn in her drink, she had even helped the plan along by giggling and pulling Charlotte towards her and down on to the cushions. Jules had kissed her. Receiving that kiss had taken some acting. Her mouth still felt violated, but the intimacy had been crucial to getting Jules into the bedroom and into her bed. She had been so dopey, she had been easy prey – easier than Charlotte had anticipated.

The rest was history.

Chapter Twenty-Four

Last night's seduction might be history now, but sealing the Family's future this afternoon was not going to be so simple.

Pulling up at the cottage, Jules limply got out of the car to open the five-bar gate. After manoeuvring the car up the gravel sweep, Charlotte finally switched off the ignition. Her mind was in over-drive. Jules had already gone into the cottage and was opening windows, her body language reflecting her mental distress. She was still tormented by what she thought had happened last night.

Biding her time in the driver's seat, pretending to fumble around for her handbag and bits and pieces, Charlotte was confident about the final part of her plan. The last twenty-four hours had been somewhat precarious – she had not felt fully in control, had had to rely on an element of luck. Would Jules willingly come to London? The final part of her plan was, she knew, watertight – finely honed and crafted. Mentally, she went through a check-list. She had everything.

The really tricky bit had been getting Jules up to London, and upsetting her so much she could coerce her into accepting a lift she did not want back to Sussex.

Charlotte had to act this weekend or never. Time had run out. Last week, Barty had let slip that Portugal was her last assignment before they started on two months packing up and finalizing the letting of the cottage before the move to America. That innocent remark had made Charlotte realize she would never again have the opportunity to get Jules on her own. Today was the only 'window'. It had to be done today.

She had known that during this crucial last-chance weekend – with Barty returning after a week away – Jules would *never* invite her to Midhurst. Barty always returned from shoots exhausted, drained, and needing 'a bit of space'. The first part had been easy. She had been able to get Jules to London with the 'carrot' of a secret. The problem had been how to inveigle her way into the cottage where she knew she was not wanted. A fake seduction, to reduce Jules to a guilt-ridden pulp, had been the only answer she had come up with. Short-term planning was not her strong point – long-term planning was her *forte*.

This morning, over an embarrassingly quiet breakfast, Jules had wanted to take the train back, as Charlotte had known she would. She had been ready for that one.

'Jules,' she had pleaded, 'don't be silly, darling. Don't let's flush our long friendship down the drain. I couldn't bear it. After all, you're off to the States and I'm going to miss you both so much. Let's forget about last night. Let me drive you home. It's ridiculous for you to go by train, especially when I'm having tea later today with friends in Pulborough.'

She had invented the imaginary friends on the spur of the moment.

It had worked. Jules had been cornered by her logic. Although desperate to get to the anonymity of Waterloo Station, she had reluctantly given in. For Jules, the one-night stand had been a disaster. All she wanted to do was to distance herself from the physical reminder of the other body – and her own guilt. But good manners had forced her into submission.

Charlotte had won – again.

Now, if Jules was looking out of the cottage window, wondering what had happened to her, she would only see Charlotte combing her hair in the car mirror. So far, so good.

In a moment, Jules would invite her in. Desperate to wave her goodbye, she would be too well mannered to treat her like a chauffeur. It was lunchtime. Feigning hunger, Charlotte, and her all-important handbag, would get into the house.

Chapter Twenty-Five

As she entered, Jules was opening the doors to the patio, saying reluctantly over her shoulder: 'D'you want a coffee? Or something stronger – a glass of wine – before you go?'

'A coffee would be lovely,' Charlotte said, adding casually: 'Could you rustle up a sandwich? It seems a long time since breakfast, and I won't be having tea until four-thirty.'

She hoped this sudden interest in regular meals did not sound too out of character. Jules was obviously dying to get rid of her, but again courtesy won the day. Charlotte knew for certain her relationship with Jules would never be the same. She had played her hand, and like a poker player had to carry on the bluff – but not for very much longer.

Jules crossed to a kitchen cupboard and got out a jar of honey.

'I'll make us Barty's famous banana-honey-mush sandwich,' she said flatly.

With only a hint of bad grace, she started mashing two bananas, raisins and honey together.

Finally, mugs in hand, they moved out on to the patio. Despite the sunshine, the atmosphere was strained. Charlotte suddenly couldn't think of anything to say – and neither could Jules. Last night had put paid to the friendly past. She alone knew they had no future. The garden, she thought, would be safe neutral territory. She looked at her watch – it was just on one o'clock.

Jules was setting out the loungers.

'Are these new?' Charlotte asked conversationally.

'No,' Jules said curtly, unenthusiastically scattering geometric black-and-white padded cushions around the newly installed swimming-pool.

Charlotte felt uncomfortable, knowing she was not wanted, but with her secret agenda had to fake the building blocks of normality after last night's so-called 'events'. She knew she had briefly to resurrect their friendship. It was crucial to the next two vital hours. She had to lull Jules back into feeling easy with her again – 'mistakes of the night', 'water-under-the bridge'. She made a real effort to lighten up.

'The garden looks great – really coming along,' she said, carefully removing her shoes, keeping her handbag close by. 'I love lilac. Remember I gave you that three years ago?'

Jules, uncharacteristically quiet, nodded disconsolately, nipping the tops off a few dead pansies. She was still hurting about last night – her body-language bewildered and wary.

Charlotte noticed the July sunlight picking out tints in Jules's Titian hair. Pretending to look around the garden, she said: 'Is Barty helping more these days? She's just about the right age to start taking an interest in all things green.'

It was such a preposterous suggestion, Jules summoned up some energy and retorted: 'Can you see Barty in gardening gloves? That girl can't even spell secateurs. The only thing *she* understands is cameras.'

Almost on cue, inside the house the phone rang. Jules looked at her watch, flustered.

'Talk of the devil . . .' She paused, looking disturbed and frightened. 'I'll have to speak to her. God, I hope she doesn't pick up anything in my voice.'

She fled to the phone.

This was not part of the plan.

Slightly rattled, Charlotte got up and walked around the paved surround of the small pool. Only a blip, she reassured herself. A blip. But was it? Would Jules tell Barty she was here in the cottage? No, surely not. There were a couple of wasps struggling for life in the shallow end. A dog barked next door. How long would Jules be? She looked back to check her slouch handbag. It was there, in all its Gucci luxury, draw-string tightly closed on its secrets. Was she really able to go through with this? Several times in the past she had given destiny a successful tweak, but what she was about to do was a hefty push. This was in a different league. Even as she hesitated, her conscience pricking, she knew she could – and would – do it.

Jules would come back after the phone call even harder to make relax, but nothing would be lost – she *could* do it. She had to do it now. Walking round the pool, she closed in on her bag, feeling for the small plastic container. It was there. Relieved, but knowing she had to move fast – Jules could emerge any moment – she removed the lid, and slipped the pill into Jules's coffee cooling innocently on the patio table. Bless India – bless that crooked doctor. She gave the drink a furtive but vigorous stir. It would do its work. It had last night. All Jules had to do was drink it.

The summer sun was now high. It was a perfect July day. The butterflies were flitting around the buddleia. A bird on the wing took a sip from the swimming pool and swished up into the beech tree. A nearby thrush was knocking hell out of a snail. A normal Sussex summer's day, but she knew there was nothing normal about today – nothing normal at all.

Five minutes later, Jules re-emerged into the sunlight and slumped down by the pool. Charlotte looked at her. Hearing her lover's voice had banished some of last night's distress. Jules's relief was tangible.

'It's all okay, Charlie,' she said, looking happier. 'She didn't suspect a thing. She's been partying all night with the other clicks. There are three of them out there.'

This was the first time, she noted, Jules had called her by her name since the early-morning drama.

'You didn't mention I was here, did you?' she said, her eyes on the cooling coffee.

Jules raised her eyebrows and shook her head. 'I didn't think that would be a great idea . . .'

Perfect. Perfect. She watched mesmerized as Jules sat down and picked up the mug, cupping it in her hands.

'Barty's home tomorrow,' she said, managing a smile. 'Apparently, she's got some brilliant shots.'

The muddy liquid would *not* taste funny.

Charlotte could hardly bear to watch. It was a Family joke that Jules was a gulper. Tomato juice, tea, brandy – all went down in one go. No sips for her. True to form, she downed the tepid coffee. Watching as the mug was put back on the tray, Charlotte was flooded with relief. Jules had swallowed it – literally. The first part was done. Everything inside her tightened. Now all she had to do was wait.

Slightly disliking herself, but *only* slightly, she mentally moved forward into Phase Two. Don't weaken now, she thought, this is the girl who's taking Barty away – separating us. And, once in America, they might just stay there. Good for Jules an American, but not so good for Barty. Or for her.

'The sun's really hot,' she said, falsely bright. 'I'm going to lie down and shut my eyes for five minutes.'

'Yeah,' Jules said, more relaxed now and settling down on the second lounger. 'Why not? Let's take five.'

Eyes closed, Charlotte thought of Barty – her dancing hazel eyes, lovely long fingers, wicked sense of humour. *No! No! No!* Justifying the contents of her handbag, she summoned up all those years at St Margaret's. Barty was after all quintessentially English. *This* was her place, *her* country. She had such brilliant contacts here. Wherever Barty went, so did her bulging black Filofax, contacts built up over so many painful years. Seduced to America, she would have to start all over again. That prospect was unthinkable. Barty did not realize the seriousness of the situation – she *did*. She *had* to act for Barty.

Echoing around her brain was that call from Barty: 'The clever girl's got it! She's got it. She's got it. We're off in September.' Then the PS-afterthought: 'And, you're coming over for a Californian Christmas.'

No. She didn't want to be left alone – one of her two crucial Family props hijacked from her. Since Christmas, she had never once articulated her feelings of desperation and trauma. And, anyway, nobody had bothered to ask her. If she had said anything, she would have sounded selfish, childish, pathetic. She would have given herself away. She shuddered. *No!* Unthinkable. She had *never* given anything away since the duckling incident.

It would have been unthinkable then to say how she felt: mortified, the beginning of a lifetime of Catholic-style mortification and secrecy. It would be unthinkable now to reveal to Jules how she truly felt about Barty.

However ghastly the next couple of hours were going to be, her way was best. The secrets of her handbag.

Chapter Twenty-Six

'Can I sunbathe for a couple of hours?' Charlotte queried gently. 'It's so nice here . . . I don't have to be at the Mortons' till much later,' she lied.

Casually, she looked across at the white face opposite her. Jules yawned. The drug was beginning to work.

'I'm knocked out,' she said. 'It's my own fault. Why did I drink so damn much last night? What's the time? I really ought to get back to my kiln and finish that order.'

She was beginning to look slightly bleary-eyed, stretched out on the cushions.

'Oh, come on. An hour's sleep will do you good. And I'd much rather stay here than kill time in Midhurst.'

Jules had closed her eyes.

'Why not?' she said. 'We can sneak an hour. We don't get many sunny days in this goddam' country of yours.' She just managed to open her eyes again to look across at Charlotte. 'God, I really feel out of it. You know, whatever I say, I'm really going to miss England. Yorkshire pudding, Radio Three, the brilliant T.V.' She paused. 'And I do want to say sorry about last night. I feel . . .' She hesitated. 'I feel, you know, *really bad*, Charlie.'

She put on her most comforting of comforting expressions.

'Darling, forget it,' she said, raising herself on to one elbow. 'Look, we've been friends for so long, a night's silliness ... let's just forget it.' She homed in, lightening the moment, looking closely at Jules. 'You already have, because you don't remember it anyway.'

Jules flinched. 'How could I have been so badly behaved?'

'It takes two to tango.'

Jules smiled ruefully. 'Sure.' She shut her eyes.

A swallow flitted down and up, a rose petal floated gently to the ground. Unreal.

'Forget it, Jules,' she said again. 'I have. Honest, it's gone. It never happened. Barty will never know. The last thing I want is to cause trouble between the two of you. I *love* both of you. You know that.'

'Gee, Charlie,' Jules said, her eyes still shut, 'you're being great about this. But I still feel sorry.' Her voice was beginning to slur.

'Don't be,' Charlotte replied. 'It'll look good on my sexual CV. My first woman ...'

They were back on safe ground – apparently friends again. All defences down, Jules, her eyes desperately trying to focus, just managed to mutter: 'I never thought of that. I'd like to think something good came out of it – your first woman.'

Her last words were: 'You'll never look back.'

Charlotte waited – one of her skills. She could not make a mistake at this point. Jules had to be out, completely out, for what was about to happen. The drug had bought her the time she needed. Don't mess up, she instructed herself. Steady. Steady. There's no need to hurry.

Barty was still in Portugal, blissfully ignorant. She didn't know Charlotte was here in her home in Midhurst. It was the weekend: silent, solitary, sleepy Sussex; no threat from the cleaning lady. Unless there was a totally unexpected curved ball, Charlotte was safe.

Getting up, she crossed to Jules and looked down on the sleeping body.

The girl did not stir. Such a shame she had to die.

Why am I doing *this*? Charlotte asked herself. I could just drive back to London now. But that would not change anything, would not stop Barty going to America. If she left now, Jules would wake up with a hangover. Nothing would have been achieved. She mustn't weaken now. Barty in America? Disastrous. She checked her handbag.

God, she needed a drink. Could she allow herself – a small one? She moved into the kitchen, opened the fridge and clinked ice into a glass. She poured a vodka – larger than she had planned. Her hand trembled. She realized she was very, very nervous. She had never done anything as ghastly as this before.

She was boosted by the glass in her hand, the sight of the lurching liquid somehow giving her strength. She bit her index finger, nearly made it bleed, but forced herself to return to the sleeping body. The drink was a mere prop. Later, she would realize she hadn't even sipped it. She left it abandoned on the green garden table.

Concentrate. Focus.

Double-checking, she gently prodded Jules, saying her name loudly enough to wake a normal sleeper.

'Jules . . . Jules . . .'

She was out – comatose. Just to make sure, Charlotte shook her. Nothing.

The drug had done its work.

Hunkering down, Charlotte made ready to do *her* work.

All doubts fell away. She felt propelled by a strange force – a current of energy. Swiftly, she removed the surgical gloves from her handbag, struck by the smell of rubber. They were sticking, resisting. She tugged and eventually won. They were on. She looked down at her white fingers – condom-clad. Sinister. She flexed her hands – she was ready. Her body gave a momentary shudder.

Steady. *Steady.*

She looked down at the sleeping Jules, this time noticing a tiny mole on her cheek – she'd never noticed that before. Jules's white face was framed by that wonderful coppery hair. She looked so peaceful, like Ophelia floating down the river.

Charlotte wouldn't need the jar of honey she had brought and left in the boot of the car. Jules had picked a useful choice of sandwich filling. It would be better to stick with her jar of honey. She retrieved it from the kitchen. Carefully, back by the pool, she half unscrewed the lid, steeling herself.

A cow in the next-door farm, separated from its calf, mooed

plaintively. There was no compromise. She didn't *want* to do this, she *had* to. Jules's chest was undulating – gently and monotonously up and down.

Charlotte shifted position. Catholic echoes: 'May this cup pass from me . . .' If she was not careful, she would weaken, cry and run. Savagely this time, to a Shakespearean echo in her head, she unscrewed the lid fully. *Screw* your courage to the sticking place – this time Jules's lips. *Concentrate. Focus.* She was wasting precious time, delaying the inevitable.

She dipped her rubber-clad finger into the jar. The honey trickled down the glove, staining the cuff of her white shirt, and she cursed inwardly.

'Fuck.'

Concentrate. Focus.

Leaning over Jules, knowing this was it, she smeared the open lips with honey. It was vital to the Plan that the sticky liquid should remain not just on the lips. It had to penetrate inside Jules's mouth. It did. Charlotte made sure it did – her rubber-covered finger massaging the honey into the pink oral vagina.

Jules did not stir – her life about to be sweetly sealed.

Knowing she had to move quickly, Charlotte seized her open slouch bag, taking out the muslin-covered jar.

Buzz. Buzz. The bees were still alive. Relief.

There had been so much in the papers recently about allergies – the unexpected peanuts in a curry, powdered walnuts in a cake – a few poor sods were allergic to modern-day life. But for Jules, poor hypersensitive Jules, the killer was to be bees.

Oh, yes, Charlotte had plotted this one well; done her home-work with an innocent call to an old bee-keeping friend. She had transported the bees, on that ninety-minute journey from London to Midhurst, keeping them alive in a muslin-covered Kilner jar with sugar-water.

Opening the jar, she clamped the rubber rim over Jules's mouth.

Angry, hungry, the tired, frenetic bees went naturally about their business. She watched, fascinated. The bees generously moved her plan along, plopping hungrily on to the prepared honeyed lips. Jules's mouth was obligingly sagging open. The bees, *busy, busy, busy,* found their target. Slightly bewildered, but relishing freedom and the welcoming honey, they crawled in.

How would she know if they had stung? She had to be certain – *had* to provoke them into their deadly stings. Two bees were buzzing around on Jules's lips. Others were busy inside the girl's mouth. Still gloved, careful not to get stung herself, Charlotte closed Jules's mouth with one hand and pumped her cheeks with the other to agitate the bees inside. They would finish the job.

Moments later, the comatose girl twitched convulsively from multiple stings. Charlotte knew Jules would never wake again. Looking down at her, she anticipated the inevitable swelling. She knew what to expect. She had read the medical books. The girl's throat would eventually close. The lungs would still pump, doing their essential work, but the life-giving oxygen would be cut off by the swelling. Her breathing would become stertorous. She would fight for breath . . . but would suffocate. Eventually, her face would turn navy blue.

Poor, poor Jules – but she didn't know anything about it. Charlotte comforted herself with this thought. Picking up her bag, she started clearing up. She couldn't bear to watch. The job was done. She would cover her tracks, making sure nobody could get her for this one – not neglecting the least the detail. The gloves, the drinks, the honey, the jar, the muslin, the all-important bees.

She forced herself to look back at Jules. The swelling was beginning.

A cock crowed fields away – the biblical signal of betrayal.

It really was done. *It was done. It was done.*

Chapter Twenty-Seven

❦

Shakily, Charlotte let herself out of the cottage, closing the door on all those familiar objects – the school clock found on a trip to Maidstone, the antique chair in the hall, the carpet Barty and Jules had gleefully bought at auction. Somehow all these items, once friends, were now her accusers. She was relieved to shut the door on what she had done. The next time it opened, it would be Barty's key in the lock; Barty expecting the usual open-armed welcome: 'How was it? You look great. New shoes? What, more duty free? We're awash!' Lots of hugs.

She was limp from what she had just done.

Desperate not to be seen, she moved swiftly to the car. It had only just had a £500 service. Why shouldn't it start? It had *never* let her down before. Why was she panicking? She was pathetically relieved when the black Audi fired at the turn of the key. Cars don't recognize their driver's guilt. Would a policeman? She made a mental note to drive with extra care – ridiculous to be caught out for some minor traffic misdemeanour.

Cautiously, she pulled out of the drive, stopping to close the five-bar gate behind her. She had lied to Jules about having tea with the imaginary Mortons. But why go back to London? It actually made sense to stay in Midhurst and pick up her answer-machine calls on her bleeper. If she hacked back to London now, she would only have to return to comfort Barty tomorrow. She was not looking forward to *that* phone call – Barty in hysterics. Feeling as she did, Charlotte decided she would stay at that ivy-covered hotel in Midhurst. Under new management, it was being hyped up – Barty and Jules had talked about it, had had lunch there. She'd read about it in the hairdresser's. They wouldn't know her from Adam. She would simply be a single-woman on an overnight stop. Mentally she checked, was it Goodwood races? No. She looked at her watch. It was early, twenty-past four. Unless the hotel had a wedding party, they'd almost certainly have a room.

Stopping off at the chemist to get a toothbrush and toothpaste, she was desperate for the anonymity of a hotel room . . . the fake chintz, the pallid characterless prints and, above all, the mini-bar.

There was only a small wedding reception going on. A few select hats and confetti were floating around the car park. Charlotte's voice sounded steady as she asked for an *en suite* room.

'Yes, there is one,' the receptionist said. 'But it's a double room only so there'll be a single-person supplement.'

The badge on her lapel said she was Debbie.

Perfect – except Charlotte's stomach was feeling like curdled milk and she was shaking.

Once in the room, she sat on the end of the bed and, after a couple of minutes, opened the mini-bar. There were lines of miniatures and cans of fruit juices, even a bar of Toblerone placed seductively for the sweet-toothed traveller alongside the peanuts on the bottom shelf of the fridge.

She crossed back to the bed, took off her shoes, and threw herself back on the generous pillows. The backward movement rebounded on her. Rattled delicate insides came up to meet her mouth. She clasped her hands over the dribbling saliva.

She was going to be sick. Jerkily, she sat up. Mentally locating the bathroom, she stumbled across the carpet to the security of the white bowl and dry-retched. Nothing came but guttural sounds.

Eventually, she held the hotel's white laundered flannel across her mouth. Somehow this reminded her of Cook. Her mind flashed back to herself aged ten. How nightly she had padded down those endless draughty passages, clutching the wet flannel, ready to flop it on to Cook's crumpled sleeping face. The tired over-sixty lump in the bed had always stirred as the water trickled down her neck on to her nightdress. Charlotte had had another of her nightmares. For a time, this had been an almost nightly occurrence, and Cook had always been there for her: 'My little Trickle . . .' she would wake up mumbling.

From being Grizzle in the nursery, Charlotte had inherited yet another belittling nickname. Cook had not realized that her studious little helper in the kitchen *loathed* this endearment. At the huge wooden table, she would concentrate on the jam tarts – jam tarts to keep her quiet, jam tarts that were *never* eaten. Trickle – the nickname – had stuck for three years.

The hotel room chair looked more inviting than the bed. Charlotte did not want to upset her delicate stomach again. A drink was out of the question. Mentally, she checked where she had put her bag, and only then looked back over the day's events, dissecting what had happened and what was yet to be.

She was *truly* dreading picking up her answer-machine messages tomorrow. There would be one from Barty.

The change of plan, her staying in Midhurst, meant she could ring Barty, not wait for Barty to ring her at home. She could be there first – to give comfort. Barty would never know that she had spent the night in Midhurst, only fifteen minutes from the cottage. She would be totally in control of tomorrow's events. That was the way she liked it.

She looked back on the day.

She had cleaned up, focusing her attention on every detail. She had taken Jules's pulse. She was *certainly* dead. Charlotte had heard echoes of the oh so recently silenced voice apologizing for the night before, but hadn't been able to look at Jules's navy-blue face.

The bees, having suicidally administered the one sting Nature allowed, had died. And so had Jules – *unnaturally*. But nobody would know.

Charlotte had risked leaving one bee in the girl's mouth, but had removed the others with her eyebrow tweezers, scattering the tiny bodies in the hedge. The honey in Jules's mouth would be linked with the innocuous lunchtime sandwich. Charlotte had artfully left only one plate and knife – one set of crumbs – on the tray on the green garden table. She had dipped a corner of Jules's bathing towel into the water jug and wiped all excess honey from the girl's blue lips. She had hated doing this, but too much honey would have been a mistake, a give-away – as would the second lounger. Charlotte had replaced that in the pool-house. She had then collected up the jars, and returned them to her bag. Finally, she had emptied and washed the glass of untouched vodka and her coffee mug and plate, and took them back to the kitchen with the jar of honey. When she was sure everything was done, she had unpeeled the rubber gloves and put them in her handbag. She was safe.

On the journey through the countryside, she had carefully disposed of the incriminating containers and the rubber gloves.

Yes, sitting in the security of the hotel room, she was certain she had done everything. It was most *unlikely* that foul play would be suspected, but, if it were, she had disposed of all the forensic evidence.

Despite feeling confident, she shifted uneasily in the chair. Out in steamy pot-holed Lisbon, Barty would be blissfully ignorant of today's events – murder. Charlotte flinched, preferring the description 'today's events'. In her mind, she reiterated 'today's events', as if the bees could have struck without her.

Today was behind her. She was longing for a bath, a long comforting soak.

Focus. Concentrate. Plan.

Tomorrow, a happy Barty would be on the early-morning plane back from Portugal – shots in the can incarcerated in silver boxes in the hold. *Adeus* to Lisbon and Portugal. She'd sit on the plane, watching the clouds and the still snow-flecked mountains down below, thinking about home. She would drive herself from Heathrow back to Midhurst. Two leafy lanes away from the cottage, she would be smiling, anticipating the usual disembodied arm, proffering a glass of Southern Comfort through the cottage door. Cued by the sound of the car on the gravel, the once jokingly proffered amber gift had now become a tradition, followed by Jules's 'Welcome home, honey'.

In the morning, Charlotte would ring Arrivals at Heathrow. If everything went according to plan, Barty should be home by midday. Feeling slightly calmer, she allowed herself a whisper of congratulation, and padded over to the mini-bar. Her stomach was still not ready for the Toblerone – suddenly sweetness equalled deadliness. She took the miniature vodka and tonic, noticing there was no Slimline. A drink might make her feel better. She turned on the television to take her mind off . . .

She still couldn't face the bed. Looking down at it, she thought: Is it going to be a night in that bloody chair? She felt flustered, couldn't quite come to terms with what she had done. But she had had no choice. The two girls would have gone off to the States, and she would have been abandoned. It had been a gruesome afternoon, but a necessary one. Did she regret the last few hours? No. But she would never see Jules again – her coppery hair, her flowing skirts, her clay-splattered hands . . .

She shook herself. She couldn't face a bath. She took up defiant occupation of the bed. The screen was flickering with the usual Saturday afternoon crap. For once, immediately understanding the remote-control, she flicked and zapped from one channel to another – *not* Mickey Rooney again. Gone. Despatched. On Channel 4 there was racing. Gone. Despatched. Disenchanted, she turned off. The little white light obligingly faded into the distance, just as, this afternoon, Jules's life had also ebbed away.

Hating herself, Charlotte reached for the phone and ordered cigarettes from Room Service.

A moment later, she burst into tears. Getting off the bed, she threw the untouched drink at the newly decorated walls. Some of it landed on the dreary utilitarian carpet. It did not make the impact she had expected, just a small wet patch.

The slice of lemon, still half frozen from the fridge, slid down the wall.

Room Service knocked at the door. Charlotte put on her shoes and, carefully keeping the door half-closed, took the cigarettes from a smiling Italian. Closing the door on him, she lit up immediately. The desperate gulp of nicotine made her feel green again. She persevered, throwing the hotel matches on to the Room Service menu. It wasn't any good – she'd be back in that bathroom again. She broke the cigarette in half and stubbed it out. She hadn't thought it would be like this – hadn't expected to be so upset.

She ripped off her clothes, leaving them in a heap on the floor. When had she last done *that*? Probably the night of that horrible hunt ball when that prat had squeezed her breast so hard it had seriously hurt. Keep it all in, she reminded herself, then you are safe. No one truly knows who you are. Only one person had ever got through her armour – Felicity. Don't think about *her* now – don't think about bathrooms.

Was it safe to take a sleeping pill? She always kept a couple in a pill box in her bag. Would she need one? She was in control. She had achieved what she had set out to do – had given life a hefty push. She had actually done it. She forced herself to remember *she* knew nothing about today's events – everything that had happened today had happened to Jules and Barty. She would be the sympathetic listener in the morning.

Tomorrow would be Barty's day and Charlotte would be there to catch her.

No drink, no cigarettes, no bath, no food could comfort her. She drew the curtains, shutting out the day. There was nothing else she could do today. She was empty. It was only six o'clock, but she had to sleep, rest, forget. She took two sleeping tablets.

She needed ten hours of oblivion to be able to face tomorrow. The crisp hotel linen was welcoming, but she knew she was going to have a nightmare . . . the flannel . . . jam tarts . . . Cook . . . swimming-pools . . . bees . . . Jules's face . . . the smell of the rubber gloves.

Chapter Twenty-Eight

Fear had over-ridden the sleeping tablets. They had given Charlotte three hours of deep sleep. The rest of the night had been spent sweating, turning, shifting position. Anguish had twisted her backwards and forwards, at one point the sheets nearly strangling her in a sausage-like grip. Her mind was like a kaleidoscope – yesterday's events whizzing and whirling around, constantly changing their interweaving patterns. There was some comfort – it was all over. She had done it. She would never have to do it again.

Charlotte opened her eyes to the harsh light of the bedside lamp. God, it was only four a.m. The pile of clothes on the carpet were witness to her panic of the night before. She snapped off the light. Hell. Was this what they called a living hell? She should be feeling happy, jubilant, but she wasn't.

Stay calm.

Lying there in the dark, she felt a trickle of sweat between her breasts and reached out for the glass of water on the table. She knocked it over. Shit. Had all comfort deserted her? There were two wet stains now, one on the wall, one on the carpet, but at least she hadn't wet the bed. Yet.

It was so quiet. There was only the noise of a distant train for comfort as she fell back, hoping for more sleep. The train's echo was fading. Her last dipping thoughts were: What would today bring? Now, she *must* sleep, or she'd be no good later. Turning over, rearranging the pillows, she *knew* she had done the right thing, and Barty would never never know. With Jules out of the way, it would be Barty and Charlotte on the patio – in Midhurst, Italy, France, wherever Barty wanted. After yesterday, she would always let Barty make the decisions – the choice. For Charlotte, the setting would be irrelevant. The place didn't matter, the person did – Barty.

By six a.m., she couldn't shelter under the sheets any longer. Better get up. Take everything slowly. The bath. Barty's arrival. She had six hours before that. Make-up. Hair. Force down some fruit and coffee. Must eat. Be ready. Be everything everybody expected her to be. Elegant. Composed. Calm. Ready to catch Barty, like a wicket-keeper, but without the big white gloves.

Naked on the side of the bed, Charlotte felt her mind swim. Her hands in those white rubber gloves . . . She shuddered, got up and made herself run the bath. Where would Barty be now? Still in the air, with the duty-free trolley trundling down the aisle, the cabin crew with smiles plastered on their faces, longing for the Tarmac and the Captain's words: 'Cabin crew, doors to manual'.

She took her time in the sudsy water. The gloves. If only she could get rid of the vision of the gloves . . . the smell of rubber. Even the hotel's smellies couldn't banish it. Getting out, she avoided her reflection in the mirror. Why did hotels have all these mirrors? The harsh light exposing the body's inadequacies. Towels. Deodorant. Talc. Eventually, she forced herself to look in the glass. A totally normal Charlotte. How could she look so normal? 'Eyes are the mirror of the soul,' people said. But nobody, looking into hers, would have a clue about what she had done yesterday.

She hauled herself back to the present. She was in Midhurst. This was reality. A Sussex Sunday morning, with a crucial day's acting ahead. Today, she knew, would take her in deeper. She could back off now, just get into the car and leave. No one was forcing her to go through with today. She could see Barty in a couple of days' time. After all, she could have been away for the weekend in Truro, Manchester, anywhere. But she knew she had to go through with today; had to be the one controlling events, making things happen. She looked at her watch. Yes, however painful, she would go on.

She crossed to the telephone, pressed 9 for the outside line, dialled her own number, and cued up the three waiting messages with her remote. Brian Stewart – boring – inviting her to an auction of Old Masters; the BBC wanting a date for a planning meeting, and warning: 'We're moving to Studio B6 for next week.'

She was *not* prepared for the next message. Barty's strangled voice, howling down the line: 'Charlie. Come. Jules is dead. Charlie, you must come down.' Her voice broke and trailed off. Had Charlotte faintly heard a male voice in the background? The line went dead.

God! She put the phone down. Why was Barty home already? She shouldn't be home. What had gone wrong? Hell. She must have got an early plane. Who was the man? A policeman?

Charlotte redialled her number, and jabbed 3 again on her remote. The appalling message repeated in her ear: 'Charlie. Come. Jules is dead. Charlie, you must come down.'

Again, she could hear a man in the background – could definitely hear a man in the background.

Barty *must* have come home last night.

Steady. Concentrate.

Appalled, she reached for last night's gaping packet of Marlboros. Hell! She knew that voice belonged to a policeman. The police were there. Barty had found the body. They had been there all night.

Charlotte slumped back on the bed, visualizing and hearing sirens and bright lights. She could 'see' the solicitous WPC, asking questions. She gasped. The whys, the wherefores. The initial sympathy. Comfort for the bereaved. Then the gentle probings while they tried to establish cause of death. Endless cups of coffee. Token arms around Barty's shoulders. Sudden death is never easy to understand.

Charlotte stubbed out the cigarette, instantly lighting another. The police would have to make the cause of death neat and tidy. There would be forms to fill in. What had happened while she had been asleep? Yet another car would have forced its way up the drive, edging its way past the patrol car. This one would have contained the police surgeon, summoned by the first policeman on the scene. 'Don't touch the body,' followed by the official 'please'. Barty would have been hysterical – or would she?

Charlotte had a sudden mental image of TV's Inspector Morse, his grumpy acknowledgments of the police surgeon called out from a dinner party, going through the professional motions with his doctor's bag.

Focus Concentrate.

After all her meticulous planning, she didn't deserve this curved ball. The wicket keeper's gloves loomed back into focus. She cringed. She was out of the game. *No, she wasn't.* She would *not* walk back to the pavilion. All right, it had gone wrong. But she could still stick to her plan. When you're out, the next man pads up. Why was she dwelling on the vision of Midhurst's cricket pitch? For God's sake, why at a time like this did her mind go off to white figures against the green? Maybe Henry was right, maybe she was stupid? She was irritating herself. But she couldn't shift the cricketing metaphor. After Barty's message, she knew she had to be the next man in. Did it really matter that the police had got there first? With any luck, they would be gone before she got there. She nearly picked up the phone, but stopped herself, realizing she had to rehearse her shock, her sympathy and possibly being questioned by officialdom: 'When did you last see Ms Hardaker . . . ?' She knocked that one to the boundary.

Surely, by now, the police surgeon would be thinking what *she* wanted him to think. Jules's death was an accident – an allergic reaction to bee-stings.

She was chain-smoking, but this was understandable surely, after what she had done yesterday.

Barty – and the police.

Today, she would need to be very good at acting out the horror of losing one of her closest friends in such appalling circumstances: 'What a dreadful accident.'

Just for a second, Charlotte didn't like herself. But only for a second.

Chapter Twenty-Nine

꘎

At the funeral, she knew she had got away with it. She *really* had done it.

The ceremony, a week later, had a dream-like quality. There were so many familiar faces – older, perhaps through grief? Pops had come over from America. He looked utterly devastated and was walking with the help of a stick. Everyone was whispering the same thing: 'What a tragedy.'

Barty's face ... Charlotte couldn't afford to think of Barty's face.

Barty had written a farewell poem to Jules especially for the service. The congregation had been reduced to tears by the intensity of her emotion and her reading.

It had been a terrible moment for Charlotte, too. But then why shouldn't she, the oldest friend, put her head in her hands, tears flowing in rivulets on to her carefully selected suit? Like Barty and Pops, she had to be helped out of the church. In the summer sunshine there were gay couples, a sprinkling of heterosexual friends, the occasional American, all united in tears for Jules. Her flourishing talented life had been cut short by a terrible accident.

Bee stings. How could it have happened?

'Jules had been working so hard to finish an order before we packed up for the States,' Barty had told the mourners. 'She worked incessantly that last week, sometimes through the night throwing pots. On the phone from Lisbon I told her to ease up, take some time by the pool.'

In the cemetery, the coffin alongside her bearing a single red rose, Barty's mouth had moved courageously while silent tears witnessed her anguish.

Tiredness, they all agreed, had contributed to Jules's death. Worn out after working through the night, she had had that fatal banana and honey sandwich then, taking Barty's advice, had fallen asleep by the pool where she had been stung by some bees. That was how the Coroner had seen it. And that was precisely what Charlotte had planned from her armchair. Now, that was how everbody saw it.

But: 'How could it have happened?' they kept saying.

Over drinks, the mourners had speculated as to how Barty would cope. She and Jules had been so happy. Everyone knew for certain the two of them would have been together all their lives. What a dreadful shock, finding Jules's body in the dark. Poor Barty.

Pops sat looking sunken and skeletal in the corner, having just buried his only daughter.

The WPC who had looked after Barty had come to the funeral and then back to the cottage. Charlotte had spotted her immediately and warily kept her distance a rectory table away. They acknowledged each other with a sad smile and Charlotte remained only too aware of the slight sandy-haired figure making one glass of white wine last a very long time. Did the policewoman suspect anything? Charlotte, of course, had met her when she went to comfort Barty that Sunday lunchtime. She would never forget the sight of her friend with that professional blue-gabardined arm around her shoulder – counselling time.

That Sunday, Charlotte had forced herself to wait in her hotel room till eleven before steeling herself to pick up the phone. This had been one of *those* phone calls – like arranging a rather appointment or the dentist, filed under phone calls you'd rather not make.

On the phone, there had been tears, wails, self-recriminations. 'If only I had been there,' Barty had sobbed, ending with: 'Charlie, please come. Come now. Come as soon as you can.'

She recognized the irony of the situation. She had caused all this – brought this misery on Barty.

She had masturbated on the bed.

Then, getting up, she had checked out of the hotel and gone to the rescue.

Chapter Thirty

After the funeral, Charlotte had thought normality would be restored relatively easily and quickly. She had been wrong. It had taken weeks before she was sleeping, eating, and feeling calmer. Then, she had stopped smoking and felt triumphant.

Now she rarely saw the ghost of Jules or smelt rubber.

Sitting in her plotting armchair, she thought back to Barty's obsessive 'clicking' at the funeral. Most of the time she had literally ignored the guests. *Click. Click. Click.* The wreaths. The hearse. *Click.* She had shot the coffin from every angle. *Click.*

Charlotte remembered feeling embarrassed for her. It was so morbid, so ghoulish – Barty couldn't give Jules up. *Click.* She had clung on to the last vestige of Jules. *Click.* This was their last chance to be together. *Click.* She had been in her own world. *Click.* Cremation. Curtains.

After all that, Charlotte had certainly needed a holiday and had pressurized Barty, for her own good, to come too. She had taken her friend to the Maldives and vainly tried to interest her in snorkelling, the exotic fish and the secret world of the coral.

All Barty had wanted was to drown – to be with Jules. For her, the trip had not been a success. It had been much too soon. She was hurting – the pain appallingly raw. She had lost nearly a stone, was not the Barty of old – her career on hold. The commissioning editors were still ringing, their priority to get top-calibre shots.

'C'mon, Barty. You can't sit and mope. The front-page won't wait. And it'll be good for you. Jules wouldn't have wanted you to stagnate.'

They had persisted in trotting out the helpful, but hurtful inducements.

Barty had flinched at every call, dead voice repeating: 'I'll start again in January.'

To Charlotte she had said: 'The photography can wait, Charlie. My personal life . . . *that* part of my life . . . is over. There'll never be anyone like Jules.'

The burning sun had intensified the blues of the sea and the sky, and the green of the lolling palm trees. The beauty of the backdrop had seemed to exacerbate Barty's grief rather than assuage it. The sunsets were particularly spectacular in the dribble of islands and sand-bars that were the Maldives, and Charlotte always tried to keep Barty in the bar at sun down.

One afternoon, Barty had rolled over in the sand, biting her discarded flipper, and just howled. The languid sun-worshippers all about had looked up from their airport novels and ordered another rum punch. Misery was not part of their package holiday deal. They had enough of that at home. Charlotte, as ever, had stretched out a comforting arm and the honeyed words had flowed easily.

'Barty . . . this is going to take time. You can't just spring back to normal overnight. You lived with Jules for nearly ten years. But the sun will shine again . . .'

'I *hate* the blasted sun,' Barty had said, stabbing her toes into the sand and kicking up the fine white dust. 'I *want* Jules . . . I want Midhurst and everything we had there. I *want* to see her come through the door flecked with clay, her hair all messed up, asking is it time for supper?'

There had not been very much Charlotte could say to that.

She hated seeing Barty so destroyed, so desperate. Normally, she could fix things with her money and contacts. But time was the only healer for this one.

At least, in this state, Barty would not be falling in love again.

For Charlotte, the trip had been a success. Barty was currently bumping along on the bottom, but she would eventually heal, the emotional scars would fade. Anybody who had been bereaved always told you that. In two years' time, she would be back to her old self and still with Charlotte in England. Then they would have some really good holidays. In the meantime, Barty could lean on her full-time. The coffees, the lunches, the overnight stops, the key in the lock at Eaton Square, would continue as they always had for the past twenty-five years. Thanks to a weekend's work, their Family life would remain intact.

It was she who would now be by Barty's side. The pecking order had changed again. She, Charlotte, was in pole position – number one again.

The planning, her lack of sleep, the irritable bowel syndrome, her lack of appetite, had all been worth it.

Chapter Thirty-One

It was nearly three years since Jules had died. Charlotte had just come in from a long tedious meeting for a charity ball, planned for two months ahead.

She went into the kitchen, made some tea and settled down to watch the six o'clock news. The 'soap' was still running. Committee meetings were a nightmare, with everyone throwing in their penn'orth. Who was donating the car? Had they got a good royal? The seating plan always turned into a Semtex plot. The great and the good committee members jostled for position.

Why did she do it? For three reasons, Charlotte supposed. It filled the time, it was expected of her, and often the Good Works were rewarded by: 'You're marvellous, Charlotte. You're such a lovely person. You do so much for charity.'

The news had begun, but was drifting over her head.

So many committees, so many secret agendas of the ladies-who-lunched and schemed, hell-bent on promoting their husbands and, of course, themselves.

'Still to come on the early-evening news,' John Suchet intoned, 'social security scam . . . possible release of hostages in Papua New Guinea . . . child abuse horror in a children's home in Coventry . . .'

Charlotte wasn't concentrating. She had heard the headlines so clicked off the set.

She knew she should open the post, check the fax and messages. She'd do it in a minute. She was tired. Being the Chair of the committee and carrying the can was exhausting. She abandoned her cup of tea and poured herself a vodka, then found herself wondering what it would be like to come home to somebody who poured out the drink for you? Somebody who said: 'What sort of a day have you had?' and put an arm around your shoulder?

She thought back on Barty and Jules.

'She's cool, supportive, the light of my life,' Barty had once said. 'I feel, Charlie, as if I've met my other half. It's a dreadful old cliché but that's what I feel about her. Totally comfortable ... The "in sickness and in health" syndrome. She makes me laugh and cooks a brilliant clam chowder. What I can do, she can't. And vice versa. I suppose we complement each other – and isn't that what it's all about?'

Barty had suddenly realized that saying this to Charlotte was insensitive. She had no one in her life. Hurriedly, knowing she had sounded smug, Barty had added: 'Oh, Charlie, you'll find the right person one day.'

Somehow they had both known she wouldn't.

The world, she thought feeling sorry for herself, was peopled with couples. Her thoughts turned to Therese and Mick. Therese had always been very discreet, very protective of him. Anything Charlotte knew about Mick, she had had to winkle out slyly over the years.

She went into the kitchen, opened a packet of crisps and leaned back against the dish-washer. Suddenly, she found herself wondering yet again about Therese's partner. Mick had been fostered, not very successfully, apparently. Therese would not be drawn on that. He openly said he had been to the LSE. Had he? Therese had once mentioned he'd been quite wild. She wouldn't be drawn into how wild, but Charlotte could imagine. Occasionally, after several beers, Mick would talk about the Berlin Wall coming down, his disillusionment with Communism, his hatred of the Tories, and, after a few more beers, his hatred of just about everything. His loathing of Thatcher, Major, the Church, Royalty. If it was Establishment, he hated it.

Therese adored him, was more than willing to be his meal ticket. He was genuinely devoted to animals, but had Charlotte sensed a crack in his commitment to Therese and the endless round of mucking out and mending broken animal bits and pieces?

Perhaps she was imagining it? Therese had found her niche and so long as Mick was there, the strong man by her side, she would be happy. But was Mick happy? The last time Charlotte had been down there, she had sensed he was outgrowing the sanctuary. Her instinct told her he was restless – wanted out.

And Therese? Charlotte sipped her drink and thought back over their lunch last week. Therese had been unusually quiet. Just about to pay the bill, £28 for some mediocre dried-up macaroni cheese, a salad, and a bottle of dreadful wine, Charlotte had probed: 'C'mon, Therese, what's the matter?'

Confronted, she had given up pretending everything was all right and the tears had started to flow. Stewed-up anxiety had broken out in sudden sobbing.

'Charlie, he's gone all funny . . . he doesn't talk to me like he used to . . . and he's become so secretive lately.'

She had listened, noticing Therese's worn hands and ragged nails clutching her temples. She was beginning to go grey. Charlotte had felt a vicious stirring of anger towards Mick.

Therese had raised her head, her eyes streaming.

'I feel so left out, Charlie. I feels he's plotting and I'm not part of it.'

She had used the paper napkin to blow her nose.

'I know you've never liked him, but you've never really understood him. You see, Charlie, he's not like us. He's so clever, so political.' She sniffed. 'He's always one step ahead of everyone else.' Her body slumped, and she put her head in her hands, whispering: 'I think he's going to leave me.'

They had outstayed their £28-worth. The waiters had disappeared into the back for their own lunch. Charlotte waited for the sobs of despair to subside. Seeing Therese brought to this, she hated the man who was causing such distress to a member of her Family.

Eventually, they had had a medicinal brandy, and a closet cigarette sponged from an emerging waiter. Therese, comforted by Charlotte's sympathy, had been a bit brighter when she was dropped off at the sanctuary.

'Thanks for coming down and taking me out to lunch. I know you've got a lot on with this Ball thing, but I *really* needed you today. You're the only person to have around when I'm feeling so low. I can't talk to anybody else.'

'I'm sure all this will blow over, darling,' Charlotte had said. 'You know what men are like. He's just going through a bad patch. It's probably nothing to do with you at all.'

Therese had not looked convinced.

As they kissed goodbye, Charlotte had glimpsed Mick across a field with the usual bucket. He had given her a cursory wave.

You pig, she had thought.

On the drive back to London, she had promised him: If you hurt Therese, I'll hurt you.

Chapter Thirty-Two

❦

Spring was slow into its stride this year. Outside, it was chilly enough to be autumn. Actually, it was late May, and, thank God, a day with no meetings, no charity committees and no BBC.

Relishing the thought of a free day, Charlotte pulled a cardigan over her white nightdress. Elegant she was not, but it was only seven-thirty in the morning. She would have a bath and make herself presentable after checking the fax and the answer-machine. It was such a luxury, anticipating a no-hurry day – a day just for herself.

In the study she switched on the radio, and decided it was a Radio 3 morning. Wagner. She couldn't cope with him this early in the day. She switched to Radio 2 and some Country and Western singer, who apparently had just had a mild heart scare and been told to diet. Just for a moment she thought of Felicity in the bathroom – but she wouldn't dwell on that.

Charlotte gave a cursory glance at the faxes, and shivered. It really was cold enough to be November. Poor gardeners, preparing for tomorrow's opening of the Chelsea Flower Show. Her paper was always delivered, and today's *Times* was lying on the mat. Picking it up, she noticed the front-page headline: 'Cold Shakes the Buds of Chelsea'. The picture showed a woman using a hairdrier to keep warm her rare Malaysian Anthuriums. All the prize flowers and exhibition gardens had to be at their peak for this one week of the year. What a nightmare for the green-fingered! They hadn't reckoned on being clobbered by freak winds from Siberia.

Last year, as a guest, Charlotte had gone to the private view. It had been seventy-nine degrees at six o'clock in the evening. The great and the good had been in their panamas and summer suits – all very civilized. It would not be like that tomorrow.

She rewound the six messages on her answer-machine. While it was spooling back, she thought, yes, it had definitely been in the late-seventies last year. She had worn that floral pink frock, and had taken a straw hat. This year, she would need thermals, balaclava and a horse-blanket. Such a shame.

While the tape spun backwards, she retreated to the bedroom and pulled on a pair of warming socks. She remembered Cook's words: 'Always look after your extremities, Charlotte.' At seven, she had not known what extremities were, but it had seemed an important word and good advice to be stored away.

The machine had sorted itself out, and was automatically spewing forth messages from the bank manager, the BBC, her dress designer asking her to come for a fitting on Friday. Then, as she bent to rearrange the heel of her sock which was rucking, she heard Therese's voice. There was something about the sound that made Charlotte freeze. Something had happened. Her friend's voice was strangely manic.

'Charlie, it's me. Ring me. Ring me! I've got some simply wonderful news. I want to tell you first. I can't wait to tell you.' Therese had paused from her bubbling, sense prevailing. 'It's Tuesday, eight o'clock. I'm just off to lock up the animals. I know you're out to dinner. You'll probably pick this up first thing Wednesday. Ring as soon as you can.'

Good manners meant Charlotte never rang anybody before nine-thirty. The message was already eleven hours old. Another two wouldn't make any difference. She sensed the message was not going to be good news for her Family. She had heard that tone of voice before – the day Barty had telephoned her with the news of the exodus to America. Charlotte shivered. She would have the promised bath to warm up and prepare herself for a shock.

She loved baths, but this morning the suds seemed empty. The temperature was wrong, and she noticed two ominous cracks appearing in the sealant around the bath.

Inside herself, she knew the politeness of not ringing before nine-thirty was a sham – a total sham in this instance with a very dear friend. But she needed time to think. Lying in the water, she envisaged the scene in Surrey. It would be the same dawn chorus, the same date. London and Surrey were probably sharing the same weather. But the actors and the backdrop were so totally different.

Charlotte looked down at herself. The body in the bath. Beautiful surroundings, shiny taps, immaculate white towels. Her morning was one of opulence, privilege, protected from the real world by thousands of pounds worth of locks, burglar alarms and security grilles.

Out of the bath, she glanced at the bedside clock. God, the daily drudge of everyday dressing. What would be happening in Surrey at eight-fifteen? Mick and Therese would have been up since six. The cooing doves and pigeons would have seen to that. Charlotte remembered only too clearly the early-morning din when she had once been persuaded to stay the night at the sanctuary.

The next morning she had been red-eyed, mentally and physically drained by the night before's battlefield supper with Mick. After a fitful sleep on a ghastly lumpy mattress, she had been no use to anybody the next day. She had been woken around five by Jack-the-Ripper-ish death-calls from two mutilated pheasants wandering willy-nilly around the sanctuary. This chorus had been joined by the baying of abandoned seaside donkeys – obviously love-sick or mating. The cockerels and dogs had joined in. What a night. What a morning. Never to be repeated.

Here in her SW1 postcode she felt safe and imagined Mick pulling on his revolting jeans and the top he had left in a pile the night before, filling the troughs – being a man. Charlotte knew exactly what Therese would be doing. She was always hopeless in the mornings. Sleepily, she would be filling a kettle and doing her rounds in that awful smelly pullover, jeans and black wellingtons, carrying a mug of tea into the sharp spring air.

Charlotte put on some moisturizer and foundation, and thought how different their lives were. They shared the same spring morning, the same country, the same nationality, and yet they were worlds apart.

And now Mick and Therese would be up, mucking out and getting on with their day.

What would the so-called 'wonderful news' be? Obviously good for Therese and Mick, but Charlotte sensed she might not be so thrilled at what she was about to hear. She might not figure in the new plans. It *had* to be about new plans. It all felt so *déjà vu*.

As she crushed an obstinate coffee granule against the side of the cup, she knew she did not want to go down that road again. She was still not ready to pick up the telephone. If she left it another twenty minutes, she might get Therese on her own in that shambolic little kitchen.

Sitting at her own kitchen table, Charlotte re-ran their lunch of three months ago through her mind. She remembered how Therese had broken down, whispering: 'I think he's going to leave me, Charlie . . .'

Therese had not said anything about the future then. She hadn't, had she? There had been no future. Both she and Therese had thought that Mick was going to do a runner.

This telephone call meant something had changed dramatically. But what?

Charlotte heard an open-and-shut noise from downstairs, followed by a light flop as the mail dropped on to the mat.

It was no good, she couldn't delay ringing a moment longer. She prayed Therese would be there, making lists in that filthy kitchen.

She would ring now.

Chapter Thirty-Three

Bip ... Bip ... Bip ... The number was engaged.

Charlotte blamed the negative irritating bleeps on Mick up to his normal early-morning wheeling-and-dealing. She felt sick, instinctively fearful for herself.

Sitting on the side of the bed, she ticked herself off. Why was she panicking? The call could be about a legacy from one of the fluffy ladies. Therese could have won the lottery. Mick's hair could have stopped falling out. Why was *she* so worried?

Charlotte redialled. Therese answered: 'Surrey Animal Sanctuary.'

'It's me.'

'Charlie! God, I thought you'd never ring.'

'Sorry,' she lied. 'I was very late in last night and only got your message this morning. What is it? You sounded quite like your old self. Have you won the lottery?'

'Better than that. We – Mick and I – are going off to live in Madagascar.'

Charlotte stood up, pacing around the bedroom, changing the remote from ear to ear. She caught sight of herself in the mirror. The foundation provided no mask – her panic was transparent, thrown back by the mirror.

'That's wonderful,' she mustered the words. 'I can't keep up with you two ...'

Therese laughed down the phone.

'Hang on a minute, Charlie. Gobble's just come into the kitchen.'

It was the usual phone call with Therese – animals in the kitchen. Why did she always have to vie for her friend's attention? It was her versus a turkey.

'Come on, what's going on? What's the news?'

She could hear the sound of a kettle coming to the boil and imagined the coffee routine: milk from the fridge, coffee from the cupboard. She waited for the cry: 'The milk's off.' Heard Therese say, 'Damn!' Then: 'Right, Charlie, I'm sitting down – black coffee . . . milk's off as usual. Here goes. It's been the most amazing twenty-four hours. Yesterday morning, Mick – completely out of the blue, typical of him – just announced he's got this conservation job in Madagascar of all places.' She giggled. 'Honestly, Charlie, I thought of you when I rooted around for my school atlas. D'you remember the one we had with the globe on the front? There it was – "Therese Allinson-Smith, Edith Cavell House" written in my squidgy fourteen-year-old writing. Bet *you* don't know where Madagascar is?'

Charlotte did not care where it was. Wherever it was, it was too far.

'I've got the atlas here,' Therese burbled on. 'Listen, it's an island in the Indian Ocean, renowned for its unique fauna and flora. French influence. Lemurs and Ploughshare tortoises . . .'

Charlotte could not respond.

'Are you still there, Charlie? It's off Mozambique . . . near the Seychelles. I've got a cutting Mick's given me,' she droned on. 'Farming is the occupation of eighty-five per cent of the population, only three per cent of the land is cultivated. Can you imagine that?' She did not wait for a response. 'We'll be living in a tropical rainforest. It says here coffee and rice are the main products . . . Oh, and vanilla.'

America. Madagascar. Barty. Jules. Pottery. Honey. Vanilla. Charlotte's mind was in turmoil. This time it was Therese, not Barty, who was going. This time it was Mick, not Jules, who was taking one of the Family away. She needed time to think, before she could sound normal, but Therese could not wait.

'Doesn't it sound marvellous, Charlie?'

She knew she had to make an attempt, however pathetic, to match her friend's mood.

'Therese . . . it's wonderful.'

'You can come out for our usual New Year.'

This time it was New Year not Christmas that was being offered.

'Yes, and I could have a holiday with you in the Seychelles.'

Charlotte knew her enthusiasm sounded hollow. What the hell was going on?

'What are you and Mick going to be doing out there in this tropical rainforest?' she added snidely.

Therese was oblivious of the dig.

'Well,' she cantered on, 'it's the old story – poaching. The Ploughshare tortoise is a deeply endangered species, and recently – you've probably read about it, Charlie – a quarter of the entire population of tortoises was snatched in a midnight raid from this remote breeding station, and that's where Mick comes in. The authorities know that the babies will be put on the black market for endangered animals. It's perfect for him,' she gushed, 'he will be a kind of conservationist policeman. "Protect and preserve", that's his brief. Black-market tortoises are big money in Holland, Japan, Slovenia and the Czech Republic.'

Charlotte heard Therese gulp her coffee, and could envisage the smile on her face. Her own instinct had been right: this *was* bad news – *very* bad news indeed.

Things, she thought, like buses, often come in threes. She had been here before – faced other threats to the break-up of her Family and her own stability. To her own cost, she had managed to see off two threats and get away with it. She had despatched Felicity . . . well, Felicity had despatched herself. The grey face in the grey bathroom loomed before her eyes.

She batted the vision away. Felicity had been easy. Jules had been another matter. Occasionally, she still saw the girl's sleeping face and needed tablets to obliterate memories of a summer afternoon. Jules had been a friend, but she had been a threat. No longer.

'Who will look after the sanctuary?' Charlotte heard herself ask, weakly.

Therese had her old confidence back.

'I've got it all sorted, Charlie. You know Janet, the one with the long hair and the ghastly mother . . . she's going to take over. It will probably be for two years. But isn't it *exciting*?'

'When are you going?'

'A month's time . . . It's all so quick. Isn't Mick clever? I didn't know anything about it. All those phone calls – and I thought it was so sinister . . . I was like a horse seeing paper bags in gates – him leaving me . . . sinister plots . . . I feel so stupid now. And all the time he was going for interviews and doing it for *us*.'

Not for me, thought Charlotte.

'Mick's contacts have really paid off here,' Therese added. 'Charlie, I'm longing to tell you more about it at a farewell lunch. Obviously I can't have lunch next week because I've got to start packing and getting the jabs.' She paused. 'But you *will* come out for the New Year, won't you?'

June. July. August. September. October. November. December. January. That was eight fucking months, with only one farewell lunch in between. Damn Mick. Damn him. Damn him – and his Ploughshare tortoises!

She knew at this moment Therese did not care if she was there or not.

Left high and dry.

The hurt burned into her.

Chapter Thirty-Four

Charlotte had very little time and much to do if she were going to put an obstacle in the way of the Madagascan bandwagon. Therese was calling her less frequently, and, when she did ring, there was a strong impression that she had better things to do than chat.

'I'm up to my ears packing up here. You know what a squirrel I am – I seem to have kept everything! There's only three weeks to go to get rid of it all. We can't take it with us. Mick's having a daily bonfire.'

One day Charlotte just sat and looked at the wall. She had discarded Plan A, then Plan B, then Plan C – too messy, too risky, too dangerous. Lateral thinking – what were her strengths and Mick's weaknesses? The wall did not deliver any answers immediately, but, by three o'clock she had arrived at a possible solution. She knew it was three because the church clock had chimed.

The success of Plan D would depend on the results of the phone calls she was steeling herself to make. Why had she not thought of this before? It might *not* work, but then again it just *might*. With all his foxy cleverness and dodgy background, Mick might just have dug his own grave. All she needed now was luck on her side.

Charlotte picked up the phone. It was always embarrassing calling in favours, but this was an emergency. Old money, contacts and family could be relied on to close ranks when necessary – and to open doors.

She had finished the four calls by six. She had stressed the urgent time factor. No one had said no. By tomorrow she would know whether she could put a stop to this Madagascan lunacy. There was no time for sophisticated plans. Jules came to mind. Mick was different. This had to be quick, sharp – and it had to work. Would her instincts about him be right? Only a night to wait . . .

Twenty-one hours later she knew all she needed to know about Mick Davies. She had her dossier, had all the information she required. Exactly as she expected, she now had a fighting chance. For the first time since Therese's phone call, Charlotte felt confident and in control. She was ready to play chess with Mick. She didn't know much about chess but, looking through the dossier she had compiled, knew she had some major pieces, including the King and Queen. She smiled. Mick had never thought much of Royalty, and in the past had spent a lot of time pushing her into a corner.

This time, Charlotte would checkmate him.

Therese and Mick believed they would be flying to Madagascar and its beastly insect-ridden rainforest in under a month. Therese, she thought, might have to live in a tent. Cockroaches. Bats. Natives. Therese trusted everybody, thought the best of them. Mick might go off with God knows what. There could be dead-beats on drugs – and where there was drug-trafficking, there was also violence. She panicked – Therese could be mugged or raped. Conveniently, she tossed aside Madagascar's stunning flora, fauna and history.

She didn't want to go out this evening. She wanted to stay in her robe in the stillness of her house and go over her plan for tomorrow. But she couldn't get out of this charity evening of music and fireworks at Hampton Court. Cream suit . . . the jacket could come off if it got too hot. She went through the motions of dressing, make-up and hair.

Mick had now become dangerous and she nagged herself not to underestimate him.

Concentrate. Focus.

Mick was the consummate weasel, and she was about to shut

off his tunnel. People like Mick always had an escape route – somewhere to hide. Therese's voice came back.

'He's always one step ahead of everyone else, Charlie. So political, so clever . . .'

On the side of the bed, she ran through her plot until she was satisfied she had missed nothing. Thanks to her phone call, Mick would be here in her house for the first time tomorrow night. By Monday, he would be gone for ever. Relieved, she realized that in forty-eight hours she would never have to look at him again. Ever.

Dressed and waiting for the car, she picked over the details. Yes, Mick had to be winkled out of Therese's life. Her plan had used up considerable resources and contacts – favours she could call in only once in a lifetime. The dossier had needed some fleshing out and she had leant on brother Henry. He went fishing with the Police Commissioner at Scotland Yard. That contact had proved invaluable.

Charlotte reflected on today's phone call to Mick. She had been apprehensive, but had surprised herself with her quiet, confident voice. Did she feel guilty? No. Mick had been a bad boy. Yes, of course she was interfering, using information, changing the course of two people's lives. But she was making necessary things happen.

She checked her watch. Her driver was not late. Yet. Bloody fireworks. Today was Saturday. Mick, curious and anxious, and probably furious, would be here tomorrow. By lunchtime on Monday Therese would be safe from his influence.

Charlotte anticipated Monday. Therese would no longer need the boxes labelled Madagascar. Instead, there would be a Thamesworth of tears. Confusion. Betrayal. A sleepless night when her man didn't come home – and then, she, Charlotte, would make it all better.

The doorbell interrupted her. There was a long way to go yet, she reminded herself, before she could congratulate herself.

She picked up her handbag and put on her professional face. You should always keep a driver waiting. She did a final check in the mirror.

It had been a short but successful telephone call to Mick, hopefully with devastating consequences for him . . .

'Mick, I'm so relieved I got *you* and not Therese. It's Charlotte. This may sound very odd, a rather strange request, but could you come to see me in London tomorrow, around seven-thirty? It really is *crucial* you come and even more *crucial* for you not to mention this call to Therese.'

There had been no immediate response at the end of the line, but she could hear him breathing.

'What's this all about? Have you gone mad?'

'Mick, it's about you.'

There had been another pause.

'It *really* is important.'

'What's it all about?' he had repeated. 'It's a hell of a hack up from Surrey to London ... and we're up to our ears down here. Can't you tell me on the phone?'

'D'you really want to talk about the Trafalgar Square business on the phone?'

There had been another long pause. The stop-you-in-your-tracks factor had worked, as she had known it would.

'Trafalgar Square,' she had repeated. 'And, Mick, don't forget, not a word to Therese.'

Hurriedly, afraid he might just say 'Yep' and put the phone down, she had added: 'I know something you need to know. And, just as a precaution, I think you should bring your passport.'

This had thrown Mick, as she had known it would.

'Why should I bring my passport?' he spat back.

'You'll regret it if you don't, Mick. See you tomorrow night.'

Swiftly she had put the phone back on its cradle.

The mention of his passport had hooked him. She prayed that tomorrow she would reel him in.

Hampton Court had been built by the great Cardinal Wolsey in celebration of himself some 500 years ago. Now, as Charlotte arrived, it looked so innocent in the sunshine: cheery red bricks, its box maze and tennis courts where Wolsey's one-time friend and boss, Henry VIII, had beaten his opponents at real tennis. Perhaps they had let him win, preferring to keep their heads?

Hampton Court had probably seen more political and religious plots hatched on these immaculate lawns than any other palace in the land. In Tudor Britain, the Tower of London had always been the end of the journey. Traitor's gate and the executioner's block. But the seeds and whispers of jealousy, ambition and deception invariably began here at Hampton Court.

Charlotte had never been particularly interested in history, but had always been fascinated by plots and plotters. Poisoned food. Poisoned books. Even poisoned gloves. They certainly knew how to despatch each other in those days.

It was an outdoor concert. For once, thank God, the weather was perfect. The musicians were gently dripping in the heat but were bowing and blowing, drumming and clashing, as one. As the white-jacketed conductor turned to the audience, sweat was running down his face.

She hadn't registered much of the concert, had continued thinking about Mick through most of the performance, and had only been defeated by the sawing of violins.

Her mind continued to run over tomorrow's plan, ticking off minor details. She had his favourite brand of beer. Yes. All the stuff she needed was locked in her safe. Yes. Her arguments were sound, lucid and well rehearsed. Yes.

At that moment, relieved at the prospect of cool beers and the journey home, the orchestra erupted into a finale. The fireworks went off. The charity's host, sitting next to Charlotte, turned and said: 'Perfectly splendid. At least we Brits are still good at something. Fireworks, eh? Splendid!' His perspiring face was beaming. It was very humid.

'Yes,' she agreed, echoing his words. 'Perfectly splendid.'

What if Mick didn't come? But she was certain he would.

Chapter Thirty-Five

Charlotte had made a bet with herself Mick would be late. But she had been mistaken. The prompt ringing of the doorbell had wrong-footed her.

Now he was sitting in front of her, barely able to contain his anger and frustration. Charlotte watched him, thinking he looked rather silly in her surroundings. Denim, stubble and rough hands looked incongruous against the walnut inlay and rosewood marquetry of her furniture.

'What's this all about?' Mick stood up. He was controlling himself but only just.

She handed him a can of beer and a glass.

'Don't need the glass.'

The widget in the can flicked froth on to his jeans. He ignored it and came closer to her.

'What are you playing at? Why did you get me here? What about Trafalgar Square?'

Suddenly noticing his surroundings, he seemed to run out of steam and returned to his chair deflated. He sat there, watching her warily. It was seven-forty and she registered the noise of Concorde going over. She twiddled the stem of her sherry glass.

'Did you bring your passport, Mick?'

He raised his eyebrows, glaring at her.

'Yes. I had to find it when T wasn't there.'

Thank God! Charlotte concealed her relief.

'What the hell are you up to?' His face was contorted in anger. She had expected him to be edgy, but was suddenly frightened by his sheer male power, heightened by belligerence and fear. She wouldn't stand a chance if he lost control and went for her. He'd been brooding for twenty-four hours, storing up his fear, having to conceal his anxieties from Therese.

Trafalgar Square. For Mick it had been deeply buried for decades, but, thanks to Charlotte, it had now resurfaced.

It was time for her to speak. Although she was frightened, she realized she was savouring the moment, this reversal of their roles. This time it was Mick in her space. She held the cards. He needed her.

'Another beer?' He had drunk the first one.

He nodded sulkily.

'Okay . . . So, Trafalgar Square?'

He pulled the can open. More foam on his trousers. He was oblivious of the creamy mess adding to the stains on his jeans.

'What d'you wanna talk about, then?' He paused. 'What have you been poking your nose into? Listen, I've only come up here because you're T's oldest mate and I don't want anything to rock her, to . . .' he hesitated '. . . to shock her.'

Well, she thought, at least he cares about Therese and wants to protect her. This was the first sign of softness she had ever seen in Mick. Charlotte warmed to him slightly. But it was a bit late for that. She had to go for it.

'Mick,' she said, 'I hardly know how tell you this . . . and I can't explain how I know . . . but I've seen a file which perhaps I shouldn't have seen. I know what happened in Trafalgar Square. But I'd like to hear it from you, not a police report. What do *you* say happened that night?'

Mick looked at her coolly, said nothing for a few seconds, then asked for the toilet.

After five minutes he came back. His mood was different. He crossed the room.

'Sod the beer, I need something stronger.'

He plonked the can on the sideboard and poured himself a whisky from the cut-glass decanter.

Looking very tense, he turned and walked back towards her. She recognized that walk – the animal sanctuary walk. No deviating. The man with a knife at his belt who always knew exactly where he was going.

'Seems I've underestimated you, haven't I, Ms Twinset and Pearls.'

'Sit down, Mick. Just tell me your version and then I've got something to tell you.'

He put down his drink.

'No. Why should I tell you anything? You tell me first.'

Charlotte took a packet of Camels and some matches out of her handbag and offered them to him: He took one and lit up.

'Mick,' she said, 'there's no time for games. You don't realize it, but your time is fast running out. You really have got to trust me . . . talk to me.'

She wasn't stupid, but she must never forget Therese's words: 'Charlie, he's always one step ahead of everyone else.'

Would the words 'trust me' do the trick?

The grandfather clock chimed eight o'clock.

Mick reluctantly started to speak.

Chapter Thirty-Six

'For God's sake, I was only nineteen, just started at the LSE. It was a Friday morning. We'd been larking around, Tony and I . . . been on the piss all night. I think it was his birthday. About four in the morning we ended up in Trafalgar Square, eating a burger and chips sitting around the lions. It all happened so fast. Tony chucked the burger wrapper at a pigeon. The guy was in the wrong place at the wrong time – probably been working all night.'

Mick was blank-faced. She said nothing to interrupt his flow.

'I just remember the Suit. It was like a red rag to a bull for Tony. Then the Suit made a fatal mistake, saying: "Why don't you put your litter in a bin? There's one over there." Next thing I knew Tony had him by his tie, was shoving the burger wrapper in his mouth and frog-marching him to the litter bin. The Suit fought back. Tony yelled to me: "Get my knife!" He always kept one in his boot. I grabbed it. He had the Suit face down on the pavement. Tony shouted: "Do him! Do him!"' Mick paused, head bowed. 'I've regretted what happened next for twenty-one years. I don't know what got into me – I just slashed at him. And then we ran. It was only meant to teach him a lesson, shut him up . . .'

He broke off, choked, and moved to the sideboard for another whisky.

'Next day, the incident was reported on the news. I'd severed his spinal cord. He was a wheelchair job for life.'

He threw back the whisky, and refilled his glass.

'I've had to live with that all my life.'

And the Suit, she thought, had to live with a wheelchair for the rest of his.

'I did it,' Mick mumbled. 'Tony was in the clear. It was summer . . . no other news. The papers went to town on lager louts, skinheads and hooligans. And, to make it juicier, the Suit turned out to be a reporter's brother.'

He looked up at her.

'I'm not making excuses, but I was only nineteen . . . and very drunk.'

Like now, she thought.

'The police swept up everybody, including us. There were endless identification parades. But in those days we all looked and dressed the same. The Suit didn't pick us out, but somebody who had been in Trafalgar Square did. We'd had time to fix our alibi with some of Tony's mates. We said we'd been at the flicks . . . the Gate at Notting Hill. The truth was we'd seen the film the night before. We stuck to our story. The cops had no proof. We got off. They knew we'd done it. We knew they knew. Nothing they could do, though. I've never told Therese. Never talked to anybody about it till now.'

This time, Charlotte poured him the Scotch.

He drank it down in one.

'How did you know? How did you find out?'

She took her first sip of sherry.

'It doesn't matter, Mick, does it?'

She did not want to give him any unnecessary information that might be embarrassing later. She waited a second, adding: 'The fact is, you're on police files . . .'

'And with all my political protests,' he interrupted, 'I suspect the bastards have kept an eye on me all right.'

'Then you must already know . . .' She paused, wanting her next sentence to have an impact. 'They're closing in on you—'

It was clear from his expression he was rattled. He was chain-smoking now. With a cigarette between his fingers, he moved across the room to refill his glass.

Number four, she thought, wishing he would slow down.

'Closing in?' he said, moving back to her. 'What are you talking about? What else do you know?'

He was so close, she could smell the whisky – and his fear.

'*Who are you?*' he snapped. 'I just thought of you as T's old schoolfriend – rich bitch, to be honest. And here you are, dishing out all this stuff about me. How do you know? Are you a spy or something – undercover fuzz?'

'Mick, sit down. Rich bitch, yes, and Therese's friend, and yours, which is why you are here. I know a lot of people, Mick. The sort of people you despise – Establishment figures. And let's put it like this . . .' She paused for effect. 'I don't know all the details, I don't pretend to, but the police know the Animal Liberation Front is planning a big coup and the authorities are pretty certain you're a part of it. Has somebody been putting pressure on you? Is it Tony? You're still in contact with Tony, aren't you?'

Opposite her, Mick sighed. It had been an inspired guess. He didn't deny anything, blurting out: 'Well, he's got something on me, hasn't he? And, yes, you're right, he's fucking using it. I put the knife in. He can't be got for it.'

He looked her straight in the eye.

'But what do you know?'

She met his stare, slowly replying: 'You're in a mess. I know it's to do with the Government.' She paused. 'And it's to do with a woman.'

Mick slumped in his chair.

'How do you know all this?'

She ignored him. Saying nothing paid off. Having confessed to Trafalgar Square, he couldn't stop.

'Oh, God! I didn't want anything to do with this kidnap thing. The animal sanctuary has been like a penance for me. I've purposely kept my head down. Other ALF people have done the messy work: releasing the beagles, the break-ins at the animal labs, the hunt saboteuring . . .'

He shook his head.

'I'm not one of the front men. Never have been.' He tugged his hair. 'I've kept out of it all, done my bit on the phone. I'm only a fixer. After Trafalgar Square I couldn't afford to be a front man. It's Tony – you're right. He's become a really hard nut, a fanatic, like the suicide bombers – only the Cause counts for him. You know what they're like. Now he's putting the squeeze on. He wants me to do this big one. He doesn't trust the young ones – all enthusiasm and cock-ups. Oh, yes, Tony's putting on the screws all right. He thinks it's perfect timing putting me up-front. I'm meant to do the difficult bit, nab the woman then bog off to Madagascar. Therese doesn't know a thing about all this.'

'Who are you supposed to be kidnapping?' asked Charlotte, although she already had a good idea.

He got up, crossing to the sideboard again.

'God, I underestimated you, didn't I? I shouldn't have been so nasty to you at the sanctuary, should I? Well, since you seem to know everything . . .' He shrugged. 'No point in me shutting up now. In a month, the plan is to kidnap the Minister of Agriculture's wife. Tony thinks we'll get at least three bites of the cherry with her. It's all arranged. We know how to do it, where to keep her and what we want. We'll dangle her in front of the Government and get the concessions the ALF wants. It's the best way to get to the Minister. It's taken a year's planning.' He looked genuinely distressed. 'Look, I love animals, feel passionately about animal rights, but after Trafalgar Square I've always stopped short of hurting people. I'd never blow up an animal researcher, though they have. I just couldn't do it. I ruined that guy's life . . . just a normal bloke and he was reduced to being a telephonist in a wheelchair.'

He went quiet, dragging on his cigarette.

'Mick,' she said, 'knowing what you know now – that the police are closing in on you – may I suggest something? This is where your passport comes in. You weren't lying to me? You have got it, haven't you?'

He nodded, stubbing out the cigarette and lighting another.

'You don't have to go down this road, be blackmailed and bullied by Tony and end up in prison with Therese visiting you . . .'

The alcohol and adrenaline were taking their toll. Suddenly he looked defeated, and sighed. 'I'm prepared to listen.' He shrugged his shoulders. 'Seems I've got no choice.'

'I've got a plan. Would you like a cup of coffee?' she asked, trying to avert another trip to the decanter.

'I'll stick to whisky,' he said.

'Mick, I have to be blunt. I've been thinking about this.' She paused. 'You don't have a choice. Listen to me. You have to leave the country. You can't wait for Madagascar, the police could pick you up tomorrow.' She watched his face. He was listening. 'You have to leave tomorrow. If you wait any longer, you won't be able to break away from Tony. You'll be forced into the kidnap, if you're not picked up first, and you'll end up in prison. M15 knows everything. You're a marked man.'

Now that she had named M15, he looked stunned.

'I know you're right,' he said desperately. 'But . . . what am I going to do? We can't just leave . . . we haven't got any money. And how would I explain the change of plan to T?'

This was her cue. These were the questions she had hoped for. Silkily, she moved on with her plan, and opened her handbag.

'Money,' she said, 'is *not* a problem. Indeed, it's the least of your problems. You've got me.'

She pulled out the ticket and the bundle of cash, and carefully laid them on the coffee table. Bait.

'It's your choice, Mick,' she said slowly.

'What is it?'

'It's an open ticket and £60,000 – your passport from the police and from prison.'

Mick looked totally confused.

'That's a hell of a lot of money. Why are you doing this for *us*?'

She had always known the 'us' would be the sticking point.

Mick leaned forward and picked up the ticket and the money. He sat, flicking through the cash. The moment he touched it, she knew she had got him. He opened the ticket.

She had to say it now.

'Not *us*, Mick. Just *you*. Therese stays here. It's a single ticket with just your name on it. That's the deal – and you go tomorrow.'

He was not looking at her, his eyes still on the money. Then he looked up.

'What about T?'

'Come on, you were bored anyway, weren't you, Mick? You'd had enough of the sanctuary – enough of Therese. Now you've got a choice. This is the time to move on. I'll look after her. You look after yourself. You'll never get another offer like this.'

Charlotte waited. She knew fear and greed would win over honour. He had the money and the ticket in his hand. Could she risk a further push?

'Where do you want to fly to tomorrow?' she asked quietly.

'South Africa? South America?'

Disingenuously she kept one continent to herself.

There was a long pause.

'Australia,' he mumbled finally.

Victory.

With that one word he had chosen the destination she had always known he would. She'd learned enough about Mick over the years to gamble on Australia. She had already checked out tomorrow's departure times.

Chapter Thirty-Seven

Thirty pieces of silver, thought Charlotte. Mick was betraying her friend and his lover.

In the kitchen the kettle boiled for coffee. In her moment of triumph she loathed the man still slumped in his chair. He was starting to get maudlin, and she had needed to escape to another room for some space and thinking time. He had given in remarkably quickly, turning his back on Therese almost without a second thought – too intent on saving his own skin.

She made her coffee, and, as she poured in the milk, suddenly realized Mick was watching her from the doorway, another whisky in his hand. He moved towards her.

'Is this all about you, Charlotte?' he said suspiciously. 'Are you trying to get Therese for yourself – get rid of me using all your money and contacts?'

She knew she had to be careful and guided him gently to the kitchen table.

'C'mon on, Mick,' she said, sitting down with him. 'Of course I care desperately for Therese. But I would have thought everything I said tonight shows I care about you, too. I don't want you to go to prison.' Smiling at him, she tried to lighten his sudden belligerence. 'With you inside, Therese would be distraught. No, this is about the two of you.'

He swigged his whisky, lit another cigarette, and managed a slight smile.

'I know, I know. I'm drunk. Don't get me wrong, Charlotte. I'm grateful. I wouldn't have been tipped off without you. And you're right, I could end up in the Scrubs. But it shouldn't have ended like this,' he slurred. 'What you said has given me a bit of a jolt. I'm not really fed up with the sanctuary or T but I've often thought recently I couldn't take another six years, doing the feeds, mucking out . . .' He paused, looking red-eyed and sorry for himself. 'When I met her, she was a stunner. I'm just finding it all so depressing – the pressure from Tony.'

Then the tears started. 'Six years ago T was gorgeous. Now look at her. She's lost it.' He stubbed out the half-smoked cigarette, and groped for another. 'Perhaps I should never have given her my sodding phone number.' He took another gulp of whisky. 'Without me she could have been married to some county nob, with two kids and a horse.'

Charlotte reached for his hand.

'Look, Mick, I've known Therese for over thirty years. She never had any purpose in her life. When she met you, you gave her a reason for living. You gave her a cause.'

He was sobbing now, roughly brushing away the tears. She squeezed his hand and reassured him. Why was she suddenly feeling so anxious?

'Honestly, Mick,' she said, 'you gave her a reason to get out of bed in the morning.'

'And into it at night,' he snivelled. Standing up, he added: 'I'll catch the last train home. I'll go back to her tonight. Tell her everything. Tell her how brill you've been. Tell her about the ticket and the money. Tell her, when all this has blown over, she can come out to me. Thanks to you, it's all going to be all right.'

Charlotte's instinct had been right.

He was intending to go home. No. That was not part of her plan. She mustn't allow that. Therese must never know of her involvement, and of this meeting with Mick. No, he could not be allowed to go home. It had always been part of her plan that Mick would meekly stay the night in one of her guest rooms. She had intended to keep control of his ticket and the £60,000, then escort him to the airport first thing in the morning and wave him goodbye at departures.

Now, teeteringly drunk, he had it in mind to go home to Surrey and tell Therese everything. And that could *not* be allowed to happen. That would blow everything.

Mick was stroking her arm, becoming amorous under the influence of the drink.

'You're fabulous. You've got me out of a right hole. Me in prison? Oh, hell . . .' He picked up her hand and started kissing her fingers. 'Why don't we seal our little bargain by going to bed?' His words were running together. 'I've seen you in a new light tonight. I can get a later train. It's only nine. A farewell fuck.'

This, she thought, was *certainly* not on her agenda. But at least it would keep him here. Once horizontal, he would never get up again. Could she cope? Given what was at stake, she decided she could.

'How about one last whisky?' she said seductively. 'And this time I'll join you. A toast to your future – safe in Australia.'

She stood up, pandering to his physical and mental surrender. She was winning.

'Why don't we have our drink in bed?' she added casually.

'In *your* bed?' he said, trying to stand up. 'Me and Ms Twinset and Pearls in bed?'

He laughed, staggering across the room. Leaning heavily on her, he pushed her back against a cupboard, burying his head in her neck. He could hardly stand up. Kisses dribbled on to her skin.

'I'm sorry, I'm a bit pissed,' he muttered.

'What are friends for?' Charlotte managed. 'If you can't get pissed with friends, who can you . . .'

She left the sentence hanging, extricated herself and went out of the kitchen.

Shakily, she crossed the smoke-filled drawing-room to the depleted decanter. God, he had got through nearly a whole bottle. What a horrible obscene five minutes! She took a few deep breaths. She could do it for Therese. Charlotte took a sip of the whisky, took the pill from her pocket and took care of Mick's drink.

Now all she had to do was to get him upstairs, and keep him there until tomorrow morning.

Simple really.

Chapter Thirty-Eight

He smelled, not just of whisky – he had a sweaty, bonfirey smell. Without her, he had managed to find her bedroom and undressed. He was already on the bed – naked. On the floor was the usual Mick pile of clothes.

Charlotte stood just inside the door, looking at him. He had his eyes closed. Nice arms, she thought – strong from all that bucket-carrying and landscaping. Therese was very proud of their mini-lake. It had helped bring in the visitors.

'Punters equal donations,' she had joked at one of their lunches. 'Some people like to spend all day here. They eat their sandwiches around the lake. We might even get some bequests from all those dotty old ladies.' Realizing she had sounded mercenary, she had added: 'I love them really.'

Concentrate on Mick.

It was going as she had planned. He would not be going home to Therese tonight – or ever, if she had her way.

He was lying on the bed, legs apart, brown against the white linen.

Oh, God, she thought, why were men so vain? So little to brag about and obsessed with five inches of taut pink skin.

He opened his eyes.

'Take your top off, Charlie.' He had his hand between his legs.

'Don't be so school-marmy,' he added, catching the expression on her face. 'C'mon. Come over here. Take that thing off. Put my cock between your tits. Touch my balls. Touch me.' His voice was thick and urgent.

He was gross. She could hardly bear to look at him, but had to act out touching his balls with a fair display of enthusiasm.

'I shouldn't have drunk so much,' he slurred. 'I won't do you justice.'

She noticed the hairs in his nostrils and turned away.

'Get undressed. I want to see you.'

She crossed the apricot carpet to her bathroom, half closed the door, and slowly started to remove her designer suit. Mick's voice just reached her.

'Come back quickly.'

She looked in the mirror, realizing she was very nervous and trembling. Can't fake love in earrings, she thought. If she had got it wrong, she had got it *very* wrong. Had she got it right? She sat on the edge of the bath, lingering, calculating how much he had drunk, how long the Mickey Finn would take to work. She heard him call out again, but continued to take her time. Then, when she was ready, she quietly opened the bathroom door and looked across to the bed.

Her timing was perfect. She had left him just long enough. Mick, oblivious, had just snored his way from between her thighs, snored his way out of Madagascar, snored goodbye to Therese. Mick had snored his way into oblivion.

Poor Mick. A bottle of whisky, one of those pills she had got in India, and all she had had to do was squeeze a pair of balls.

She looked down at his body. It had been a mucky business, but a relatively cheap price to pay to keep the Family together. He would feel like hell in the morning.

Poor Mick. Penises lead to so much trouble.

Chapter Thirty-Nine

The next morning Mick was hungover and subdued. Charlotte had already been up for two hours. In another twenty, she thought, sipping her tea, Mick would be history and on the other side of the world.

She had half expected him to renege but he had been totally submissive, giving the impression he wanted to leave the country as soon as possible. He had not changed his mind overnight and, miraculously, considering the amount he had drunk, had retained most of their conversation. He hadn't mentioned his sexual failure. She suspected he couldn't remember whether he had or hadn't done it. In the state he was in this morning, he certainly wouldn't ask. His only question had been: 'What time's the flight?'

'I rang them last night,' she lied. 'BA 11 London/Perth, midday. Check-in ten o'clock. We'd better get a move on.'

She was not fussed, knowing shaving would not be on his agenda.

Still red-eyed and armed with a cup of tea, Mick had allowed himself to be bundled, a shambolic mess, into the bathroom.

Charlotte drove. Considering it was rush-hour, it was an unusually quiet journey down the M4, interspersed only by Mick's sighs. He was uncommunicative, deep in his own thoughts, and did not mention Therese once. She appreciated things had moved very fast.

In thirteen hours the man's life had changed completely. No home, no country, no lover, no stability. Now he was a suspect, on the run. The way out of his problems was her £60,000 and the prospect of a twenty-hour flight to safety.

She felt smug and confident in the driving seat and turned on the radio to catch the eight-thirty news. The whir of the aerial broke the silence of the journey. By extraordinary coincidence, the lead report mentioned the Minister of Agriculture's name and quoted from his speech the night before on animal transportation.

In the passenger seat, Mick flinched.

'It's getting a bit close for comfort, isn't it, Mick?' she said.

He shrugged.

'Well, I'm out of it now. But you certainly gave me a scare last night. I'm still taking it in. I'll only feel safe when I'm on that plane. I can't even think about T. You were dead on last night when you said, "Think about yourself".' He sighed. 'I could do with a beer.'

Despite herself, Charlotte joked: 'You're going to the right country for that – home of the amber nectar.'

The news item had shaken him. Not the time for jokes.

Nearing the end of the journey to Heathrow, with all its familiar promise of change and adventure, he remained impassive. He did not register the concrete blocks of the airport hotels, the replica Concorde, the vulgar hoardings advertising cars and booze. Even the high-octane rumbles of the one-a-minute take-offs and landings failed to stir him.

In the car park, he was out of his seat before she had even closed the sun-roof. Mick wanted to be away. The events of last night had emasculated him. Charlotte had checkmated him. She knew what he was thinking. He was desperate to get to departures, beyond her control, and out of the unholy mess she had convinced him he was in.

Their goodbyes were stilted – embarrassing for both of them.

'Mick,' she said as a parting shot, 'remember – the deal is you've chosen Australia. You mustn't contact Therese to tell her any of this. It's our secret, in exchange for your ticket and that briefcase full of money.'

'Don't worry,' he said, cutting her short. 'I know the deal. I know I can't contact her. And, anyway, how could I come back

here . . . to the police . . . to T? There's nothing here for me now . . .
I've just got to start again.'

He did not bother to insult her with the hypocrisy and false
courtesy of a kiss, just turned his back on her. She watched his
familiar walk as he went through departures. He had swopped the
bucket for the briefcase.

She turned away, knowing her job was done. She sensed Mick
would be a good boy. Yes, he felt guilty about leaving Therese. But
did he have a conscience about believing he had slept with her best
friend? Charlotte would never know and certainly did not care.

Now she needed time for herself. She glanced up at the airport
clock. It was time to get home. She had an overwhelming desire
to shower, air the house, strip her bed, change her clothes.

She had not told Mick, of course, that in two hours' time she
would be lunching with Therese.

Chapter Forty

She had really cut this fine. No time to spare. If Mick had been stubborn, hadn't believed her, had thrown the money back in her face, hadn't got drunk . . . if there had been a delay at the airport . . . Yes, she had been very lucky. Plans like hers always needed an element of luck.

Predictably Therese was distraught. The familiar Italian restaurant, the scene of so much shared happiness in the past, was now a setting for high drama. On their way to the tapestried confessional banquette in the corner, Therese could hardly contain herself.

'Charlie,' she sobbed as they sat down, 'he didn't come home last night. He's left me. I know he's left me.'

'Darling, shush . . .'

Since her mother's all too public outbursts, scenes had always embarrassed Charlotte, but she knew this one was inevitable. Trying to keep it as private as possible, she reached for Therese's hand, at the same time catching the waiter's eye, requesting their usual bottle of white wine. They had been coming here for ten years.

'Sweetheart,' she said, 'keep your voice down. What on earth has happened?'

'I need a cigarette,' Therese replied.

Charlotte had anticipated this and lit one for her. The wine came, and was poured. Therese took a large gulp and twiddled with her napkin.

'Mick's never done this before. He .didn't come home last night . . .'

'Well?' Charlotte shrugged it off. 'He probably just had a night out with the boys. Maybe he fell among thieves and was having a farewell bash before Madagascar. It doesn't mean he's left you.'

She thought she sounded convincing.

'But he's never done anything like that before – ever. He would always ring. I've had a sleepless night, didn't sleep a wink. I went round the woods with a torch. He's not at the sanctuary.'

Charlotte assumed a look of concern. 'He could have had an accident. Would he normally have rung?'

'Always,' Therese said. 'But not last night. And he's not in the local hospital, I've already checked that. I haven't rung the police. He would kill me if I did. You know his phobia about the police.' She broke off as the waiter arrived with the menu.

'Will you be having your usual, ladies?'

Charlotte decided for them both. 'Yes, please – and some mineral water.'

That got rid of him. They could deal with the vegetable risotto and spaghetti carbonara in their own time. Therese needed to talk, comforted by wine and cigarettes.

'Charlie, what I haven't told you,' she broke off sobbing, 'is that I had a call last night. It was meant for Mick, but of course he wasn't there . . .'

'What was it about?' she interrupted, still holding Therese's hand. 'Who rang you? Who was it?'

'That's the whole point. It was about Madagascar . . .'

'But, you're going in three weeks. That's all on. That's all right, isn't it?'

But the anonymous dossier sent to Mick's prospective employers had obviously worked.

Therese sobbed into her napkin and looked up, red-eyed.

'We're not going anywhere. No one's going anywhere. And it's certainly not all right.'

Charlotte knew she had to remain composed.

'Darling, calm down. Explain it to me. Who was the call from? What did they say? And when did they say it?'

She refilled Therese's glass. Her friend stared back at her.

'Sorry . . . I know I'm not making much sense.' Her face looked empty and terribly strained. 'I'd done the feeds. I was just going to have some beans on toast. I'd just opened the tin when the phone rang. I thought it was Mick.'

'Who was it, then?' For once Charlotte really wanted to know.

'I didn't take in his name . . . it was someone called Simon, or I think he was called Simon. He just wanted to speak to Mick. He said it was very important. His voice was so urgent, Charlie, so serious. I said I didn't know where Mick was. He said it was confidential . . . he obviously didn't want to talk to me, but as Mick wasn't there and he knew I was going to Madagascar with him, he said . . .' She broke off, trying to keep control. 'He said . . . he would have to speak to me. Apparently, the charity had received some information . . . information that made it impossible for them to send Mick to Madagascar.' She started crying again. 'They had to act very fast, get someone out there in three weeks' time, stop the poaching. They had no option but to give the job to somebody else.'

'What are you talking about? What sort of information? What did he say? What could Mick possibly have done that could cost him the job?'

'I remember the word. I'll always remember the word negative, they had received "negative" information . . . confidential information. He wouldn't tell me what it was, but said Mick had withheld things about his past at his interview. He'd got the job under false pretences, and so they couldn't go ahead. He wasn't the man they'd thought he was.'

'What on earth could they mean?' Charlotte interrupted. 'Is there anything in his past – anything that could be true? Mick must have talked to you, Therese – must have pillow-talked.'

'You know Mick, Charlie . . . he never talked very openly about himself, even to me.'

'All right, he's lost the job – we don't really know why. But it doesn't mean he's done a runner and thrown himself off the Forth Bridge, does it? Let's be realistic, you could be making a storm in a teacup. The facts are he's been away one night in six years. You said it . . . just one night in six years. Anything could have happened. You could be jumping to conclusions. If he hasn't been home, he doesn't know about Madagascar. Darling, it could be anything. Do you know anything damaging? Anything you haven't told me? Perhaps something you haven't even thought about?'

Therese ignored the logic and the questions.

'I just know in my heart, Charlie, he's gone. I've lived with him twenty-four hours a day for six years. I know every twist and turn of that man's brain. You can't live with a man all that time, under the same roof, in those conditions, and not know when he's doing something out of character. Something has definitely happened – I *know* it.'

She knew she had to get her friend out of the restaurant as soon as possible. Heads were turning, ears sensing a juicy drama unfolding.

'Here we are, ladies – vegetable risotto and your usual carbonara. Black pepper. I'll bring the Parmesan.'

'Sorry, Alfredo,' said Charlotte, reaching into her purse. 'We have a problem. We're going home. This will cover it, won't it?'

Alfredo looked dismayed.

'Is there anything wrong with the food?' he queried, carefully ignoring Therese's tear-streaked face.

'No,' she said. 'It looks as lovely as ever. We just have a few unexpected problems to sort out in private. C'mon, Therese,' she coaxed. 'Let's go.'

They got up. Charlotte held Therese's arm, purposely ignoring the curious glances all around them. She moved her friend to the door, out into the sunlight and the short walk home to privacy.

'I'll get you a brandy,' said Charlotte as Therese sat with her elbows on the kitchen table, head in her hands, sobbing quietly.

'Did I make a fool of myself in the restaurant? I did, didn't I?'

'Darling, they were all much too busy feeding their faces to notice us.'

Therese saw through the lie.

'Sorry about the food. What a waste. And I'd been so looking forward to seeing you – our farewell lunch before Madagascar.'

The word Madagascar brought on fully fledged, uncontrollable howling. Therese's body shook with sobs. She got up and moved quickly to the kitchen sink.

'Sorry,' she said, standing there. 'For a moment I thought I was going to be sick.'

'C'mon,' said Charlotte, gently leading away her from the sink. 'Sit down. Take a sip of your brandy.' She was aware her voice was taking on a comforting nannyish tone. 'Why don't you ring home? He's probably there.' They looked at each other. By tacit agreement, Charlotte picked up the receiver. 'I'll dial for you.' She punched in the familiar numbers, made sure it was ringing and passed it to Therese encouragingly.

'He's not there. It's the answer-phone – just my message.'

'C'mon, dumbo,' said Charlotte, smiling. 'Give it to me. Get your bleeper. He's probably left a message. Let's ring again.'

She repeated the procedure, and once again handed the phone back to Therese. The messages would doubtless be about abandoned puppies and orphan squirrels. Therese listened for thirty seconds, then shrieked.

Straight away Charlotte knew that Mick had betrayed her at Heathrow. Having got rid of her, he had gone straight into the departure lounge and, with her £60,000 in his hand, the bastard had rung home.

Therese threw down the phone.

Practical as ever, Charlotte remembered to switch it off.

Bastard! she was thinking. He rang her. I know he rang her. Therese's face confirmed this.

'Was there a message from Mick? Is he okay?'

'I was right,' Therese replied in a dead voice. 'He's gone.'

What the hell had he said? Had he implicated her? Shit! This could blow everything. She managed a genuine-sounding: 'What did he say? Where is he?'

God, she thought, he could have come back out of departures after she had left the airport. He could still be in the country.

Therese swallowed her brandy, extending her glass for another. She had gone very quiet and controlled, her voice a monotone.

'He said: "By the time you get this, T, I'll be out of the country and out of your life."' She paused. 'That's what he said, Charlie. Then he said: "Something's come up . . . I can't talk about it. It's better this way. I'm just sorry – *really sorry* – leaving you and the animals like this. Please look after old Beano. Stupid, I really loved that nag . . ."' And Therese broke down again.

Charlotte couldn't push her into the rest of the message. That would have to wait. She crossed over and put an arm around her friend's shoulders. After a few minutes, she said gently: 'Did he say anything else?'

'He said he loved me. I know he was at an airport, Charlie. I could hear the background noise – the bing bongs.' Therese fell quiet again and didn't say anything for a few minutes.

She waited for the remnants of the message. Had he betrayed her? Had he mentioned her part in it all? So far, she had not been implicated. So far, so good. She realized she had her fingers crossed behind her back.

'So,' Therese sobbed, breaking her silence, 'he's gone. After all these bloody years he's gone ... just walked out. I told you, Charlie. You didn't believe me ...' She broke off, looking angrily at her friend. 'I've told you three times now. You heard it, but you didn't listen.'

Charlotte understood Therese's anger – understood why she was taking it out on her. And she realized the irony of the situation.

Disappearances happen all the time, she thought. A so-called normal day begins; the husband – or wife – burdened with secret problems just never returns to the nest. Escape. A new start. The John Stonehouse syndrome ... clothes left on the beach. No explanation. No goodbye. No responsibilities. Another family abandoned.

Bastard! He had promised her he wouldn't ring Therese. That was their deal. Within five minutes of leaving her, he had broken their bargain. But, at least ... her body flooded with relief ... it appeared *she* had not featured in his message. She was dying to ask if her name had come up, but realized this would be a give-away. No. No. Stupid. Don't bring *yourself* into it. No need. Mick would surely never go that far. He had her £60,000. That should buy some loyalty – even from Mick.

She turned back to Therese and, standing behind her, gave her a hug.

'Therese, we've known each other for – what is it? – thirty-plus years? We've gone through hell and back before. Remember our dreadful mothers, the school dinners, the bullying? Now it's Mick. C'mon, we can get through this. I'm taking charge, just for the day. You're going to have another brandy and then I'm going to give you a sleeping tablet. While it's working, we'll talk. I'll ring the sanctuary.'

Therese did not demur. Her body was like stone.

'Janet of the greasy hair will cope. You'll sleep. And tomorrow's another day. How about that, then?'

To her relief, Therese limply stood up, saying: 'I feel totally out of it. I'm not used to drinking. I've already had two. Honestly, Charlie, I know you mean well but I don't want another drink. I just want oblivion. Where's that sleeping tablet? I can't believe he's done this ... I really loved him ... I thought he loved me ... I thought we had a good chance of being together for ever ...'

Delighted, Charlotte noticed Mick was already relegated to the past tense. Therese's tears flowed silently as she was gently guided upstairs to Charlotte's own room.

'Darling,' she said, 'sleep in my bed. It's only five or so and it's coolest in here. My room's got the thickest curtains ... they'll keep out the light.'

Therese lay down on the bed.

'C'mon, don't be a slut,' said Charlotte gently. 'Take off your clothes. Look, you're emotionally drained. With the tablet, you might even sleep through till tomorrow.'

Mechanically, Therese started to undress.

Charlotte could not help noticing that the sundress was at least eight summers old. She helped Therese take off her shoes and gave her a nightie.

'I'll put another sleeping tablet here on the bedside table. You'll probably wake up in the night,' she said. 'You will take it, won't you? I'm not working tomorrow, so I'll be here when you wake up. Darling, forget everything.' She looked at Therese. 'He wasn't worth it, was he?'

Therese shivered, pulling the duvet up around her neck.

'Charlie,' she said, in a dead voice, 'I don't want to talk about him. I don't want to think about him.' She managed a faint smile. 'I don't know what I would do without you ... you're such a lovely person. I'm exhausted. I'm out of it. How could he have done this to me?' She closed her eyes, and sank back.

God, if she hadn't changed the sheets, Therese might have smelled Mick. She bent down and kissed her.

'Sleep well, darling.'

Tiptoeing across the room, she gently closed the door.

Therese's head was now resting on the same pillow where Mick had snored his way into oblivion the night before.

Chapter Forty-One

✧

Therese had never really recovered from Mick's disappearance. Thank God he hadn't tried to contact her again. He was probably deeply into Australia and Therese number two by now. Charlotte was seriously concerned about her friend. After three months, she was beginning to realize that Mick had been pivotal to Therese's life. She had really loved him – still really loved him – and, emotionally, was not getting better.

Charlotte had tried her best and made all the right sounds. Nobody could have cared for and cosseted a best friend more, but Therese had never regained her equilibrium. After six weeks in a clinic, where Charlotte had insisted on paying all her bills, Therese had slowly started to pull herself together. In truth, the psychiatrist had said that Mick's departure had left her clinically depressed and totally uninterested in life. Time and medication would help, but it would be a long process.

Six months later the animal sanctuary had closed and Therese had been forced to make things up with her anxious mother. She had returned to live in her old wing in the family house.

Charlotte had saved Therese from worse: Mick . . . Madagascar. She could easily have turned into a Wormwood Scrubs' widow by now.

In her own black moments, she recognized there were very

distressing negative sides to what she had done, but she had always been there for Therese. Since Mick's flight, she had rung Therese twice a day. Their fortnightly lunches had continued, indeed had become weekly. Despite Mick's treacherous telephone call she, Charlotte, had won. She liked that.

The holiday they had taken together had not been a success, even though Charlotte had planned the trip meticulously. Innocently, she had suggested going to the Maldives.

'It'll be a first for both of us,' she had lied to Therese.

Charlotte had wanted the security of knowing where she was taking her friend and how to fill every day. She could then play the role of leader and be confident and self-assured. They would be sharing the same *sand* and coral reefs that she had shared with the grieving Barty, but the little collection of beach houses was under new management. She had carefully checked that before booking.

During the holiday, there had only been one moment of panic. Freshly showered, she had come down at seven, ready for her sundowner, and found Therese casually dressed in a sarong at the reception desk, idly leafing through the huge leather-bound Five Year Visitors' Book. Charlotte's arrival, thank God, had caused the necessary distraction. What if Therese had leafed back three years?

Offered a rum punch, Therese had instantly forgotten the Visitors' Book and they had strolled out into the sunshine to watch the fishermen unloading a few more lobster-red guests.

After Therese had gone to bed, and the reception area was empty, Charlotte had crept back. Her little nail scissors had carefully removed the relevant page that revealed the Honourable Charlotte Pierce and Barty McClaren had stayed there three years ago. Fate had a nasty habit of catching you out, but her good luck had continued.

She had needed the holiday as much as Therese did. The cost had been high for a damaged Therese, but the price of keeping the Family together had been even higher. Charlotte knew her own smoking and drinking had escalated. She hardly slept any more. The memories refused to die: the body in the bathroom ... Jules and the bees ... drunken treacherous Mick in her bed ... the plotting ... the planning ... the dossier.

Her public face was intact, but making things happen and giving destiny so many nudges had certainly taken their toll.

She was spending less and less time at Eaton Square and more and more time at the other place – the place nobody else knew about.

Chapter Forty-Two

❦

It was the last place anybody would expect to find the Honourable Charlotte Pierce, but that was why she had bought it and kept it secret for fifteen years. She *loved* it here. It had been Cook's flat when she retired from service. The Pierces had bought it for her. After Cook had died Charlotte had secretly bought it for herself. She had shared many happy visits here with Cook, and couldn't entertain the idea of strangers trampling over it.

Outside it was grubby, with peeling white paint, broken steps to the basement flat, the kind of house you would expect south of the river – the kind of divided up house everyone walks past. It was a high-crime area. No window boxes to attract attention, the net curtains obscuring anything of interest. The bunch of alcoholics at the end of the road were happy just sitting on the wall, swaying gently, anticipating their next Giro-bought can of beer.

Charlotte let herself in, ignoring the junk mail lying on the mat. She closed the front door on the gentle vibrations of her neighbours' guitar practice, and the twenty-four-hour smells of spicy cooking. She always trod carefully on the pavements round here, stepping over squashed drink cans, take-away containers, and the inevitable dog mess. Her neighbours were big shaven-haired men with Rottweilers and Staffordshire bull terriers, modern-day versions of Bill Sykes. This was a pooper-scooper free zone.

The women always looked run down – in need of some fresh vegetables. Strangely none of these things offended Charlotte's normal obsessive cleanliness.

The door clicked to behind her. This was her way of shutting out the world she had been born into. There was no telephone, no casual visitors, nobody expecting anything, no duties, no BBC pressures. This was where she could be herself, free from Pierce family echoes.

Despite the unsavoury exterior, the inside of the flat was spotless. After all, she did her own cleaning here. She thought back to the first time she had gone to a supermarket. It had been fun looking along the unfamiliar lines of polish, dusters and bleach. Charlotte had loved cleaning up and decorating for herself. Paranoid that the inevitable flecks of paint in her hair and under her nails would give her away to the Eaton Square set, she had called in at her health club. The steam-heat treatment had freed her of the smell of turps, meths and paint.

As basements go, hers was spacious, a large sitting-room big enough for a sofa and two armchairs. Stupid really. Nobody but she ever sat on the plumped-up cushions. On her visits she alternated between sofa and armchair, armchair and sofa, hugging the thought that nobody, *but nobody*, knew she was here.

Once in this house her movements were predictable. She would toss her handbag on the floor, allowing some of the contents to spill out on the green carpet. She would giggle out loud, relishing the silence. No high-pitched: 'Charlotte, don't do that.' Or the admonishment: 'Pick it up.' Sometimes she would even bend down, pick up the handbag, and, just for the hell of it, throw it back again on to the carpet. She loved watching her keys, credit cards, small change, make-up and comb all tumble out. There was nobody here to tick her off.

After bouncing on the sofa, with her shoes on – the ultimate childhood sin – she would scoop up as many jelly-babies as she wanted and stuff them in her mouth. En route to getting changed, she would pour herself a ginger beer and carefully draw the green curtains in the sitting-room.

The ritual was always the same – done in the dark. Around three times a week, she would let herself in. This home reminded her of a burrow – she had seen enough rabbits bolting for home, escaping the family guns – and that's what she was doing every time she came here. She had painted everything green – sage green, moss green, leaf green. It all blended perfectly, and was all her own work.

'*Run rabbit, run rabbit, run, run, run. Don't let the bastards catch you with their guns. They'll get by without you in their pie. Run rabbit, run rabbit, run, run, run.*'

She had altered the rhyme to suit herself. She bolted whenever she could.

The hanger was behind the sitting-room door. She took down the lovingly pressed clothes and laid them carefully across the back of the sofa. She needed to get changed. It was urgent now. It would only take a minute. Soon she would be out of her summer Liberty print frock, infernal tights, uncomfortable heels, and into her other clothes . . .

'*Run rabbit, run rabbit . . .*'

She was down to her bra and pants. She tugged, pulled, buttoned, zipped, and expertly laced up.

When this ritual was complete, she always experienced enormous relief. Her breathing quickened. She rewarded herself with some more jelly-babies. The familiar sugary shapes in her mouth calmed her. Henry's voice: 'Bite the head off first! Bite the head off first . . . and you won't hear it scream.'

Her panic was subsiding. She asked herself the familiar question: was she ready to open the curtains yet? The reliable Victorian full-length mirror was perfectly positioned, waiting for her. There was one thing left to do. She always left this till last. It was part of her ritual to leave the rubber bands next to the jelly-babies on the table. They were there, but then they always were. No interfering cleaning ladies here.

Picking up the rubber bands, she slowly did her hair. When she opened the curtains, she would be ready. But before she did this, she always closed her eyes. Then, like a blind person, she moved unerringly past the side-tables, over the rug, and positioned herself in front of the mirror.

This was the moment she longed for . . . the elusive bliss that always evaded her. Adulthood, for her, had meant making things happen. No one looked after *her* – her parents had hardly acknowledged her unwanted female gender. She had always looked after Barty and Therese – had always been 'such a lovely person' for them. Now this was her moment – her own private moment, just for her. For a few treasured hours, she could blot out her adult life.

She opened her eyes.

Gone was grown-up Charlotte. There, smiling back at her, was Charlotte, hand up, aged thirteen: 'Present.'

There, reflected in the mirror was Charlotte Pierce . . . her hair in two neat bunches, wearing a green school blazer with badge, cream shirt, green skirt, striped school tie, white ankle socks and Clark's lace-up shoes.

PART TWO

———— •◆• ————

'I have spread my dreams under your feet;
Tread softly because you tread on my dreams'—

W.B. Yeats,
'He Wishes for the Cloths of Heaven'

Chapter Forty-Three

꩜

After Jules's death, Barty had loathed the holiday with Charlotte. It had happened too soon.

Now, three and a half years later, she was certainly not happy, but was coping. After the accident, she had just existed. Work calls had been left unreturned. Nothing gave her pleasure – reading, music, swimming, food. Without her partner, life had lost its lustre – everything was meaningless. She dreaded waking up, saw nobody, except Charlotte – and even did that reluctantly.

She recognized she was depressed and becoming a bit of a recluse, but needed time to be alone and cherish the memories of Jules and their time together. She had blown up every photograph she had taken of Jules, in life and in death, and they were all over the cottage. Barty had dreaded those first anniversaries and had asked for assignments to deaden the pain of those special occasions. At Christmas, she had photographed reindeer in Lapland, Easter she had been with the Christian Arabs in Jerusalem. On Jules's birthday, declining Charlotte's kind invitation to dinner at the Savoy, she had drunk and blubbed herself into oblivion at the cottage. On her own birthday, she had sat rocking Jules's last present in her lap and had not moved for four hours.

The rest of the time, she knew she should be working, but she didn't. The commissions were coming in, along with the bills, but she had no appetite for work. The silver boxes containing her camera, light metres, lenses, fast-and-slow films, had lain untouched, with the exception of anniversaries, since the day of the funeral. Despite her grief, it had been a knee-jerk reaction to lock away the tools of her trade safely in the old sea-chest. Since turning the key, she rarely thought about them.

She had, of course, thought about herself. A successful photo-journalist, beating men at their own game, reduced to staring at blank walls and cuddling a partner's unwashed, still scented nightshirt. It was the fragrance that undid her every night, no matter how controlled she had been during the day. However hard she tried, she could not let go, still reached for the nightshirt under the pillow, deliberately making herself cry.

Days that used to fly past in a whirl of deadlines, airport check-ins, anxieties about fading light, now hung long and heavy. All she felt able – and wanted – to do was to complete ordinary everyday tasks that she and Jules had planned – the new herbaceous border, the garden pond, cutting back those irritating trees.

Making herself cross the lawn with the saw, she could hear Jules's voice saying: 'Those goddamn trees have got to come out, honey.'

Annually, through her tears, she had planted more and more memorial bulbs – Jules's favourite flower. Every spring, the garden bloomed with brilliant yellow tulips.

Bath, bed, sleeping pills, oblivion. Sex? Barty never thought about it.

With bank statements unopened, the call she had been dreading had eventually come from the bank manager.

'Time to go back to work, Barty,' he had prompted gently.

He had known her through many years of feast and famine. She recognized from his tone that this was famine.

Not totally irresponsible, she had bought herself time by selling off the grandfather clock and a couple of antique mirrors. The one piece of furniture it had been too painful for her to part with personally was the table she and Jules had fallen in love with at an antiques fair. Charlotte had been wonderful and had found a buyer for her. A man had come in a van. The other bits had gone to auction. If she wanted to keep the cottage and its memories of Jules, she had to go back to work and was forced to say yes to the next assignment – a dreary trek to photograph nothing special in Newcastle-upon-Tyne. Having been off the circuit for a while, the plums were going to her rivals.

Once they knew she was back, however, and still as good as ever, the phone had never stopped ringing. Soon, she had started picking and choosing again.

After Jules's death, she had need tranquillizers, but had loathed their after-effects which made her wander about like a zombie until midday.

Work was now beginning to take her away from the cottage and was numbing her grief. Midhurst was replaced by Rome, Florence, Paris and Bruges, and a three-week assignment in India. One day, stuck at Delhi airport at two o'clock in the morning, she had sighed that Jules had been right about not getting a dog. She could hardly look after herself, let alone a dog. The heat, the saris, the striking airline, her sulky camera assistant, were suddenly too much. She desperately wanted to be home again in the cool of the cottage at Midhurst. Amid the mêlée of assorted turbans and high-pitched babble, she reminded herself she was *freelance* and could do whatever she wanted. Her bank balance was in the black. The bank manager was off her back. It was her life.

Back at Heathrow, the assignment over and done with, she cancelled the next job.

'A ghastly case of Delhi-belly,' she said apologetically down her mobile phone and went home to the empty cottage, three glasses of Southern Comfort and Jules's waiting nightshirt.

That night she enjoyed being in her own bed. The next day she took the phone off the hook and slowly dealt with the dust and weeds. To her surprise, she prepared and cooked a meal in her own oven. She had binned the kindly meant book from a friend's mother, Delia Smith's *One Is Fun*. One was never fun. The light was fading. Now, sitting at the long pine table, over rice and spicy prawns, glass of wine in hand, Barty realized her life wasn't good, but it was getting a little better.

After a long weekend, she found herself automatically putting the phone back on the hook. It rang after lunch.

'Fishing ports,' Harry's familiar voice said. 'I didn't think I'd get you. How does six weeks roaming around the coast grab you? Or are you a bit above all that – addicted to the foreign?'

'You've caught me on the right day,' Barty replied, still in her gardening gloves. 'I've had enough of airlines and dodgy food.' She almost believed her own lie. 'I want to enjoy the spring in this country. Six weeks? What's the deal?'

'Good,' he said. 'I'm glad I rang you. It's a colour supplement job – everything on expenses. The editor specifically asked for you.'

They clinched the deal. She would have to leave the cottage in a week.

Cockles at Leigh-on-Sea, fish and chips in Mallaig, cod at Southwold, the wonderful characters at the Port of Grimsby – then the highlight of the trip, down to the West Country, to St Ives and Padstow. It would be like a holiday.

For the first time since Jules's death she felt a glimmer of interest and, professionally, looked out of the window at the weather.

It was fine.

Chapter Forty-Four

Back again at the other place, Charlotte was sitting on her tiny patch of lawn, feeling pensive. She had gone through her usual rituals but was feeling strangely anxious. In private, she was chain-smoking.

She looked down at Kevin the tortoise on her lap. Cook had given him to her as a gift to take as a pet to St Margaret's.

'He'll keep you company – remind you of me,' she had joked.

He hadn't always been called Kevin. She had changed his name from Sam when Therese had a crush on one of the gardeners who was called Kevin. She remembered the ghastly series of lectures on Tuesdays when, school-uniformed and white-socked, they were all herded into the auditorium. Fish farming – that had sent them all to sleep; life in Bolivia; medieval cathedrals. At thirteen, everything and everybody seemed crashingly boring.

She looked back on the two hundred squirming girls. None of them had listened to those lectures. All of them had wanted to be somewhere else – preferably outside on the sunny lawns.

Kevin was on the move, slowly and laboriously, using her skirt as a chute, trying to get back to his grazing. Charlotte's moment of triumph had come during the last lecture before they broke up – Looking After Your Pets. They had quite liked that one. Lucy had demonstrated her Angora rabbit, Fiona had shown off her guinea pig, Katy's canary had sung, and Charlotte had held Kevin aloft.

The lecturer was from the local zoo. Charlotte remembered three facts from his talk – one that Kevin was identified as a Hermann tortoise, two that tortoises loved tomatoes but should never eat them, and three that Captain Cook in 1773 had given a tortoise to the Queen of Tonga that had lived until 1966. It had been 200 years old.

As Kevin – who could actually be a Kate – lumbered off, she reckoned he was nearly forty.

She realized, watching him, that her stomach was still feeling curdled, like a ploughed field. She had lived with this feeling since puberty when it had slowly dawned on her that her parents with their huge house and subservient staff were not the average even by St Margaret's affluent standards.

She was pleased brother Henry could not see her now – in a house on the wrong side of the river, crying, with only a tortoise for company.

If he could, he would say, as he *always* did: 'Have you taken your tranquillizers, Charlotte? You know what happens, if you don't . . .'

She stood up, shook the grass from her skirt and felt like kicking something . . . but there was only Kevin. She knew she could never kick Kevin. Henry was right, she had not taken the pills, had not taken them for some time. Was that why she was feeling so anxious and depressed? It could be the weather – thundery and heavy.

Having got rid of all her problems, all the people who had threatened the Family over the years, she should be feeling jubilant. After Mick's departure – and his one telephone call – Therese had received no news from Australia. Thank God. Charlotte had felt home and dry, and so confident that one Sunday morning six months ago she had played doctor and scaled down her own medication. Recently though she had been waking up with the heeby-jeebies, and today had excused herself from a charity committee meeting and bolted for the other place. It was not working its usual magic.

Kevin had disappeared under a shrub. It really was getting thundery – she could hear distant rumblings. Shivering, she moved back into the sitting-room. The usual jelly-babies and glass of ginger beer lay untouched where she had placed them on the table.

She didn't want anything. She just wanted to be happy, but had she ever been happy? Was she capable of happiness?

She knew she was important to Barty and Therese, but knew too she was not as important to them as they were to her. They had lives. She just existed on the margins of theirs. The awfulness of this truth perhaps explained the empty void she was experiencing now. She had never faced up to it before.

She had to do something. She would put on some music, resurrect some happy memories, work her way through the nursery rhymes she had sung with Cook, *The Mikado* which she had shared with the girls, and their teenage pop heroes when the threesome had been a gang and they had been all of sixteen: Elvis, Cliff, Fleetwood Mac, Cilla, Lulu, Credence Clearwater Revival, and the Beach Boys. Years ago, she had painstakingly put together a tape of them, so that she could play it at times like this. At Eaton Square, she only played the Three Tenors, Bach, Monteverdi, Vivaldi and Mozart, as was expected of her.

Putting on the tape, and sitting down on the floor with a jelly-baby in her mouth, she knew she had been lucky – lucky that Felicity had had the heart attack in her bathroom. That had been very lucky indeed. She had been lucky that Jules had been hypersensitive – and that she herself had cleverly stored this fact away until it was useful. Lucky that Mick had had a dodgy past and been so susceptible to money. Lucky that she had learned so early in life how to make things happen. Lucky that people were so malleable. Lucky that she had money and contacts.

These thoughts, like everything else she tried today, did not comfort her.

She moved into the bedroom and lay on the bed, looking up at the ceiling. She did not *feel* lucky. She was feeling vulnerable, pathetic, depressed and alone. She tried to sleep. Her body lay down, but her mind kept fizzing.

How long would her luck last? Luck always ran out, didn't it?

Chapter Forty-Five

Therese, dressed in chef's blue-and-white checked trousers and white top, was concentrating on the herbs lying on the marble slab. Chop. Chop. Chop. They had just done thirty-seven lunches – up on yesterday. Today had been drizzly and the tourists, as one, had deserted the beaches and dived into the pubs and restaurants circling the harbour.

Looking out of the kitchen window, she noticed the rain was slowing down. Typical Cornish weather – strips of blue sky were hustling the clouds away. Waterproofs, buckets and spades were trickling out again. Dads were eating Cornish pasties out of paper bags. Mums walked with one hand on the pushchair, the other keeping track of stumbling toddlers on the look out for ice-creams. She chopped on, thinking a few idiots would soon start throwing their bits of uneaten rolls and hard bits of pastry to the gulls, ignoring the notice: *Please Do Not Feed the Gulls – they become a nuisance and are aggressive.*

She would just finish off the marinades and dressings for tonight's sitting and then go out and get some air.

Lydia's fraught phone call had been well timed.

'Therese, can you come down, just to fill in? My chef's got to go back to Scotland – his mother's died. And . . . well, basically I need another pair of hands.' She had sighed. 'Sorry it's such short notice, but I'm desperate for a vegetarian cook immediately. Can you come? You can stay with me. It's the height of the season – we're heaving,' she had groaned. 'Chef promises he will be back on the 20th.'

Therese had not hesitated. This was manna from heaven. Two weeks in the West Country with an old mucker from St Margaret's running a veggie restaurant. *Yes. Yes. Yes.* She had put down the phone and immediately started packing. She had had enough of her mother hijacking her life – the subtle but determined attempts to win her back to old family values and ways, and more than enough of her mother's enforced eating policy: 'You're like a stick insect, all skin and bones.' She had had enough derogatory comments on her personal appearance to last several lifetimes: 'Darling, your nails . . . Daddy always said you had beautiful nails.' And then there were all the pathetic attempts at matchmaking: totally unsuitable hunting, shooting, fishing types, all terminally tedious. She had overheard her mother talking to a friend over six o'clock sherry: 'Before *Mick* . . .' Then the friend's muted response: 'Daphne, I never met him but he sounded *awful*. You poor thing. I know how you must feel . . . Amelia is going out with someone Ralph can't stand. We don't say anything, of course, when she brings him down, but Ralph would die if she settled for him. He would never fit in.'

Yes, Therese had been very glad of the rescue call. Now she was here in Cornwall – away from the finger-wagging and the 'I told you so's.

She was even temporarily rescued from Charlotte's kindly meant calls and, at times, cloying concern. This small and spotlessly clean kitchen was, in a way, her passport back to the real world. Here with divorced single parent Lydia, sharing her twin-bedded room above the tiny restaurant, working all hours but laughing through the washing-up, she felt liberated.

In a way it was back to the old routine of constant feeds, but this time around the hungry mouths belonged to tourists, not animals. Thanks to Lydia's chance phone call, she had stopped idling about in her stately Berkshire home and was back with real people, having fun on their bikes, in their shorts, with their ubiquitous chips and snotty-nosed children.

She moved on to the fennel and cabbage – she might as well get those done before tonight. Chop. Chop. Discard the unwanted bits. Suddenly she thought about Mick. Where was he? Since the message on her answer-machine, and the give-away airport sounds in the background, she had heard absolutely nothing. She was certain he was far away. Chop. Chop. More leafy green bits hit the bin, ready for the compost heap. She seasoned the vinaigrette and gave it a spiteful shake. Tonight was pasta with pesto – Lydia's home-grown basil; chickpea and broadbean salad; spinach filo parcels; vegetarian shepherd's pie with horseradish cream potatoes. That was already done, and Lydia was looking after the vegan dish. She would be in later.

This was her break-time. She would go out now, have a walk and do the potatoes for the chips when she came back. She was enjoying herself. It was good to be away from south-east England . . . away from the incessant hope that Mick might try to contact her . . . away from obsessionally scouring the television and newspapers for news of animal rights activists.

She had never really come to terms with why her life with Mick and the sanctuary had come to such a sudden juddering close. No letter. No goodbye. Nothing. What had happened to his covert plotting – the Madagascan job, their life together? What had happened? It had been like a sudden death, but worse because she had not even got a body. No explanation.

It had all stopped that day she had lunch with Charlotte.

She took off her chef's bottoms, cling-filmed her work and put it into the fridge. The next couple of hours were her own. Locking the kitchen door, she went out of the restaurant in search of some much-needed sea air.

She stood on the quay, looking across the walled harbour. She knew she smelled of cooking oil. The tourists were wandering around, happy that the sun had come out. People were standing outside with pints of beer, risking their toes as inconsiderate motorists inched their cars around the harbour. A couple of fishermen walked past in their black waders, carrying blue buckets. She noted her favourite rusty fishing smack. Would it ever go out to sea again? Whole families, including grandparents, clutching plastic carrier-bags dawdled aimlessly by. Everyone seemed to be armed with a lolly or an after-lunch ice-cream. Avaricious gulls were everywhere, screeching indignantly. Empty sailing boats bobbed up and down at their regimented moorings. A man the colour of a conker was rowing slowly and rhythmically in a dinghy towards his sail boat.

She started to walk, feeling as carefree and aimless as the holidaymakers. It was turning into a lovely afternoon, with the promise of a beautiful evening.

For the first time since Mick had left, she felt relatively at ease with herself. Across the quay, she could see a person with a tripod setting up a shot. The silver tripod glinted in the sun. The biggest ship in the harbour was a battle-grey coastguard vessel. A man in a blue jersey was climbing aboard, joining his colleague silhouetted in the wheelhouse. As she watched, one of the gulls mugged a small boy, separating him from his Cornish pastie. The boy's ear-splitting screams made everyone turn round. Even the photographer, she noticed, was momentarily distracted.

Therese stopped. She had intended to turn left here and walk up along the cliffs, but something made her turn right and walk on round the harbour towards the small boy, his parents . . . and the photographer.

Chapter Forty-Six

Negotiating a path through the ambling tourists, Therese was aware
of the queue waiting for the incoming ferry from Rock, the village
over the estuary. On the other side of the harbour were cyclists
in sunglasses and hardhats, and holiday-makers with their dogs,
children and pushchairs. The photographer – she could not see
from the denim and cropped haircut if it were a man or a woman
– was clicking away. Therese fancied an ice-cream, and headed for
Martha's gift shop.

She loved watching the ferry decanting its passengers every ten
minutes or so. Sometimes faces she'd seen during the day turned
up that night at the restaurant.

The photographer was fiddling around in a silver stock box. It
had clouded over again. The slack halyards were tinkling away
in the watery sunshine. The ferry was edging its way past the
sandbank, through the shallow waters, to the concrete ramp.
Therese decided to watch the wind-blown arrivals – her ice-cream
could wait five minutes.

The photographer had obviously tired of taking shots of the
ferry, and had now turned round and was concentrating on the
gulls hovering over the coastguard vessel. The two men in blue
jerseys were deep in discussion on deck. When she next looked
the photographer had abandoned the tripod and was taking shots

of people strolling about. There were enough of them, Padstow was heaving with holiday-makers. She knew the locals were already anticipating September – the slowing down of the season, when they could start to call the town home again. But business was business.

As she lingered, she noticed that the photographer had stopped working, the camera had been lowered and was swinging loosely against the denim shirt. A pair of arms waved wildly in the air. She heard a cry – and then a shriek of excitement that silenced gulls and tourists. For the second time that afternoon heads turned. Still waving madly, and bellowing something inaudible, the photographer was weaving through the tourists, running towards *her*. She was the object of attention.

She heard her name.

'Therese . . . Therese . . . Therese . . .'

It was Barty.

Chapter Forty-Seven

On the quay, Therese and Barty just stood there, looking at each other, grinning stupidly. They had years of catching up to do. They hadn't seen each other since that last traumatic day at school. Individually, they were taking in the changes.

Barty noticed Therese's hair was peppered with grey, and her once pretty mouth was more downturned than she remembered from their schooldays. She looked older than she should.

Barty, Therese was registering, was unashamedly androgynous in her denims and workmanlike boots. She was still very slim. Her dark chestnut hair was expensively cut, squeaky clean and feather-fringed around her face.

After the excitement of the unexpected reunion, they were both disappointed they couldn't meet up that night. Each had prior commitments – Therese to the restaurant, Barty to a night-shoot.

'Oh, c'mon, Therese,' she said excitedly, 'we've *got* to see each other. Can you do tomorrow?'

Juggling with what she had to do, Therese said: 'Look . . . see that restaurant over there – the one with the green-striped awning? D'you remember Lydia Grainger from school? It's hers, I'm just filling in for a couple of weeks. We could have a late lunch there tomorrow, around half-past three, when we close.'

Barty had instantly agreed, and they had said simultaneously: 'I can't wait. After all these years . . . what a coincidence.'

They had hugged each other and, splitting up, reluctantly walked back to their separate responsibilities. Halfway around the harbour, they had spontaneously turned, grinned at each other and waved. The gossip and news would have to wait until tomorrow.

The next day, at the Green Café, there were two lunchtime lingerers wanting a second cappuccino and a brandy. Therese cursed them. She was so wanting to flick the 'Closed' sign on the door and join Barty who, bless her, had arrived early and was nursing a glass of wine at the corner table.

The last two customers did not outstay their welcome by too long. By three-fifteen, Therese was pulling the cork on a bottle of Lydia's best white wine. She sat down opposite Barty and they grinned at each other.

'I'll get us some food in a minute,' Therese said.

'You go first,' Barty said, inviting confidences.

'I don't know where to start . . .'

Three hours later they had progressed from a tentative trot, to a canter, to a gallop through each other's lives. It was as if the past gulf between them had never happened. They realized they still liked each other enormously. Therese found herself crying when Barty told her about Jules, and Barty was sympathetic about the Mick saga and equally bemused by the man's sudden disappearance. Somehow, it had not come as a surprise to Therese that Barty's great love had been a woman.

Lunch had become irrelevant. Instead, they picked at cheese and biscuits, and treated themselves to another bottle of wine. They gabbled on, swopping schoolday reminiscences – about the teachers and the other girls – and ended up in fits of giggles.

'What a pity you lost contact with Charlotte Pierce,' Barty suddenly said, as they poured another glass. 'She's been such a *marvellous* friend to me all these years. I don't know how I would have coped without her.'

Therese froze, a water biscuit in her hand.

'But I don't understand,' she gasped. 'I thought it was *you* who had lost contact with her? *She's my best friend.* I see her every week.'

It was Barty's turn to gasp.

'But she's *my* best friend and she's never mentioned you, ever.'
They sat looking at each other, bewildered.

'But I don't understand,' Therese kept repeating. 'Why did she
never mention you? Why didn't she say she had kept in touch with
both of us? I don't get it . . .'

Their fingers collided over the shared cigarette packet. Barty
flopped back in her chair.

'How extraordinary. She's never mentioned you. Well . . .' She
looked embarrassed. 'Since that last day at school . . . You've been
a non-person all these years. I had *no* idea you two were still
in touch.'

Therese drew on her cigarette.

'Barty, I promise you, your name has *never* cropped up, *never*
in all those years. But,' she queried, 'you've truthfully kept up with
her all these years? And she *never* mentioned me?'

'*Never*,' Barty said, looking astonished. She crossed herself in the
old St Margaret's way. '*Never*. I'm as staggered as you, Therese. I
can't understand it. I really do speak to her several times a week
and we see each other as often as we can.'

'But so do I,' Therese said. 'Certainly every fortnight and
sometimes every week.' Her voice trailed off.

They sat looking at each other, baffled.

'But . . . but . . .' Barty said. 'Why did she *never* tell me about
you? Whenever I mentioned your name . . . she always, sort of,
blocked you out.'

'She did the same whenever I mentioned you.'

They sat in silence.

'But why didn't she say anything? Why didn't she tell us about
each other? Why would she keep it a secret? Why would she
want to lie?'

Neither knew the answer.

At that moment the kitchen door opened and Lydia appeared,
clearly wanting to say hallo to Barty who was sitting with her back
to the door. Therese gave a tiny shake of her head. This was *not*
the right moment. Lydia tactfully retreated into the kitchen.

'I *can't* believe this . . .' Barty was repeating. 'I just *can't* believe
it. You're telling me she's been in constant contact with both of
us, and neither of us knew it!'

'It doesn't make any sense, does it?' Therese said. 'Why would she be so deceitful? Why would she . . .'

Barty raised her eyebrows. 'I don't know.' She paused. 'Jealousy?'

'Jealous of what?'

They sat silently, each with their own thoughts.

'She was always a bit of an oddball at school, wasn't she? Always very secretive,' Barty said.

They both nodded.

'She was *certainly* always very highly strung. D'you remember that business at open day?'

'And how mystified we were,' Barty interrupted, 'by her invisible parents who never turned up for anything?'

'And d'you remember how she always wanted to come and stay with us during the holidays?'

'And,' they said together, '*we* were never invited back.'

The next fifteen minutes passed in a multitude of questions, but no obvious answers. There was a mutual dawning of animosity towards Charlotte, but at the same time their negative emotions were tempered by memories of her having been so supportive. When they had needed her, she had been there – a true friend and lovely person towards both of them. Separately. Thoughts of Charlotte hovered over the silence that grew between them, posing uncomfortable questions. *Why* had she lied to them – deceived them both? *Why* had she wanted to keep them apart? *Why?*

They agreed only one person could answer those questions: Charlotte herself.

Chapter Forty-Eight

Their quest for answers in the Green Café had fizzled out. Until they challenged Charlotte there could be no answers. The mystery had certainly spoiled and subdued the effervescence of the reunion lunch. Barty and Therese parted with a promise to challenge Charlotte as soon as possible.

Barty wrapped up her shoot in Cornwall; Therese left her apron and a slightly tearful Lydia behind, and returned to her mother. The week's gap since their reunion in Padstow had only heightened the tension and their urgent need for answers.

Their agreed rendezvous was outside Charlotte's home in Eaton Square.

When the day came, as they met they were nervous and excited, but at least nearer to some explanation for Charlotte's extraordinary behaviour. Or so they hoped.

Back in Padstow, they had promised each other: 'Look, it's going to be difficult for both of us when she calls, but we won't say a word to Charlie. We won't say we've met.'

That had been their pact.

On their return, as anticipated, they had found Charlotte's interim calls tricky to handle. It had not been easy to sound normal and cover up their momentous meeting on the harbour wall. With Charlotte on the end of the phone, unspoken thoughts and words had troubled them both. They had never before had to conceal anything from her. They had always been honest.

Now, standing on her spotless doorstep, they were expecting answers.

'Miss Charlotte left an hour ago,' Josefina said helpfully.

'Damn! Sorry, Josefina ... Have you any idea when she's coming back?' Barty asked, adding: 'We really need to see her.'

She and Therese looked at each other, flatly.

'She said she was going to see Cook,' Josefina said, beaming back politely.

Josefina had been with Charlotte for as long as they could remember.

She knew them both individually, but before today had never seen them together.

'Is it worth our waiting?' Therese asked.

Josefina shook her head, then shrugged.

'I really don't know when she'll be back. Sometimes when she goes to see Cook she doesn't come home.'

They thanked her, exchanged a few pleasantries and went back down the steps on to the pavement.

'Oh,' Barty said. 'Bugger. What a disappointment.'

Therese looked at her.

'I'm a bit confused ... I'm sure Charlie said her old cook had died. You know, Cook practically brought her up? She must be nearly ninety, if she's still alive.'

'I remember going to her place with Charlie,' Barty said. 'She did the most marvellous teas ... baked for Britain. The last time we visited her ... we must have been about seventeen.' She paused. 'Did you ever go to her flat? The one the Pierces bought her when she retired?'

Therese shook her head.

They stood aimlessly on the pavement

'Well ... what are we going to do now?' Barty asked.

'We'll have to call it a day. D'you fancy a pizza?' Therese replied. 'Then we could come back later.'

'No,' Barty said, 'don't let's give up so easily. I'm in Iceland next week on a shoot. I want to get this cleared up.' She screwed up her eyes, thinking. 'I'm sure I can remember the name of the road.' She put her hands on her temples, concentrating. Therese smiled. She had seen that gesture many times at school.

'The road had something to do with a flower – something Lily. I remember . . .' She had got it, almost shouting: '*Langtry Road*. I remember it quite clearly. We'd just done the Prince of Wales and Lily Langtry in History. Yes, it's Langtry Road. I even remember the number,' she said triumphantly. 'It was 39.' She beamed at Therese. 'I remember because that was the number of our house in Streatham. Charlie and I laughed about the coincidence. I bet you anything I can find Cook's flat.'

'But should we gate-crash on them?' Therese asked.

'It's not a question of should . . . we *will*.' Barty's jaw jutted out determinedly. At that moment she spotted a black cab with its yellow light on and hailed it. 'Therese, we're not going to be fobbed off. We'll be perfectly polite but that girl owes us a few explanations. I, for one, can't bear to wait till after Iceland. I want to know today. Now.'

Therese was not feeling as bullish as Barty. Talking turkey with Charlotte was one thing, but with a ninety-year-old witness . . . She was not at all happy about that. She wished Barty would back off and take up the more comfortable option of lunch.

Barty was having none of it and hustled her into the cab, saying to the driver: 'D'you know a Langtry Road?'

'Yep . . .' he said. 'Langtry Road. It's just over the river. Take you fifteen minutes.'

Sitting in the back of the cab, they moved off on their quest, heading for Chelsea Bridge, Charlotte . . . and some answers.

'D'you realize we've known each other since prep school?' Barty said, turning to Therese.

'Since we were eight. Charlotte didn't come into our lives until we were thirteen,' Therese said. 'D'you remember, she turned up all on her own that first day of term in that huge car? It was a Silver Cloud. We were just standing there waiting for Matron.'

'I remember her funny, vulnerable little face,' Barty added.

'She was so white and frightened-looking,' Therese recalled. 'It was all right for us, we knew the ropes. We were just moving up from juniors to seniors.'

'I resented her latching on to us like a limpet at first,' Barty said, adding: 'D'you remember, we used to giggle behind her back, saying "two's company, three's a crowd"?'

'But we were nice to her, weren't we?'

'Eventually!'

Therese was regaining her confidence: 'Of course we were.' She took Barty's hand. 'It will all be all right, won't it? This afternoon, I mean?'

'I don't know. I honestly don't know what she will say to us. Something's going on.'

The taxi swung round a corner.

'I'm certainly bloody confused,' Barty added, looking at Therese. 'I've thought about this since Cornwall . . . I just can't come up with any plausible reason why she would want to be *your* friend and *my* friend – and not tell us she was friends with *both* of us. I'm totally baffled.'

'So am I.'

They moved past the Battersea Dogs' home, past the derelict power station, past Nine Elms vegetable and fruit market, into some grimy side streets . . . and a different world.

Chapter Forty-Nine

The taxi driver was as good as his word. He deposited them outside 39 Langtry Road. Barty was so chuffed she had been right about the address, she gave him a generous tip. On the pavement, they stood looking over the rusty railings, down into the well of the basement flat.

Facing the reality of what they were about to do, Therese said: 'I think I'm losing my nerve. We could find somewhere better to do this – so it would be just the three of us.'

'Oh, c'mon, Therese,' Barty said, 'don't be so wet. She's the one that's given us the shock – she split us up, kept us both for herself all these years. It's time we gave her a taste of her own medicine. She might have a turn, but she won't eat us.'

'Yes, but . . .' Therese said, seeking more excuses. 'What about the old lady? And what about Charlotte seeing us *together* after all these years?'

Barty wasn't listening, already moving down the steps to the basement door.

Therese followed reluctantly, tweaking her elbow, whispering: 'Look, Barty, I spent all last night thinking about this. There has to be some reason for Charlotte's behaviour. D'you remember that last day of term and that ghastly locket incident? D'you think it's got anything to do with that?'

Barty ignored her. 'Look,' she said pointing, 'that's Cook's surname on the buzzer – Green. She was Mrs Green. This is certainly the right place. Look . . . the door's not shut. That's a sure sign Charlotte's here.'

They exchanged glances.

'I always said at school Charlotte was born in a barn . . . she never shut doors. At home, the staff did that sort of thing for her.'

'She's not like that any more,' Therese said, loyally defending her friend. 'She's meticulous about such things now.'

'The lock's sticking,' Barty said, pushing the sneck in and out. 'She obviously thought she'd shut it.'

She pressed the bell. They could hear it ringing inside, and stood there frozen.

'You've done it now,' Therese said, anticipating footsteps down the passage. 'Hell . . . what are we going to say?'

'Look, *we've* done nothing wrong,' Barty retorted. 'Shut up and listen and see what happens.'

Nothing happened. They rang again. There was no sound from inside. Barty moved across to the window and tried to peer through the nets.

'I can't see a thing,' she whispered. 'Ring again, Therese.'

She shook her head. 'I hate this.' She had an idea. 'Perhaps Charlotte's taken her out to tea?'

Her superficial delaying tactics were obviously irritating Barty. Boldly, she pushed open the door, shouting loudly: 'Hallo . . . Mrs Green . . . Charlie . . . it's Barty.'

Nothing. The complete silence niggled her and she pulled Therese over the threshold into the gloomy passage, closing the door carefully behind her. Their eyes immediately focused upon the old bentwood hat-stand in the far corner and the thing pinned to the wall. They stood there, taking it all in.

'Bloody hell,' Barty said. 'That's Charlotte's lacrosse stick. Look, it's got CP burned into it. And that's her panama.' They looked at each other. 'She must have given them to Cook as a memento of her schooldays.'

'Barty,' Therese whispered nervously, 'I feel we're trespassing.'

Standing uninvited in somebody's else home was making them both feel uneasy. In her work, Barty was used to trampling in and out of people's lives with her camera, not even averse to standing on camera boxes and peering through windows. If there was a fee at the end of the job, she would do it. But this was different. This was personal.

Therese, innately shy, was finding the afternoon very uncomfortable. For her it was turning into a nightmare. They looked at each other guiltily. Therese's nervousness somehow strengthened Barty's resolve to go through with it.

'We're not going to slink away,' she said, 'Charlotte owes us answers.' This statement dispelled her doubts, and she shouted even louder: 'Charlie ... Mrs Green ... anyone there?'

The atmosphere and the stillness were becoming oppressive.

'C'mon, it's obvious they're *not* here,' Therese said. 'Barty ... let's go.'

Barty ignored her and moved towards the closed green door at the end of the passage. Reluctantly, Therese followed. Why was she so frightened? It was only Charlie. She had spoken to her last night on the phone – but then so had Barty. Why was she feeling this sense of foreboding? She wanted to get out into the sunlight – wanted to go home.

It was too late. Barty had already opened the door and entered the room. Therese's heart was hammering. Barty stood in front of her, silhouetted against the unexpected sunlight flooding through the french windows.

There was nobody there.

No Cook. No Charlie. No trace of a ninety year old ... no knitting, no television, no walking stick. This was *not* an elderly woman's flat. They saw the jelly-babies and the bottle of ginger beer on the coffee table at the same time. They did not speak or look at each other. Therese moved closer to Barty for comfort. They stood, side by side, looking around the room.

Very slowly and very quietly, Barty said: 'That's Jules's table.'

'That,' Therese said, looking at the wall, 'is a tapestry I sold.'

Barty moved across the room, like a sleep-walker. 'This was mine.'

Therese touched a chair. 'And this was mine.'

Barty's voice was quivering: 'And this vase was ours.'

Therese saw the needlepoint cushions. 'And these were mine.'

Barty was now holding a pair of wooden candlesticks. 'These were ours.'

Her voice broke and she started to cry. Therese dropped the cushions and crossed to her. She looked at Barty's tear-stained face.

'What's going on? I'm out of my depth.'

Barty's tears turned to rage. 'That's my mirror!' She looked at Therese. 'What *is* this bitch up to?'

They were silent again, looking around the room. Suddenly Barty let out a yelp: 'Therese, those are my feet photographs! I took shots of people's feet all over the world. I was keeping them for a one-man exhibition, but had to sell them when I ran out of money after Jules's death.'

There they were on the wall, fourteen immaculately framed prints. Ugly toes. Beautiful toes. Gnarled feet. Black feet. White feet. Yellow feet. Calloused soles. Barty had sunk into an armchair. Therese knelt down beside her at coffee-table level.

A moment later, it was her turn to be shocked. There, on the table, was her gold Elizabethan locket.

They were both speechless, sentimentally lost in reunion with their possessions. Everywhere they looked, they recognized things they had once loved and lived with – and had to part from. Rugs on the floor, paintings on the walls, furniture, lamps, candlesticks, silver picture frames. Charlotte had secretly bought up their material possessions when they were most vulnerable and in financial crisis.

She had been so helpful.

'Barty, I can provide a man with a van . . .'

'Therese, I can get that into Sotheby's for you. No problem . . .'

'Oh, darling, don't worry about that. I'll sort it out for you . . .'

She had used the same patter on both of them. At the time, they had been grateful. In reality, they had been gulled by their best friend.

'Such a lovely person' – always there for each of them.

They did not need to speak. Each knew what the other was thinking. Charlotte Pierce, their best friend, had been very busy. She had bought them up lock, stock and barrel – materially and mentally. If it had not been for chance and Charlotte's luck running out, they would have been the last to know.

The gold locket glinted in the sunshine.

Chapter Fifty

⌒⌒

Barty looked down at the locket. Neither of them wanted to touch it. 'Well,' she said flatly, 'that's one question answered. I'll *never* forget that last day of term. You'll never know how awful I felt. It was mortifying to be accused of stealing ... and from your best friend.' She looked at Therese. 'It's obvious now who planted it on me.'

Therese looked up at her, shocked.

'Oh, Barty, it *can't* have been Charlotte ... surely? *Why*? What would she have achieved by it? Why would she have done that?'

'To split us up,' Barty spat out, standing up and pacing round the room, 'so we would hate each other ... and she jolly nearly succeeded.' She paused. 'Don't you see, Therese? Buying up our things is only half of it.' She indicated the locket. 'Presumably you put that up for auction afterwards and innocently mentioned it to Charlotte?'

Therese nodded, silently concurring.

'It's not the locket, not really any of the things she wants. *It's us*. She wanted both of us for herself. She's spent all these years making sure we never met up again. If it hadn't been for Padstow, and sheer chance ... think about it ... we never would have seen each other again.'

Therese was looking bewildered as Barty's words sank in. Tentatively, she reached for the locket and picked it up.

'But those sort of feelings are the ones you have at fourteen. All that "you're my *best* friend" stuff.' It was her turn to get up and walk around the room. 'It's so childish . . . so vindictive . . . so evil to make us all believe *you* took the locket.' She was holding it in her hand. 'Barty,' she said, suddenly deeply distressed, 'I'm *so* sorry I didn't trust you. I'm *so* sorry . . . I can still hardly believe Charlotte could have done such a thing. She was our best friend . . . we were the Gang of Three.'

'Two's company, three's a crowd,' Barty muttered. 'Maybe this was her revenge for our snubs when she first latched on to us.'

'I can't believe it of her . . . *not* the Charlotte I know. I just can't call her Charlie any more,' Therese muttered. 'This is *not* the Charlotte who looked after me when Mick disappeared. Over all these years,' she sighed, 'she's always been an ideal friend. Why would she do this? Why would she want to buy up our furniture . . . our things?'

'I've just told you,' Barty said impatiently, 'she wanted to buy into our lives.'

They stood looking round the room.

'I'm beginning to hate her,' Barty said. 'This has convinced me she's a manipulative lying bitch. Just look at it all, she's obsessed with both of us.' She sank back on to the sofa. 'Look at that table, Therese. You never met my darling Jules. We bought that together. It was the *last* thing I wanted to sell, Charlotte knew that. But I was in such a mess when Jules died I couldn't think straight and couldn't work. Anything that could bring in money had to go to pay the mortgage. It would have been the last straw to lose our cottage. That's all I've got left of Jules. It was better to lose the furniture, and keep her spirit alive at home.'

Therese nodded, still struggling with herself.

'But is it possible . . . this is only an idea . . . is it possible she was just doing all this to help us?' She waved her arm around the room. 'Could she be saving all this for us?' Her voice faded. 'As a surprise?' she ended pathetically.

'You *don't* really believe that, do you?' Barty said, looking at her. 'Why didn't she just lend us some money? She's got enough of it. No, Therese, in some very strange way, since school this woman has wanted to control us. Honestly, buying up our things is just half of it.' She looked around at the furniture. 'I know I'm playing the amateur shrink, but buying all this was her way of keeping us here . . . close to her for ever.'

Therese seemed to be waking up to the truth. Frightened, she went over to Barty and tried to hold her. Barty's body was rigid.

'Therese, I am so angry I can hardly speak. No one has ever manipulated me in the way I feel manipulated by Charlotte.' She, too, had dropped the nickname. 'That locket business will stay with me for ever.'

Therese looked at her. 'You're right.' She paused. 'We have been so much more important to Charlotte than we ever knew.'

'Bugger that!' Barty said. 'I find this flat, and everything that's happened to us this week, incredibly sinister.'

Therese turned away from her, still struggling with the Charlotte she had known and the Charlotte she was now coming to know.

'But none of it adds up. It's *not* the Charlotte I know – you know. When the family cut off my trust fund because I'd been spending so much of it on the sanctuary, and because they thought it would starve out Mick, Charlotte was always there.'

'What *is* this place?' Barty said, not listening to her. She looked around. 'It's like a weird kind of museum . . . a lair . . . a rabbit's bolt hole.'

'I'm feeling very nervous,' Therese said. 'She could walk in any minute with Cook. I really couldn't cope with a confrontation now.'

'Forget Cook,' Barty said. 'I'm sure you're right . . . she died a long time ago. It's obvious, looking around, nobody comes here but Charlotte. We're probably the only other people ever to have set foot in this place.' She looked over her shoulder. 'And we're not finished yet. D'you realize? There's another room . . .'

'Oh, no,' Therese said, panicking, 'you don't think there are more of our things in there?'

They both looked at the closed door. It had to be Charlotte's bedroom.

Therese shuddered.

'Barty, I really *don't* want to go in there. Look, why don't we go somewhere else? Let's get out of here . . . talk it through?'

Barty was firm. 'No, Therese.'

'In all these years with her,' Therese said, realizing there was no moving Barty, 'did you ever see any signs? Signs of . . . What am I talking about? Did you ever think there could be something . . . ? Well, *seriously* wrong with Charlotte?'

Barty was standing by hers and Jules's table, stroking the wood. She was near to tears. Slowly she said: 'Well, thinking back . . . You said she was always highly strung at school. She was, wasn't she?' She paused. 'And there was that time when she was sent home suddenly before the end of term because she was so overwrought and excitable.'

'And what about that time,' Therese said, 'when she was supposed to be coming to me for the holidays? D'you remember? It was suddenly cancelled? And nobody said why. You were coming, too, and the three of us were going to have such a lovely time in Shropshire. Mother was furious.' She hesitated. 'But what I'm really talking about, Barty, is her adult life. Don't forget, we've both been seeing her regularly for years. To me she's always seemed incredibly smart and together. The job at the BBC . . . Sometimes she seems to achieve more in a day than most of us achieve in a week.'

'Perhaps that's the problem,' Barty said laconically.

They stood, letting their thoughts sink in.

'She must have really *dreaded* the possibility of our meeting,' Therese said.

'Yes, she's had years of good luck,' Barty retorted, adding thoughtfully, 'but I *do* remember seeing her once, by chance, when she looked absolutely dreadful. Her eyes were dead, her skin was dull . . . She looked odd. And then there was that time at the Ritz . . . that was really strange. We were having tea. I never quite understood what was going on that day, but I always felt Charlotte's strange behaviour had something to do with Jules.'

'I must say, I've never seen her like that,' Therese interrupted.

'Did she ever meet Mick?' Barty asked.

'Of course she did. They didn't really like each other.'

'She loved Jules, of course,' Barty said, turning the conversation back to herself. 'But she nearly always came to our cottage. Often I rang her from the airport, and then called in. But somehow, even though I had a key, I always felt I had to ring first. She just wasn't the sort of person you would drop in on.'

'The same for me,' Therese confirmed. 'She nearly always insisted on coming down to see us. And Mick never even went there. Sometimes she'd cancel our lunches really abruptly. At first I thought it was work. But at other times she just sounded odd on the phone – speaking very quickly, quite unlike herself. Sometimes I would even say: "Are you all right, Charlie?" She always said she was.'

'Yes, that happened to me, too. I sometimes said: "Have you been on the bottle?"'

'Oh, she's *not* a secret drinker,' Therese said, still defending the Charlotte she thought she had known. 'She doesn't take after her mother.'

'But her speech was sometimes slurred,' Barty said, 'almost as if her tongue was too big for her mouth.'

'Maybe it was her pills,' Therese suggested.

'But those were only for headaches,' Barty replied.

They lapsed into another silence. Once again it was all questions and no answers.

Barty's sudden thump on her table made Therese jump.

'But why,' she shouted, 'does she have *this* place? It's so odd and creepy – the lacrosse stick, the panama hat. I dumped all that crap years ago. And what's all this?' she said, indicating the coffee table. 'Jelly-babies ... ginger beer? It's like a time warp.'

Therese had no answers. They stood looking round the room, taking in the bits and pieces of their personal lives, loves and losses.

'C'mon,' Barty said, 'let's brave the other room.'

'I'd rather go home,' Therese replied. 'Honestly, Barty, we've been here ages. She could walk in any minute.'

Barty, ignoring this, was already by the bedroom door. She flung it open.

'Oh, my God,' she said, staring into the room and steadying herself on the door frame. 'You *won't* believe this.'

Chapter Fifty-One

Therese, terrified of what she might see, and fighting down nausea, moved slowly to the doorway. Over Barty's shoulder, she took in the small room and its contents. Like an echo, she too whispered: 'Oh, my God.' They looked at each other: 'St Margaret's,' they said in unison.

Barty, regaining some control, stepped into the bedroom and onto familiar parquet flooring.

'Therese – she's utterly barking. Look, it's a complete replica of our dorm. How did she get hold of an iron bed like that? This floor? Those awful daisy-chain curtains?'

Therese was quiet. The sight of the room had left her dumb.

'Look . . .' Barty went on, pausing by a metal bedside locker and banging her palm on it. 'This is sick.'

Therese had picked up a hockey stick with a school scarf draped around it. Shuddering, she immediately threw them down again as if they were contaminated. Barty noticed she had gone very white, and guided her to the bed.

'Sit down. Put your head between your knees,' she ordered.

Therese did as she was told. Barty tweaked the bedspread.

'Look, she's even got the green candlewick right. Colour of vomit.'

Therese was slowly straightening up, her eyes now focusing on the opposite wall: 'Oh, God, Barty, look at the photographs.'

Their eyes took in the shots of *The Mikado*, and all the end-of-term photographs of pupils and staff rigidly lined up in the hall and on the lawn. In each shot the three of them were neatly ringed.

Therese stood up and whispered: '*Why*, Barty? *Why*? What's this all about?' A moment later, she gripped Barty by the shoulders.

'Barty, have you seen these?' she asked, indicating a montage of photographs she had just noticed on another wall.

'What?' Barty said, allowing herself to be led across the room.

'She's been spying on us,' Therese said. 'That's Mick on his mountain bike ... That photograph was taken in Wales on the only holiday we ever had time for.'

'Good God,' Barty said, ignoring Therese and indicating a photograph of a Titian-haired girl in the left corner. 'That's Jules. She had short hair then. It was taken in Venice, in St Mark's Square.'

'But *why* would she have stalked us?' Therese said. 'What on earth was she doing in those places when we didn't know she was there?'

'Spying on us,' Barty repeated, quivering with anger.

'Look,' Therese said, moving on to other photographs of her and Mick. 'She was there, too. And there ... And there ... I don't understand. Why would she want to spy?'

'Because,' Barty said patiently, 'she *never* wanted us or our partners out of her sight – out of her control. Just look at these photos, Therese, it's obvious that if we did anything out of the ordinary, anything *she* wasn't involved in, she had to be a part of it somehow.'

'I never noticed a thing,' Therese said, as the truth sunk in. 'She must have taken so many risks. How could she have lived with all those lies without giving herself away?'

'She's sick,' Barty said, voicing the thought for both of them. 'Sick and mad.'

Therese met her eyes. 'I just can't believe it. What's happened to her, Barty? What's happened to the Charlotte we've both known since we were at school?'

'She never grew up,' Barty replied firmly, 'that's what *didn't* happen to her. She's stayed in a time-warp and tried to keep us in there with her. Don't you see, she's totally obsessed by us ...' She paced around the small room. 'We're so important to her, she'll go to any lengths to keep tracks on us.'

'I'm beginning to hate her,' Therese muttered.

'Me, too. But I'd lay a bet her bloody family has a lot to answer for,' Barty said, sounding suddenly deadly calm. 'A drunk for a mother. A suicide for a father. A snob for a brother. I always loathed that superior bastard. He was always reminding me I came from the wrong side of the tracks. With that lot for a family, no wonder she latched on to us. No wonder she's turned into the epitome of *selfish* love.' She paused, picking up an unshapely raffia basket and a nearby embroidered linen pinny.

Both recognized *these* items. Every girl at St Margaret's had been forced to make the same things. Both remembered Miss Strachey's perpetual cry:

'Not good enough. I'm sorry, girls, you will have to unpick it.' These crafts had been a fourteen year old's futile labour when the sun was beckoning outside during the summer term. Aprons never to be used, never to be worn, never to be wanted.

Therese crossed to a small chest of drawers.

'The mattress on that bed,' she said incongruously over her shoulder, 'is as hard as the ones we had at school.'

'Are you surprised?' Barty snapped back. 'Can't you see? This *is* our old dormitory. She's done it on purpose.' She paused and sniffed. 'Therese, it even smells the same, doesn't it?'

'Beeswax,' Therese replied, reaching for a small brown plastic container with a white lid. 'Barty,' she said reading out the long word on the label, 'these are tranquillizers, aren't they?'

'Well, they're certainly not for migraine,' she retorted, raising her eyebrows sarcastically. 'That sounds like serious stuff ... psychiatric heavy stuff.'

Therese was now crouching down by the metal bedside locker.

'It's not locked,' she said, turning back to Barty.

'Why should it be? This is her lair – obviously her secret place.' Barty knew she was snapping unnecessarily, but Therese's naivety irritated her. 'She *certainly* doesn't want anybody to see any of this.'

Therese was sitting on the floor, leafing through the buff-coloured folder she had taken from the locker. Barty moved across to the bedside table and picked up a large leather-bound book.

'Good. This must be her diary,' she said. 'This will tell us more about our friend.'

'Barty!' Therese said, shocked. 'We *can't* look at that. Diaries are private.'

'Oh, sod that! I want to know what she's been up to. We certainly know she's been manipulating us. Remember the locket? I want to know how far she's gone.'

Falling silent, Barty started to leaf through the pages.

'Barty,' Therese said nervously. 'Why don't we just take this stuff and run? We can read it somewhere else. Honestly, she could come back any moment.'

Barty was not listening.

'You read that file and I'll get on with the diary. It's only Charlotte. She's not going to come back with a meat-cleaver. And there *are* two of us.'

Therese was panicking but said nothing, her eyes superficially skimming the bundle of papers in the folder. Some of them were handwritten, some were faxes, others neatly typed.

'Oh, my God,' Barty said. 'Listen to this. It's . . . it's all about Jules.' Turning round on the bed, she read aloud:

> *'Jules is becoming a menace. At Christmas she said she's going to take Barty to America. Their departure is not imminent, but Jules definitely means it. She wants to go back and live and work in the States. Life without Barty. Oh, no! I can't allow this to happen . . . the Family has to stay together.'*

'What family?' Therese asked, puzzled.

'She means us, you idiot,' Barty replied. 'We are the Family . . . *the three of us.*'

'But we've got families of our own.'

'That's the whole point. I know it's weird, but, don't you see, we've replaced Charlotte's family? In her strange warped mind, *we* are her family. Her replacement family.'

'What else does it say?' Therese managed.

Barty had gone quiet.

'Hang on,' she said. 'I'm just reading this . . . trying to take it in. You read that.'

Therese went back to the file.

'I can't make head or tail of this,' she said a minute later. 'It's all about a stabbing in Trafalgar Square. Some guy called Tony and another called . . . I can't quite read the writing . . . My God, *it's Mick*. The other man is *Mick*. Barty,' she said urgently, 'are you listening? This is all about Mick.'

Barty was only half listening.

'This bit,' she said, 'is all about Jules. Shhh, Therese . . . I just want to carry on reading.'

Therese, ignoring her lack of interest, went on: 'But, Barty, this is all about Madagascar. How did she get *all* these details? Even I don't know all of this.' She leafed feverishly through some more of the pages. 'My God, this is all about the Animal Liberation Front . . . and a kidnapping. These look like police reports . . . on Mick.'

Barty turned round. She had never heard Therese sound so shocked. Therese was now on her feet, oblivious of her friend's equal discomfiture and anxiety.

'Listen, Barty. *Listen to this.*' The file was open in her hands. 'She's written:

> *Last night was a nightmare. He got spectacularly drunk. It was the only thing I hadn't bargained for. I told him: "Mick, you don't have to go down this road and be bullied by Tony and end up in prison with Therese visiting you."*'

Therese looked across at Barty to make sure she was listening.

> *I gave him £60,000 in cash. He promised he wouldn't go back to Therese and spill the beans. He spent the night in my bed. What a night! I convinced him the ticket was his passport to freedom. A good night's work. This morning I packed him off to Australia. Good riddance. Let's hope he'll be a good boy and stay there. T very upset . . . but I'll sort it, just like I've sorted everything else.'*

Therese could not read any more.

'Why would she want to split us up?' she sobbed quietly. 'Why would she want to ruin my life?' She hammered the floor. 'I hate her. I hate her. I *hate* her. I thought she was my best friend, but she's destroyed me and got rid of the only man I ever loved. "*He spent the night in my bed. What a night!"* God, she even went to bed with him, pretending all the time she loathed him. What *kind* of a woman, is she? Why would she want to split us up?' Her voice trailed off.

'Therese,' Barty said in a dead voice, 'I'm *truly* sorry. I really do want to listen, but I just can't. I've got to find my own answers now.' She turned another page of the diary, then another, then another.

'This is extraordinary,' she said, looking up. 'It's not a normal diary, every single entry is about us: Barty this . . . Therese that . . . She says here:

> *I had a shock today. Barty has not mentioned Therese for at least three years, then she suddenly said at lunch: "I wonder what happened to Therese Allinson-Smith?" I was so taken aback, I pretended I had hayfever and, playing for time, fumbled in my bag for a tissue. Then I said: "I never think about her, Barty. I've never forgiven her for thinking you could possibly have stolen her locket."*
> *Thank God, they never suspected me!'*

'Oh, how *could* she?' Therese said, tears coursing down her face. 'She's been *so* treacherous. *She's evil.*' Her voice rose despairingly. 'Mick . . . will I ever be able to find him again?' she said, rocking her body backwards and forwards.

'Why would you ever want to?' Barty said angrily. 'He dumped you for money. It's there in the file. Charlotte bribed him to go. Don't you ever *dare* try to find him. He's a total shit. He could have got in touch with you any time if he'd wanted to.'

'I'll never trust anybody ever again,' Therese said, choked. 'Charlotte knew all my secrets . . . all my intimacies. I told her everything, and she used it against me. I feel so stupid . . . so used . . . so betrayed. I never had an inkling . . .'

Barty, half listening, was still turning pages.

'Hell!' she said, interrupting Therese: 'Listen to *this*:

> *I've never understood passion. Instinctively, I know it's messy, smelly, damp, uncomfortable. It must be embarrass-ing afterwards. Love, yes. Passion, no. Friendship, yes, like mine with Barty and Therese. Friendship lasts. Passion, by*

*its very nature, cannot. So why choose passion – here today,
betrayed tomorrow – when there is friendship? I hang on
to my friends. And nobody, man or woman, will ever have
sex with me. I would rather die first. I'm proud of being a
virgin, in the tradition of Elizabeth I.'*

Barty looked up from the diary.

'She's mad! What a bloody hypocrite. *Friendship!* I don't think
Charlotte Pierce knows the meaning of the word. Therese ...' she
said gently, at last aware of her friend's distress ... 'at least
she never went to bed with Mick. That's something. Fancy her
being a virgin! There's no way she ever went to bed with him.
It's obvious from this,' she said, waving the diary, 'she's still a
virgin. She fancies herself as a virgin queen. It's all here, in her
own poisonous little hand.'

Therese managed a nod.

'Thank God for that,' she murmured. 'I couldn't live for the
rest of my life with the picture of Mick in bed with Charlotte.
I'm so relieved it never happened. You don't think it did, do you,
Barty?'

'No way,' she replied. 'When she wrote "What a night!" she
meant it had all been a total drama, *not* a night of passion.
Knowing her, she'd deliberately set out to get him paralytic so
he'd be incapable of anything. Then she'd have put the screws on
and got him to agree to go to Australia. That was her plan.'

'Yes, you're right ...' Therese said hesitantly. 'But what a mess.
I've still lost him.' She started to cry again.

'Oh, Therese,' Barty said, irritated, 'do stop crying. He really
wasn't worth it. He never gave you a thought, did he? From the
folder, it's clear he just left to save his own skin.'

She returned to leafing through the diary.

'It's Therese this ... Barty that. Hell!' She paused. 'This bit's
about Jules ...' She fell quiet, reading avidly. 'Dear Mother of
God,' she suddenly shouted. 'Bees! She's writing here all about
Jules's death. It's ... it's dated the day after she died. It's a kind
of check-list. Therese, listen to this:

*I remembered everything and got rid of it all. Surgical
rubber gloves. Honey. Tweezers. The all-important bees. I*

*remembered to wipe everything. And then spent a ghastly
night at Midhurst.*

'My God,' Barty said, stunned, looking up from the diary, 'she was
there in the cottage that afternoon. She was there when Jules died.'
She looked down again, reading on silently, then horrified at what
she was taking in, turned again to Therese.

'She's written here,' she said in a dead voice:

'The swelling began ...

'And she's ended this page, at the bottom here, with:

*In that stupid hotel room I couldn't get rid of the sound of
that wretched cock crowing fields away yesterday as Jules
was dying. To the world it will appear like an accident ...'*

Barty choked. She could not read any more, just sat staring at
the wall.

'*What?*' Therese said, leaping up and wrenching the diary from
her.

'Oh, my God, Barty. This is *awful*, even worse than Mick. At
least he's still alive,' she said, reading the passage herself. 'Oh, no!
I can't believe this about Jules ...'

Barty was too shocked to speak.

'We've *got* to read it,' Therese said emphatically. 'We've *got* to.
I'll do it ...'

Barty was incapable of anything.

*'It comforts me she didn't feel anything ... didn't have any
pain. I drugged her. I felt I owed that to Barty, and after
all I did like Jules. But it had to be done. And I did it.
I did it.'*

The sheer evil and hypocrisy of that self-justification overcame
Therese. She stopped reading, clamping her hand over her mouth
as Barty slumped forward on to her knees.

'I know this is destroying you, Barty, but we must get to the
end of this,' Therese whispered gently.

'Now Barty will not go to America. She will stay here with me, and the Family will stay together. I did it . . . Felicity in the bathroom and now Jules. Yes, back in London, I'm feeling tired, but quite exultant . . . once again in control of my life and theirs.'

Chapter Fifty-Two

꩜

'It was murder,' Barty said, fighting back nausea. 'She came down to the cottage specifically to kill Jules. She murdered her. It was murder ... murder plotted down to the last detail. It *wasn't* an accident.'

Therese, like Barty, was in a state of shock, but she crossed the room and sat down on the bed. Barty snatched back the diary.

'I want to read that for myself,' she said brokenly, scanning the tight handwriting. 'She *deliberately* set out to get rid of Jules. She didn't want us to go to America so she murdered her. It's all here.'

Therese put her arm around Barty. She knew her own thoughts were selfish. Jules was dead while Mick was alive. Barty was beginning to shake.

'And what about Felicity?' Therese said. 'Who was she? And what did Charlotte do to her in the bathroom?'

'Poor Jules ... my poor Jules,' Barty was moaning. 'If only I'd been there ... I *loved* her so much. If only I'd known what we know now. We've all been so naive, so stupid ... We've endangered the people we loved because we didn't know ...'

'Barty,' Therese said, 'we can't blame ourselves. How could we have known? She's been so clever.'

The diary slipped off Barty's lap on to the floor, closing on its secrets.

'Until today,' Therese added, 'neither of us had a clue what Charlotte was all about. We *really* can't blame ourselves. We mustn't.'

'I do,' Barty sobbed. 'I feel as if I murdered Jules. I feel it's all my fault . . .'

'Barty, don't,' Therese said. 'We've got to get out of here. We've got to go to the police.' She bent down and retrieved the diary. 'This is evidence . . . concrete proof of everything she's done. Without this, nobody will believe us.'

They both looked down at the diary in its innocuous leather binding. It looked so innocent, so respectable.

'She'll go to prison for a *very* long time,' Therese said. 'Can you imagine Charlotte Pierce in prison?'

'Some comfort! It won't bring my lover back. Life inside is too good for her. I'd like to see her hang,' Barty said bitterly. 'If she *ever* comes out . . . if she does . . . I'll be waiting for her.'

She looked at Therese through swollen eyes. Her face said everything. In ten minutes, the contents of the diary had destroyed her life as surely as Charlotte had destroyed Jules.

'I want to kill her. I *really* want to kill her,' she sobbed.

Therese remained silent, nursing her friend's grief. Barty's anguish had temporarily blocked out all thoughts of Mick. They sat for a long time, absorbing the secrets of the room: the horror, betrayal, deceit and treachery of their 'best friend'. The woman they had loved and trusted nearly all their lives had destroyed their happiness for her own selfish, deranged reasons.

Therese forced herself to stand up. She wanted to flee the house with Barty and the diary. Barty was repeating monotonously, like a mantra: 'I want to kill her. I want to kill her.'

Therese put her arms around her.

'What are we going to do, Barty? We can't ever meet her again. Oh, God, I just couldn't look at her. It would be a nightmare.'

'You're right,' Barty said, suddenly finding some energy. 'We've got to get out of here – and fast. She could be dangerous if she found us now. Hang on to that diary.'

Barty moved quickly to the bed and picked up the file.

It was too late. They both heard the sound. They froze.

A key was being inserted in the lock.

Chapter Fifty-Three

༤

Time hung suspended. They could hear Charlotte in the passage. There were rustling sounds. She was obviously taking off her outdoor coat. Familiar everyday noises seemed to be magnified. They heard the crackling of plastic as a bag was lifted on to a work surface, a suctioned click as the fridge door was opened. There was a metallic noise – a can being put down? They heard two bottles fall sideways, the heavy thud of plastic as one hit the floor. A tap was turned on. Water ran. And then the noises stopped, followed by more movements – mundane kitchen noises. A drawer opened, cutlery rattled. The sound of humming. They looked at each other – Charlotte was humming the school song.

Barty thought Therese was going to faint. They looked at each other again, horrified. Barty put her finger to her lips and shook her head. She was *willing* Therese to hang on, to rally, not to leave her alone. Mutual fear was holding them up – neither could desert the other now. They had their answers, but had left their escape too late. Now they would have to confront her together. They would face Charlotte with their accusations and condemnations. She had tried to split them with her lies and treachery, but she couldn't win any more. They were reunited.

They had not spoken since the sound of her key in the lock. They looked at each other again, jumping at the sound of a fizzy explosion. Charlotte was obviously pouring herself a drink. They heard a glass being put down on the table, then the movements drew nearer. She was coming out of the kitchen. She was coming . . .

'Oh, God,' whispered Therese. 'She's coming.'

They could hear her footsteps down the short passage, coming towards the bedroom. They broke apart from each other and instinctively retreated further into the room.

They stood side by side, gripping each other's hand, bracing themselves against the shock of seeing Charlotte.

Chapter Fifty-Four

⫷

They were frozen like statues, hand in hand, as the bedroom door swung open. Charlotte stood framed in the doorway. Therese and Barty were transfixed by the slight figure. They took in her white face devoid of the usual make-up. She was dressed in school uniform – *their* school uniform. Her hair was in bunches. Horrified, they took in every detail.

She saw them.

As frightened as they were, they realized the shock of seeing *them* together in her secret place, the invasion of her citadel, was even more cataclysmic for her than it was for them. Her body and face went rigid. She stood exposed – paralysed with shock. Their questions were forgotten, obliterated by the spectacle in front of them. She uttered a sound neither of them had ever heard before – like a death rattle – over almost before it had begun, and brought her arms up to shield herself from what she was seeing.

Barty suddenly dropped Therese's hand and lunged forward with a shriek – no words, just a howl of hatred. Her arms were outstretched for Charlotte's throat.

'Don't, Barty. *Don't*,' Therese screamed, running to her, pulling her back, and desperately clinging to her arm.

'Are you mad?' Barty spat, spinning round to face Therese and frantically trying to wrestle free from the tight grip. 'I'm *not* going to let her get away with this. She killed Jules. I'm going to kill her.'

They were locked together in a grotesque wrestle.

'Don't, Barty,' Therese kept repeating. *'Don't.'*

Barty was pushing and shoving, using every part of her body to free herself.

'She killed Jules. Get off me. *Get off.'*

She shoved Therese backwards, and they both crashed on to the parquet floor, their bodies still locked together.

Therese's head had hit the side of the metal locker. Blood was beginning to ooze from a cut on her forehead.

Barty, her eyes still locked on Charlotte, was scrabbling to get up. The fall had winded them both.

'You're not going to stop me, Therese,' she was gasping.

'Barty, *please,*' Therese pleaded. 'If you kill her, you'll go to prison. She's sick. Look at her. She's sick.'

Barty was beside herself, still struggling to release herself from Therese's arm lock.

In front of them Charlotte was oblivious to the threat on her life. Frozen to the spot, she was still shielding her face with her arms.

'I'm going to kill her,' Barty was repeating. 'You're *not* going to stop me.'

Therese's grip was weakening. She knew she couldn't keep Barty down on the floor much longer. She released her hold, hit her very hard around the face, then gripped her arm again. Momentarily, they were both shocked. They sat looking at each other stunned. For a few seconds there was absolute silence, then Barty raised her hand to her stinging face. 'You *hit* me. How could you, Therese? *How could you?'*

'To save you from prison,' Therese mumbled, mortified, 'I couldn't think of anything else to stop you. Sorry . . .' Her voice trailed off miserably, but she did not release her hold on Barty's arm. The room was deathly quiet. Charlotte remained frozen in front of them.

The slap had brought Barty to her senses. She was totally expressionless. Her body went limp and lifeless against Therese.

'You can let go of me,' she said eventually in a dead voice. 'I won't harm her.' She paused. 'I promise I won't harm her.'

Therese looked at her warily. 'Are you sure?' She was still on her guard.

'I'm sure.' The dead voice repeated.

Barty remained inert. As they sat there they heard a movement. In the doorway, Charlotte was slowly lowering her arms from her face. Then, as they watched, she blinked and moved out of the room.

It was as if they were not there.

Shakily, they stood up, then looking at each other silently crossed to the door. Charlotte was sitting in the other room on the carpet, calmly unlacing her shoes and pulling up her school socks. Her legs were splayed out like a typical fourteen-year-old. Oblivious of the watchers, she reached for a handful of jelly-babies and shoved them into her mouth.

Therese leaned against Barty. 'She doesn't even know we're here, does she?' she whispered. 'She's blocked us out. We've got to get out of here, and get the police.'

'And the doctors,' Barty added. Drained, she could hardly take her eyes off the schoolgirl now casually leafing through a comic on the floor.

They looked at each other's empty faces. Nothing in life had prepared them for a moment like this. Madness.

'She's crazy, isn't she?' Therese said, more in sorrow than in anger.

'Yes,' Barty replied almost inaudibly, 'as mad as a March hare.'

Chapter Fifty-Five

⚜

Of the many psychiatrists involved in the preparation of reports for the trial of the Honourable Charlotte Pierce, only Dr George Flanders interviewed the witnesses, Ms Barty McClaren and the Honourable Therese Allinson-Smith.

Dr Flanders took a particular interest in this case, fascinated by the dual nature of the patient's life: the keeping up of normal public behaviour countered by the intense need to sustain a secret life. Only his report (see below) came near to providing an adequate explanation of the cataclysmic events that took place that day in the Honourable Charlotte Pierce's flat.

... *Ms Barty McClaren and the Hon Therese Allinson-Smith were witness to the psychological disintegration of the Hon Charlotte Pierce. I believe that the unexpected sight of these two women in her 'secret home' led to the dissolution of the fantasy world which the Hon Charlotte Pierce had carefully constructed over a period of thirty years. It is clear from her diary, that these women had become her substitute family (see page 4 of this report). Knowing no love within her natural family, she could not express love in any 'normal' way. In this regard, I think it highly significant that she is a virgin (see her diary entry for 12 June).*

In my opinion, this lack of natural affection at home caused her to overvalue the friendship which she formed with Barty McClaren and the Hon Therese Allinson-Smith at the age of thirteen. I do not think it is going too far to say that she was 'imprinted' on both girls and that they became her substitute (and only) family and source of affection. It became of the utmost importance to her to control their lives. Any person or event which threatened that control was unacceptable and, in my view, this led to the alleged murder of Jules Hardaker (see page 7 of the Arresting Officer's report) and to the manipulation of the Hon Therese Allinson-Smith's former partner, Mr Michael Davies (see page 6 of the Hon Therese Allinson-Smith's statement to the police).

I believe that the Hon Charlotte Pierce's behaviour following her discovery of Ms McClaren and the Hon Therese Allinson-Smith in her flat can only be understood in the context of the completely central role which these women had played in her life. She had purposely separated them, but, by chance, they had been reunited.

In my opinion, at the sight of her two friends together in the area she had created for herself, and with the extent of her deception revealed, she immediately retreated into a state of denial which was so complete as to convince the witnesses to her behaviour that she had made them 'disappear'. She saw them but did not see them, heard them but did not hear them. In effect, the shock had made her deaf, dumb and blind. Her eyes would have been open but blank. The accounts given by Ms McClaren and the Hon Therese Allinson-Smith are consistent with this opinion.

I believe that the Hon Charlotte Pierce was never equipped to deal effectively with the world of real emotions. Instead, she created for herself an illusory world in which she attempted to control friendship and love. Of necessity, this world was a fragile thing, rather like spun sugar, and, to pursue the metaphor, it dissolved in the instant she was confronted by her friends in her 'safe' place. Her sense of self – never strong – was at that moment dealt a fatal blow.

In conclusion, it is my belief that the Hon Charlotte Pierce has no memory of the events of that day. However, she is unable any longer to sustain the fiction which has been the mainstay of her life. I think this unresolvable conflict accounts for her current mute and passive condition.

Her present mental state reminds me of those catatonic patients who used to inhabit the asylums of old. I would not care to predict how long she will remain in this state, nor what she will be like if, or when, she returns to reality.

For the Hon Charlotte Pierce the cataclysmic events of that day never happened. Her two worlds had collided.

George Flanders MB ChB, MRCPsych
Consultant Forensic Psychiatrist